Poacher's PARADISE

An Alaska Wildlife Trooper Novel

Ron Walden
Alaskan True to Life Crime Writer

ISBN 978-1-95-726311-3
eBook ISBN 978-1-95-726312-0
Library of Congress Catalog Card Number: 2013942552

Manufactured in the United States of America.

This book is dedicated to my old pal
ARTHUR T. SCHMIDT
Owner and Proprietor of
SMITTY'S SALMON SAFARI
My friend transitioned from a grouchy old guy
to a legend of the Kenai River
on
September 27, 2012

ACKNOWLEDGMENTS

The predecessor of the Alaska Wildlife Trooper was the Alaska Fish and Wildlife Protection Officer. When they were taken from the Fish and Game division and made a division of the Alaska State Troopers, they were differentiated by their brown uniforms, hence the blue shirt and brown shirt designations.

In the early 1970s, there were few officers and a vast area to patrol. Those officers established protocol that is still used today. My wife was one of those officers, which gave me a chance to meet and associate with some of the great wardens in Alaska history. Her immediate boss was Al "Bear Bait" Thompson, whose wife Joyce wrote the account I have quoted in this book about his attack by an Alaska brown bear. The Thompsons are now retired and no longer live in Alaska but remain our friends. I am truly grateful to them for allowing me to use their written account.

There were many officers now dead or retired who struck fear in the hearts of poachers on the Kenai Peninsula: Al Thompson, Dan France (who taught me about the mechanics of fabric-covered aircraft), Ed Painter, Bernie Merit, Richard Dykema, Sr., Chuck Rogers, and a long list of others. These men and women set a standard which can never be equaled or surpassed.

Today Alaska Wildlife Troopers have many of the same duties, and they do them well. Fish and game populations have changed due to habitat and regulation changes, but the officers on the Kenai Peninsula have a vast area of responsibility, as well as the most diverse venue in which to perform.

They are responsible for a commercial salmon fishery, a commercial halibut fishery, a commercial herring fishery, and other lesser fisheries. They also oversee sport fishing, in both fresh and salt water, along with overseeing both private and guided fishermen—all in addition to hunting, private and guided, trapping and personal use, and subsistence hunting and fishing seasons.

The job isn't easy, the responsibility is great and the victims cannot speak for themselves. My hat is off to all of you.

Thank you.

CHAPTER 1

Alaska's large number and varied species of animals have drawn hunters and tourists from around the world since long before it became a territory of the United States. Many species were hunted to near extinction for their furs and meat: seals, sea otter, walrus, and many species of sea birds. Wealthy Russians hunted trophies and fur, taking their winnings home by the boatload. It was thought at the time that the abundance of wildlife and the remoteness of the north would protect what remained. Time and history have proven this a false hope.

After the United States bought the territory and gold was discovered in the North Country, miners and trappers lived off the meat provided by nature, looking out for their own survival and caring little about the survival of the animals and fish. Prior to statehood only minimal care was taken to protect fish and wildlife from wholesale slaughter. Hunting guides made small fortunes leading wealthy clients from all over the world into the wilderness of Alaska to hunt world class trophy animals. The size of Alaska brown bears was legendary. Moose with antlers of six feet in width were common. These hunts commanded fees of astronomical figures and gratuities worth more than the annual wage of the average resident.

With statehood came more stringent enforcement and more careful management of the wildlife resource. State game wardens were few in the early days, but they were dedicated and energetic. Shooting of caribou or moose for bear bait is now illegal. Some of these practices live on today but are infrequent.

On a Tuesday morning, one of these game wardens, now called Wildlife Troopers, was at his desk when his phone rang.

"Will Trippet," he answered.

"Hi, Will. Gordon Ponset here. Do you have anything scheduled for today?"

"Good morning, Gordy. I don't have anything special. I thought I would go out and check some bear-baiting stations. Why? Do you have something going on?"

"Not really, but I have to go out Mystery Creek Road to the pipeline and thought you might like to ride out with me. There are usually a couple of bear-baiting stations out that way."

Mystery Creek Road is located on the Kenai National Wildlife Refuge and federal officers patrol it. Gordon worked for the feds. The two men had been friends since college. Gordon went to school at Idaho State while Will attended Boise State. Both played football and were across the line from each other on several occasions. It was there they met and became friends. Will was first to come to Alaska and go to work for Fish and Wildlife with Gordon following two years later to work for the Wildlife Refuge. Will Trippet had been with the wildlife division for just over ten years. He was still single and wanted to stay that way for a few more years while he moved from post to post within the division.

"I had better take my own truck in case I'm called back," he told Ponset. "I'll meet you at the parking area at Mile 63 on the Sterling Highway. I'll plan to leave here within a half hour. Is that soon enough for you?"

Will ran through his mental checklist to be sure he had everything he needed. He also checked the ammo supply in his truck, noted the fuel tank was full and notified dispatch where he was headed. It would take about forty minutes to drive to the meeting place. It was a pleasant May morning and the sun was beginning to hold some warmth.

Will arrived at the meeting place before Gordy, but he was not the first to arrive. There was a new GMC pick-up in the parking area. It had a small utility trailer behind and whatever had been hauled there was not on the trailer. Will wrote the license number of the pickup and trailer in his notebook and returned to his truck radio to call it in.

"The vehicle is registered to Victor Resnic of Ninilchik, Alaska," the dispatcher reported.

"Thank you. I will be out of my vehicle for two to three hours and radio reception in the area is poor, so I may be out of range for the next two or three hours."

Gordy pulled into the parking area and waved to Will who gathered his shotgun, thermos of coffee and a small daypack with emergency essentials that he loaded into the back seat of the federal vehicle before climbing inside to greet his friend.

"Glad you could make it this morning," he greeted Will. "I am scheduled to patrol Mystery Creek Road out to the gas pipeline on a weekly basis. I thought you might like the ride."

"Thanks for asking," Will answered as he fastened his seatbelt.

"Did you check the registered owner of the pickup parked over there?"

"Yes, I did. It came back to a Victor Resnic of Ninilchik. I think there are Resnics on our watch list, but I don't remember a Victor."

While Will was talking, Gordy pulled out of the parking area and drove the few yards to the gate guarding Mystery Creek Road. Will stepped out of the truck and opened the gate, closing and locking it after Gordy had passed. They passed the time during the first three miles of the drive by comparing basketball season statistics for each of their respective schools. Three miles into the trip, Will spotted something.

"Stop, stop." Gordy stopped. "Back up a little." Gordy slowly backed up until he was once again ordered to stop.

Will was looking intently up a rocky bank alongside the road. "What do you see, Will?"

"That pickup in the parking area had unloaded some sort of all-terrain vehicle. Look up at the top of this rocky bank. See the fresh ATV tracks at the top?"

Gordy stepped out of the truck to get a better look. "Oh, yeah, I see them." He reached through the window and turned off the ignition. "Grab your shotgun and let's take a look." With that, Gordon pulled his own twelve-gauge shotgun from its rack in the back seat. The two men scrambled up the steep rocky slope. Once on the top it was easy to follow the tracks left by the huge tires of the ATV. They had only walked about fifty yards when they spotted the machine parked in a small stand of willow. No driver was visible. Cautiously the two officers followed an overgrown seismic trail deeper into the spruce forest. Moving slowly and quietly, they were about 150 yards past the parked ATV when they broke out into a small clearing. What they encountered was horrifying.

The first thing they saw was massive amounts of blood over the entire clearing. A cow moose lay on the far edge of the clearing had been dressed out and some of the meat sections were in gauze meat sacks. Twenty feet to the left was the carcass of a medium size brown bear, partially skinned. Near where the officers stood was a rifle leaning against a spruce tree. Ten feet from it was the body of a man—or what was left of him.

Will chambered a round into his shotgun, immediately on edge. "I have a camera in my daypack. Get it for me, will you Gordy? I want to record the scene before we walk into it." He turned his back to Gordon for him to access his pack. Vigilant and wary Will scanned every corner of the clearing and surrounding woods for movement or signs of the bear that had attacked the hunter. After several minutes without seeing anything, he began to relax. Gordon Ponset kept guard.

While taking still and video pictures of the scene, Will asked Gordon Ponset what he thought had happened.

"I can't be certain, but it looks to me as if this guy spotted that cow moose and shot her. He dressed it out—I see the remains of an unborn calf in the gut pile. While he was working on dressing the moose, this bear attacked him. It looks like the guy made it to his rifle and shot it. While he was skinning this bear, it appears another bear attacked him. This time he didn't make it to his gun and lost the wrestling match with the second bear. And by the way, that other bear is likely to be in the area."

"That's pretty close to what I figured, too." Will paused while he finished filming. "How do you want to handle this? It is clearly death by bear. I think that we should notify both our supervisors and get some help out here. I also think it will end up as my case because of the state game laws being broken. Your violation is trespassing and using a motor vehicle on the refuge. I think the supervisors have to make that decision."

"I agree," replied Ponset. "I'll go back toward the highway until I can get radio reception while you stay with the scene. Before I leave, though let's check the ATV and make sure it runs just in case you need to make a run for it. The keys were still in the ignition when we came in."

"Good plan. I suggest that you try to find a spot to get cell phone coverage. That way we may not have so many curiosity seekers watching. You know my office number." He paused a moment, then added, "Let me see if there is any identification on the body before you leave. Have my captain check him out if there is."

Will approached the remains of the body while Gordy stood guard. He donned a pair of rubber gloves and tried to find a wallet. He found it in the rear pants pocket of the victim. While looking for the identification, Will noted the body had significant damage and that some parts were missing, apparently eaten by the bear. He wiped some of the blood and gore from the wallet and opened it to find an Alaska State driver's license that confirmed the victim was Victor Resnic of Ninilchik.

Will handed the bloody wallet to his friend, Gordy. "You had better bag this for evidence. Let's go check the ATV, then you can go make the calls. I'll stay on guard until you get back." Will smiled at his partner and said, "Please hurry! I don't want to be out here alone with a mad bear any longer than necessary."

Gordy nodded and the two men walked back down the trail to the parked Polaris Ranger XP800. At the vehicle, Will turned the key and it started immediately. Gordy continued to his truck and Will returned to the scene of the mauling. There was nothing to do now but wait until permission was granted to move the body. The next hour or so would be very, very long.

Nearly an hour had passed when Will heard a vehicle on the road nearby. The bear had not returned and, for that, he was grateful. In what seemed only moments, he heard voices coming toward him. He recognized his captain and another Wildlife Trooper, Sergeant Donavan Fleer. Fleer was a hulk of a man, six feet five and 270 pounds, in his early 40s and in prime physical condition. Captain Tom Olson was the first to speak.

"Is everything OK, Will? Has the bear come back?"

"I haven't seen or heard anything since Gordy left. By the way, where is he?"

"He will be along shortly. He is waiting for his supervisor to show up. He left a red marker cone on the edge of the road, so we found you without any problem. I need to see the scene right away. I have permission from the Colonel to pronounce this body dead, if in fact he is. How far is it to the scene?"

"Only a few yards up this seismic trail. It is a pretty gory scene." With that, the entourage proceeded to the scene. The captain pronounced the victim dead and asked Trippet what he intended to do. Will said he would salvage the rest of the moose meat and finish skinning the dead bear. He planned to use the ATV to haul the meat and hide to the road where he could load it into his truck. Fleer volunteered to return to his truck for a body bag. By the time Fleer returned, Gordy and his supervisor were at the scene. It had been determined the case would be handled by Alaska State Wildlife Troopers. Gordy's supervisor returned to town with Captain Olson.

The remaining three men had the scene cleaned up and the meat, body and hide in the truck in less than an hour. They surveyed the area looking for any items or clues they had missed. Finding none, they returned to the parking area near the Sterling Highway where the victim's vehicle was parked. They loaded the Polaris Ranger on its trailer and called a tow truck to take the vehicles back to the office for impound. Finally, they returned to Soldotna with their grisly cargo.

Fleer took responsibility for care of the victim's body while Will Trippet conferred with his captain. It was decided that Will should drive the thirty-five miles to Ninilchik to find the victim's relatives and to deliver the news of his death as gently as possible.

Will reached the Ninilchik trooper on his call phone and asked if he knew the address of the victim and whether he had relatives in town. Ninilchik Trooper Sean Adams filled him in.

"Victor Resnic has a son who lives at home. He is about 18 years old and a senior at the Ninilchik High School. My kids to go school with him and say he is a nice boy. The father, on the other hand, is another story. Rumor has it that he is poaching moose and selling meat."

"He was poaching a moose when he was attacked by a bear," Will said. "Can you meet me at the Inlet View and show me where the home is located?"

"Happy to help," Adams replied, "but you should be aware that the victim has two brothers who don't take kindly to law enforcement types. They are both commercial fishermen and, again, rumor has it that they are both renegades. The older brother, Ivan, is not a pleasant person, at least not on any occasion I had to deal with him. The other brother, Josef, isn't much better. What I hear is that he is commercial fishing and keeping a lot of the catch he nets in closed areas. We have never caught him, but the rumors persist. It might be beneficial to have me watch your back while you are down here."

"Thanks, Sean. I should be there in about fifteen minutes." Will checked his watch. It was getting late in the afternoon. Mid-May is a pleasant time in spring when everything begins to turn green and the birds return to Alaska. The world seems fresh.

CHAPTER 2

Will Trippet turned into the parking area at the Inlet View and drove to the waiting patrol car. Trooper Adams rolled down his driver side window. Will did the same.

"You can follow me, Will. The home is only a short way east on Kingsly Road."

"OK, Sean, and thanks for the help."

Adams waved, put his car in gear and drove from the parking area. As he had said, the home was on Kingsly Road less than a mile from the Sterling Highway. The house was not visible from the road due to the curving driveway. As the two cars pulled into the yard, it was easy to see that the owner cared for the place. Everything was neat with two small barn-shape buildings that Will guessed to be storage buildings. Will stopped his car and opened the door.

Adams rolled down his window. "I'll wait for you here. The boy should be the only one at home."

"Thanks again, Sean. I want to talk with the boy privately for a few minutes." With that, he climbed the steps to the porch and knocked on the door. He heard footsteps inside and a moment later, the door opened. On the other side was a tall, handsome young man. He had a dishtowel in his hand as if he had been interrupted while drying dishes.

"My name is Wilson Trippet with the Alaska State Wildlife Troopers. Is this the home of Victor Resnic?"

"Yes, it is. He's my dad." Suddenly, panic filled the boy's face. "Has something happened to my dad?" he asked.

"I would like to speak with you in private, if I may. It's about your father. Please, may I come inside?"

"Sure, come on in. What's happened to dad?" the boy asked a second time.

"Have a seat, please. I have to ask if you are his son, Vladimir?" Will was as gentle as he could be.

"Yeah, but you can call me Vlad. Everyone does."

For the next several minutes, Will told the story of the death of the boy's father. He said a bear had killed the man, but he left out the details at the site. The boy's eyes filled with tears as he heard the story.

"Can you tell me what your father was doing out there? Was he baiting bears?" Will asked.

"I guess it won't hurt to tell you about it now." He sobbed and bit his lip to control the tears. "My dad killed moose for other people and they paid him for the meat. That's how he made a living when he wasn't fishing. He brought them home and cut them up in the shed. Then he wrapped the meat and took it to whoever had ordered it. He never let me go with him. He always said he didn't want me to be involved. His brothers sometimes went along, but he never would take me."

"I know this a difficult time for you. Is there somewhere you can stay to be with someone; a family member, maybe one of your uncles?"

"Nah, I'll be OK here. Dad didn't want me to hang out with his brothers. He said they were a bad influence. He made me go to school and get good grades. He said I had to go to college and be educated properly. He said he didn't want me to grow up to be a dumb fisherman like him. I never thought he was dumb. He was the greatest dad in the world. I am 18 years old and I graduate from high school at the end of next week. I guess I will have to learn to take care of myself." This time he was unsuccessful at controlling his tears and buried his face in the dishtowel he was holding.

Just then, the front door burst open and a large man in blue jeans and a denim shirt rushed through the door. The noise startled Will and he jumped to his feet, assuming a defensive posture and reaching for the pepper spray that hung on his duty belt.

Vlad recognized the man and shouted, "Uncle Josef, stop, stop. They are here to help me."

Josef Resnic, for some unknown reason, honored Vlad's plea. He stopped inside the door. He maintained a threatening posture, but gave Vlad time to explain. "Take it easy, Uncle Josef. They just came to tell me that a bear killed Dad today. They're trying to help."

On his way into the house, Josef had jumped from his pickup truck and accosted Sean Adams. He had shoved the smaller man out of the way and kept walking. Adams had been off-balance and had fallen. Now recovered, he came into the room with his weapon drawn.

Vlad saw the gun and shouted, "Don't shoot him, Trooper. It's OK."

Josef Resnic turned to see the armed officer behind him and raised his hands. "Is it true? Was my brother killed by a bear?"

"Yes, it's true. We found him this morning on Mystery Creek Road," Will recited.

The big man's shoulders began to sag and he hung his head. "Oh, man. I'm sorry. I didn't know. I thought you were just here hassling my nephew. I'm sorry." He looked at Vlad with sad eyes. "Get your stuff, Vlad. You had better come and stay with me and Aunt Ella."

"No, I'm staying here. I've already decided on that.

"Mr. Resnic," Trooper Trippet began, "we will need to speak with the other brother, too. Where can we locate him?"

"He's not in town. He went to Seattle to help bring his fish tender back and get ready for the new fishing season. I'll call him when I get home and give him the news."

"That will be fine, but I will need your to see your identification before we leave. Vlad, here, is legally an adult and if he has decided to stay at home, then, legally, he can stay. Now, please go outside with Trooper Adams and give him your personal information. I still have a couple of items to go over with your nephew."

"OK." He turned to Sean. "Sorry I roughed you up. I just thought Vlad needed help." Sean nodded an affirmative and motioned for the big man to join him outside.

Once they were gone from the room, Will returned his attention to the young Resnic. "Now, where were we? Oh, yes. You say you will graduate from high school next week. Do you have money for food and necessities?"

"Yes," the boy answered. "I work at the Mercantile and dad always left cash in a box in the cupboard. If I need anything, I can get it from my Aunt Ella. She is really nice."

"Your other uncle, Ivan, is it true, he owns a tender?" Will asked.

"Yes, he's rich and makes a lot of money from the boat. Have you ever seen my uncle's boat? It's 228 feet, the Galaxy. Nice boat. In the summer he keeps it in Homer, but in the winter he takes it to Bellingham, Washington. They repair anything broken and keep it painted." Vlad spoke proudly of his uncle. "He always takes a load of salmon when he goes out to Bellingham. He owns a seafood distributing business there. Like I said, he is rich. He works all the time, even in the winter."

"Your father," Wilson Trippet inquired, "did he own his own fishing vessel?"

"No, he worked with my Uncle Josef. He got some kind of percentage of the catch for working on the boat."

"Do you know the name of the boat?"

"Yes, it's the Volga. The family joke is that they were the Volga Boatmen. You know, after the old movie and the song they sang. My dad had a video of the movie and sometimes we would watch it and laugh. It was a sad movie, though, but I like the song." Vlad hung his head again trying his best to hold back the tears.

"Are you sure you will be alright here alone? I could take you to town with me, if you would care to go."

"I'll be OK, Sir. I have some homework to do for school tomorrow. It just makes me sad to think about it."

"You have my card. Don't hesitate to call me any time you feel you need to talk with someone. You are a brave young man and I admire your strength. I'm not sure I could I could hold my composure as well as you are doing. Remember, call if you need anything."

"I will do that, Sir," Vlad said as the two walked to the door.

Will Trippet continued to gather information from the boy and to make notes in his notebook. After another hour, and after determining the young man was competent to stay by himself under these conditions, he closed his notebook. Will stood, found a business card with his phone number on it and, one last time, told him to call if he needed anything. Will had a genuine empathy for the boy.

Outside he met with Sean Adams. "I haven't had anything to eat all day. Want to join me for a sandwich at the Inlet View Café?"

"I'd like to eat something myself, thanks. I'll follow you there." Adams waved and climbed into his own patrol car.

There was only one other customer in the café, making it easy to find a quiet table to discuss things privately. The elderly waitress gave them each a menu, asked what they wanted to drink and went back to the counter. She found a fresh pot of coffee and filled the other customer's coffee cup before returning to take their order. They both ordered deluxe cheeseburgers. She left the table and took the order to the window for the cook.

The two men watched her go before resuming their conversation. "Did you learn anything new from the boy?" Adams asked.

Will sipped his hot coffee. "Some. He confirmed that his father was poaching for profit. Vlad claims his father had earned his living that way all winter. He must have been good at it, too. I have never seen a report of commercial poaching of moose down this way." He took another drink of the hot, tasty coffee. "Were you able to learn anything from the brother?"

"I took all his personal information, but he didn't volunteer anything. I really didn't expect him to divulge anything. Rumor has it that he is a big poacher himself. What I hear about him is that he owns a commercial drift gillnet boat and fishes Cook Inlet. They say he's not too fussy about whether or not the fishing period is open. Another rumor says he targets Chinook salmon and off-loads them on his brother's tender. Local anglers say that when the Galaxy goes south in the fall it is full of illegally caught salmon, all species, Chinook, Sockeye, Coho and Pink salmon. Ivan owns a seafood distributorship in Washington State. The locals say that is where he disposes of these illegal catches. They don't like it because when the locals take their catch to the cannery they are accountable and by taking their fish south, the Resnic brothers beat the system. I think they also beat one level of taxation. It would take a lot of money to operate this way, but it appears the Resnic brothers have it."

"I'll talk to Captain Olson, but it sounds like all of this needs to be investigated." When the waitress returned with the order, Will stopped talking and sipped more coffee. She refilled their cups and asked if they needed anything else before leaving the table.

The two men finished and Will Trippet paid the tab. They said their goodbyes and parted. Will had a lot to think about on his way back to the office.

CHAPTER 3

Trippet went to his office before quitting for the day. It took him nearly two hours to finish the reports before he went home. The following morning, Wednesday, he came into the office at 7:30—late for him. His first order of business was to review his notes and to see the captain. He wanted advice on how to proceed with the information about illegal fishing he had received while in Ninilchik. He had just finished his first cup of coffee when the captain came in, stopping at Will Trippet's desk.

"Long day yesterday, eh, Will?" he said, grinning over the top of his coffee cup.

"It sure was. My report is on your desk. There are some things I need to discuss with you. Do you have time this morning?"

"Give me a half hour to review the reports on my desk and I will call you into my office." The captain saw the sadness in the trooper's eyes. "I had a couple of phone calls late in the afternoon yesterday. They were about you." Trippet jerked up his head in surprise. "Don't get excited, it was a couple of your admirers calling to tell me how you treated the son of the bear attack victim. One of them was the boy's uncle. He said he gave you a hard time, but that you handled it well and he wanted to tell you he apologizes for his anger. The other was from Sean Adams. He also admired the way you handled the boy and how you defused the uncle. Good job, Will. Delivering a death notification is never pleasant, but you did it with great skill and compassion and defused a potentially volatile situation in the process." The captain flipped the trooper a half-hearted salute and marched to his own office.

Will was trying to organize his day when the telephone on his desk jingled.

"Will Trippet," he answered.

"Will, Sean Adams. Are you ready for the day?"

"Good morning, Sean. You're up early for having worked late last night. I didn't think you blue shirts took kindly to those long hours." Wildlife troopers were referred to in-house as brown shirts and the regular troopers as blue shirts, referring to the uniform differences.

"You guys over there are a bunch of sissies. We do this all the time." Both men laughed.

"I'm glad you called, Sean. I was thinking that it might be a good idea to stop at the school and let the administrator know about Vladimir's father. The school might just cut him a little slack. He seems like a good kid."

"Good thought, Will. I'll stop over there this morning, but the reason I called was to tell you I had a call from the other brother, Ivan. He's pretty upset about us letting the boy stay at home last night. He called from Bellingham, Washington. He said he was catching a plane home today. He told me he had originally planned to come back on the Galaxy, but changed his plan when he heard about his brother, Victor. If he comes to see you, be warned, he's a big guy. Close to six feet three and about 250 pounds. He looks like he can handle himself. I've run across him in a couple of bar fights. Luckily, I didn't have to arrest him. He has a reputation of being a tough guy on his boats."

"Thanks for the heads-up, but I don't look to have any trouble with him." Will Trippet changed the topic of conversation slightly. "I would like to talk with you about the illegal fishing down there. Is there a time we can get together for an hour—perhaps here in my office?"

"I'll be in the trooper office to see the captain tomorrow morning. I should finish my business there around 10:30. How about I meet you at your office at 11:00?"

Will's intercom line was blinking. "I have to go, but I will see you in the morning. Thanks, Sean." He hung up the line and punched the intercom button. "This is Trippet."

"Captain Olson. You wanted to meet?"

In Captain Olson's office, Will leafed through the handful of paper he had brought. Mostly notes from the night before, he searched for the page with the information he had learned from Sean Adams. "I was informed of a number of rumors regarding possible poaching by another brother of our victim. Josef Resnic, I was told, sometimes helped his brother Victor in taking moose for profit. I was also told that Josef owns a commercial gillnetter, F/V Volga." F/V is the state designator for Fishing Vessel. "Commercial fishing season is only three weeks away. I would like to investigate that rumor. Also it is rumored that his brother Ivan and his big fish tender are a cover for processing, transporting and selling the illegally caught fish." Will looked into the Captain's eyes. "All this is rumor and speculation at this point. There is no evidence any of it is true, but the opportunity and the means are there with the motive of money. What I am asking is will you allow me to conduct an investigation into these rumors. If they are true, it will amount to a major case. I think the rumors are based on enough fact to warrant an investigation."

Captain Olson sat with his thumb under his chin, thinking. "I can't give you three weeks for one investigation, but any time you can get without neglecting the daily duties as assigned you have my permission to do your investigation. Let me caution you, I do mean investigation, not witch hunt. Do you understand?"

"Yes, I understand, Captain. You know me; I always play by the rules."

"OK, Will. Keep me informed all the way. I don't like surprises. Now go to work."

"Thanks, Cap." Will gathered his papers and returned to his own desk.

While returning to his office, Will had a call on his radio that hung from his duty belt with a microphone/speaker attached to his lapel. There had been a moose hit by an automobile at Mile 76 of the Sterling Highway. These accidents were a common occurrence on the streets and roads of the Kenai Peninsula. These mishaps had slowed in recent days due to the fact the cow moose seemed to be moving away from populated areas. It was getting close to calving time and the cows usually moved into wooded areas for seclusion during this time. After the calves dropped, incidents would increase again to an alarming rate.

The Wildlife Trooper acknowledged the call, dropped his paperwork on his desk and proceeded to his truck. Dispatch had indicated there were no human injuries in the accident, but the moose was badly injured. The site of the incident was more than 20 miles from the office. He turned on the red lights and headed eastward. Pushing the speed limit a little, he arrived at the scene where he found a nearly new Ford F150 with the fender, headlight and grill all damaged. The truck was parked on the side of the highway. The moose was lying in the ditch beside it.

"Who is the driver?" he asked as he approached.

"I am," said a pretty, blonde girl. She looked to be about 25 years old.

"Is anyone hurt?" he asked.

"No, we're OK, but that poor moose is in a lot of pain. Can you do something about that?"

"Yes, I will. Please stay back by the rear of your vehicle. I'll get right back to you." He reached into his vehicle and retrieved his shotgun. He walked to the front of the wrecked Ford and stepped down the bank into the ditch. He could see the front legs of the animal were both broken and its head was badly cut. He checked to see where the two girls from the truck were standing. They were between their pick-up and his official truck. There was no traffic visible, making it safe for him to dispatch the animal. It was a sad duty, but one he had performed more than a hundred times in his career. Satisfied one shot had done the job he returned the shotgun to its rack in his vehicle. He then turned his attention to the two young ladies.

"Sorry about making you wait, but you were right. The moose needed to be put out of its misery." The girl who had been the passenger was sobbing. "Are you sure you're not hurt?" he asked again.

"No, we're fine, we just feel sorry for the moose."

"I will need to see your driver's license," Will said, "And some sort of ID from you," turning to the second young lady.

Both reached into their purses and produced Alaska operator's licenses. Will took them and called the information into dispatch. While he waited for a reply, he noted the information in his notebook. When he finished he returned the cards to their owners.

"Can you tell me what happened?" he asked the driver.

"It just happened so quickly. The moose ran up into the road and right in front of us. I tried to stop, but it was just too close and I hit it. I was afraid it was going to come through the windshield. We were scared to death."

"Is your truck drivable?"

"I think so. I backed it up to where it is now and the radiator and everything seems to be OK. The headlight is broken, though. My husband is going to kill me for wrecking his new pick-up."

"I see you were heading toward Soldotna. Is that where you live?" the trooper asked.

"Yes, we were in Anchorage for a two-day shopping trip, my sister and I."

"Do you think you will be alright to drive, if I let you go on home? Or would you rather I call someone to drive you home? I just want to be certain you are both safe."

"We will both be fine, but what will happen to the moose?" the driver asked.

"As soon as I know you two are going to be alright, I'll call for a charity to come and dress it out. Some needy people will use the meat as food. It won't go to waste. I am going to give you an accident report to fill out. You can drop it by our office in Soldotna after you complete it. Give me a couple of minutes to take some pictures and you can be on your way, but please be careful. Your truck looks safe, but if you have any reason to think otherwise I'll call and have it towed."

"Thank you, Trooper. You've been nice. I guess I was sort of panicked when I called it in."

"That's understandable under the circumstances. You're sure you're okay to drive?"

As they drove away, Trippet called dispatch to notify someone to pick up the moose. He said he would wait until they arrived. It took an hour for the recipients to get to the scene. It is required they salvage all the usable meat and take the entrails and hide away from the road. After passing on those instructions and helping with the initial opening of the cavity, Will Trippet pulled the rubber gloves off and wiped his hands with wet Handi-Wipes.

On his way back to the office, he made a stop at the Wildlife Refuge Headquarters building to see his old friend Gordon Ponset. Gordy was just exiting the office building when he arrived. He motioned to Will when he recognized his truck pulling into the lot.

"I just got a call of a brown bear at a home on the other side of the river. Want to come along and help me herd it out of the owner's yard?"

"Sure. Where is it?"

"Just outside the city limits on Keystone Drive," Ponset said.

"I'll follow you."

Ponset waved and continued on to his own vehicle. The two vehicles drove across the small town to the East Redoubt Street exit. Three miles up-river on the paved road the property owner stood alongside his car which was parked at the end of his driveway.

Ponset pulled alongside and rolled down his window. "Are you the one who called about a bear on your property?"

Will was now alongside, too.

"Kevin Thompson. Yes, I thought it would just look around and move on, but he stayed around. He tipped over my barbecue and pulled the screen off the storm door. I have had bears come here and look around, but this is the first time one tried to get into the house." He looked over his shoulder, checking to see if the bear was coming up the driveway. "He doesn't seem to want to leave my back deck. After I called you, I went out the front door and got into my car. That is when I heard a crash and I could see the bear through the living room window. He was in the house. That's when I came out here to meet you."

"I am Refuge Officer Ponset. You can call me Gordy. My friend over there is Wildlife Trooper Will Trippet. How far is it to the house from here?"

"About one hundred fifty yards. The drive has a dog-leg turn so you can't see the house from here," the homeowner said.

"Please stay here in your vehicle, Mr. Thompson. Trooper Trippet and I will see if we can get the animal out of the house. We may have to fire some shots, so please stay here at the main street."

"Don't worry, I'm curious but I don't want to get close to the bear. Once was enough."

The two official vehicles moved slowly down the driveway. The house was a large two story log structure with a separate garage. The window through which the owner had seen the bear was a large, single pane glass. There were very large paw prints on the inside of the glass, but no bear could be seen. The two officers walked side by side, cautiously, to the rear of the house. The screen was indeed off the storm door and the entry door lay broken on the floor inside. Standing close to the garage, they listened carefully. They could hear sounds coming from inside the house.

"Have you got a plan?" Trippet asked.

"Yes, I have. You go in and get the bear and bring him out."

Will laughed. "I don't like that plan," he replied.

"I didn't think you would. How about this; you go back to the front door and make some loud noises, like knock on the door or something. I'll wait back here. If this bear is bold enough to break down a door and enter, he might want to do it again. I think we are going to have to stop this one for good. Just give me a minute to put all slugs in the shotgun. I don't want to pepper his butt with bird shot."

"Good idea," Will commented. "I'll change ammo, too. Whistle when you're ready."

Trippet walked quietly to the front of the house, waiting for the signal before climbing to the front porch. When he heard the whistle, Will pounded a fist loudly on the front door. There was a loud clatter from inside. He heard movement. Carefully he peeked through the living room window. In the dining room behind the living room, he could see the head of the bear peering into the living room. He seemed curious about the noise he had heard. The head disappeared for a few seconds and reappeared as it walked into the dining room, again looking at the front door. Slowly the bear turned to make his way back to the broken door. Once on the back deck the bear stood on his hind legs, sniffing the air and looking in all directions. Will took this as his signal to rejoin Gordon Ponset to face the animal. They would not shoot until it had reached the ground. Partially hidden behind their vehicles they waited. The bear took its own sweet time getting off the deck and onto the walk. Once down on ground level, he stood up, smelling the air. When he dropped back to all-fours, both men stepped out into the open and each fired two shots. The bear dropped where he had stood.

"Go tickle his chin to see if he's dead," Will joked, allowing time for the adrenalin to wear off.

"Why do you always want me to do the hard jobs?" Ponset, too, was shaking.

"I guess we really do have to check him out. It wouldn't be right to ask the homeowner to do it. He's going to be upset as it is. The bear made a real mess of the inside of the house, especially the kitchen."

The two men approached the bear with caution. Poking a gun barrel into an open eye they were satisfied the bear was dead.

"I'll go get Thompson. I can hook a rope on the bear and pull it into the back of your truck. You can take it to your office to be skinned." Will cleared the chamber of his shotgun and returned it to the rack inside the cab. A couple of minutes later, he was back with the homeowner following. The two officers managed to pull the carcass into the back of Ponset's vehicle.

Kevin Thompson went inside the house to inspect the damage. When he came out, he was white as a sheet. "That monster tipped over the kitchen range, tore down my cabinets and emptied every cupboard in the kitchen. I don't understand why, but he didn't open the refrigerator. I guess I have to call my insurance agent. I hope this is covered."

Will and Gordy took as much information as they could get before leaving with the dead bear. Ponset took the bear to headquarters while Trippet returned to his own desk and a well-deserved Mountain Dew.

CHAPTER 4

With his notebook open on his desk, Will Trippet sipped his cold can of soda. Checking the time he was surprised to note it was only a little after noon. It had seemed to him a very long day. Checking his notebook, he began the task of writing the official reports for the two incidents he had covered this morning. An hour later he was finished and reviewing his reports while draining the last of his warm Mountain Dew. He read both reports for the third time, tossed the empty soda can in the basket used for the purpose, and stood to stretch his aching back. He was grateful for the fact no phone or radio traffic had interrupted him while he finished the paperwork. Will knew the necessity of office work but like most officers would rather have been in the field. He loved patrol. He found it a challenge to cruise the back roads and look for signs of poaching. His mental set seemed to favor the old school thought that his job was to protect the wildlife. It was his job, he often opined, to protect the animals and fish since they had no way to do it themselves.

Marcy Winston occupied the front desk in the office. She was secretary, receptionist and girl Friday. She did the filing and kept the office in an orderly condition, though an officer may come in and place a dead grouse or smelly moose head on her desk. When that happened she would protest and pretend to make a scene, but in truth, she loved the distraction.

Will stopped at her desk to deliver the reports he had just finished. Marcy was on the phone when he entered. When she finished she smiled and asked what she could do to help him. Will thought she was a very pretty girl and would have probably asked her for a date, but he made it a policy never to mix duty and dating.

"I know you're busy, but could you look these reports over and make sure I covered all points and spelled everything correctly?" asked Will politely.

"Is there anything to be filed with the court?" she asked.

"No, one is a road killed moose and the other is the bear Ponset and I shot today. The crazy thing broke down the door and went into the house. It scared the owner to death. It was a big bear. If you're interested, I'll show you the pictures later. Right now, I think I'll go out for lunch. My Cheerios are wearing thin."

"I would like to see the pictures when you have time," she said. "What happened to the hide of the bear?"

"Ponset has it at his office. They will check the bear for age and health then skin it out to salvage the hide. Like I said, he was a big bear and in prime spring shape. He was just hungry and he couldn't resist the smell of pancakes in the kitchen." Will waved as he exited the office.

Late in the afternoon, Will had a phone call from Ponset. "Hi, Will. Gordy. I just wanted to let you know we weighed the bear before we skinned it out. Actual weight is 984 pounds. The boys just finished skinning it and measuring the hide. It measures ten feet three inches by ten feet six inches. That's a green hide of course, but that is a big, and I do mean BIG, bear. The hide will shrink some as it cures, but I expect it will still square out at ten feet or more." Ponset paused a moment, then continued. "I called and talked with Ted Spraker, our retired bear biologist, concerning the bear and its measurements. He said the bear was a giant. He figures it would weigh in the neighborhood of 1200 pounds had it lived and fed on salmon all summer." Ponset paused again, reading from his notebook. "The claws measure close to five inches each. This big guy was the king of the hill."

"Too bad he was breaking and entering. He would have made some hunter a nice trophy this fall." Will was making notes in his own notebook. "Thanks for the information. I'll add it to the report. See you later."

It was getting late in the day and Will felt the need to go to the gym for a good workout. He dropped the addendum to his morning bear report on Marcy's desk and told her he was done for the day.

Early the following morning Trippet drove to three boat ramps regularly used by Kenai River guides to launch their boats. Most used twenty foot, semi-vee hull boats with fifty horsepower outboard motors. These boats are wide and stable. They easily handle the guide and four or five clients with all their fishing gear. The river is low this time of year with unusually clear water running in the glacier-fed stream. Because of the low water, most guides were launching at a state ramp called The Pillars, halfway between Soldotna and Kenai, a nice facility with ample parking and metal floating docks. There were four boat trailers in the parking lot and two boats at the launching ramp. Several clients were at the restroom to get rid of the morning coffee and the beer from the night before. Will parked and walked to the ramp to speak with the waiting guide. Will recognized him as a regular and one of the old-time guides.

"How is it going this morning, Danny?" Will said as he approached.

Danny the guide had been watching the other boat prepare to launch and was surprised at the voice behind him. He turned quickly and recognized the officer. "Oh. Hi there, Will. You're out and about early this morning."

"I'm on my way to the office and stopped to see if you guys are catching any fish yet this year."

"I only had one hit yesterday, but the day before I had four clients and we landed two fish. One was about 35 pounds and the other 42. Not bad for this early in the year."

"Are there many guides fishing?"

"Nah, the water is too low for most of them. Props cost more than they can make by fishing," Danny chuckled. "How are things with 'fish and feathers'?" he asked.

"Pretty slow right now, but with cows getting ready to drop calves and the bears coming to the river, things are about to pick up. In fact, we had a bear break down a door and enter a house in Soldotna yesterday. We shot the bear. Too bad, it was a nice bear. It measured a solid ten feet."

"That is a nice bear. Oh, gotta go." Danny climbed into the driver's seat of his truck to back the boat down the ramp. His clients were already standing on the metal floating dock.

Back in the office, he finished his morning paperwork and poured a cup of hot coffee. He was sitting at his desk pondering the problem of how to make a case against the Resnic brothers when Sean Adams came in. He had stopped at the coffee pot and poured himself a fresh cup. He looked tired.

"Good morning, Will," he announced. "Is this all you have to do is sit here and look out the window?"

"Mornin', Sean. You look terrible. Have you been up all night?"

"Nah, but you know how I hate to come into the office and face the boss. It seems he never likes my reports. It wasn't too bad today. I didn't have many reports to turn in. I told him I had been busy, but didn't write any reports about it. He didn't seem to think that was humorous." He sipped on his cup. "How is your day?"

"Just dandy. I checked out a couple of launch sites this morning. Not many fish being caught, but the river is low and most of the guides are staying away to save props and skigs on the motors. Did you bring me anything on the Resnics?"

"Like I told you before, everything I know is hearsay. It will be up to you to prove any of it. Ivan has been in town a few days. Has he contacted you?"

"No. I have been expecting a call, but so far, he is avoiding me. What do you hear about the Galaxy? Is it back in Homer yet?"

"No, but the harbormaster told me it was due in tomorrow. They called to be sure the berth was ready." He finished his coffee and tossed the cup in the trash. "Speaking of Resnics, Vladimir will graduate this week, Wednesday night at 7:00. Do you want to come down and watch? I have to attend because my oldest is graduating, too. Why don't you come down and have dinner with us and we can all go to the ceremony together?"

"I would like that," Will said as he made a note on his calendar. "Thanks for the invite."

"I have been checking around and found out that Josef Resnic is looking for a new crewman. He will be short-handed since his brother was killed. Several locals have applied, but Josef turned them down. I think he is looking for someone he can trust to work with him in his illegal endeavors, someone who will keep his mouth shut. I think Ivan will have something to say about who Josef hires." Sean was all business now without the usual flippant remarks.

"I am trying to come up with a plan to catch him, but it's tough. He will be out in the inlet all season, sometimes fishing at night. It will be difficult to catch him in the act. We will ask the fishery patrols to fly around and look specifically for the Volga fishing a closed area or with illegal gear. The pilots are looking for those things anyway, but I will ask them to pay special attention to his activity. What about the Galaxy? Will they have to put gear and provisions on board while in port in Homer?"

"I doubt it. They always do all that before leaving Washington. Some of the crewmembers will have to board, though. They have a big crew. It seems like they use the same crew every year, so they must make pretty good money. Fishermen are loyal to their wallets, as a rule."

"I appreciate all the information, Sean." Will had been looking for more specific information to use in his plan, but right now, it apparently wasn't available. "I guess all we can do now is wait and hope they make a mistake."

Sean stood to leave the office. "I know I wasn't much help, but the fishing community is a tight group and most of them are my friends. Perhaps there will be more information by the time the season opens." With that, he waved, said, "See ya," and left the office.

Will continued to sit at his desk and ponder the problem. He was no closer to a plan now than he had been before Sean came in.

>>>>>>>

Ivan Resnic is a huge barrel-chested man with weathered features. His father had used him as a deckhand, and as a boy, he had worked hard and learned the fishing trade. In those days, they fished Bristol Bay and his father had made a lot of money that he and his wife, Ivan's mother, managed to drink up. They had both died young and both from complications of their drinking habits. Ivan began to drink with his father, but learned from the deaths of his parents. He seldom drank now, and then only moderately. His brother Josef, on the other hand, drank hard and worked hard. Ivan was sure his health would suffer before long, but never mentioned it to his brother.

Ivan was at home in Homer when the doorbell rang. It was Josef.

"Come in, Josef," Ivan said when he saw his visitor. "I've been waiting for you."

"Good to see you home, Ivan. How was your winter in Washington? Made some money, I hope." Josef had not seen his brother all winter but had talked with him regularly by telephone.

"I have fresh coffee in the kitchen, come on back." Josef followed him to the kitchen after kicking off his shoes at the door, which is an Alaska thing.

Ivan poured two cups and sat at the kitchen table. "Have you heard anything more about how Victor died?" he asked in a sad voice.

"Nothing more than you already know. It was a tragic thing, two bears attacking a guy the same day. That just isn't something you see every day. Victor was cautious when he was out there, but still, the bear got him. I have been trying to keep an eye on Vlad, but he's stubborn. He's just like Victor. I offered him his father's job on the boat, but he turned me down. He said he didn't want to be a fisherman and that his dad had wanted him to go to college. I guess I can help him a little with that. The kid graduates on Wednesday. Will you be going to Ninilchik to the graduation ceremony?"

"I plan to be there. I got an announcement in the mail." Ivan smiled slightly, "You have to admire the kid's grit. The three of us have done some things we wouldn't want to see printed in the newspaper, but Victor kept Vlad out of all that. I think you're right, the two of us should help him with his college." Ivan finished his coffee and retrieved the pot to refill the cups.

"I don't seem to be having much luck finding the right person to work for me this summer," Josef announced to his brother. "There are a lot of fishermen looking for work, but I can't trust most of them to keep their mouth shut. I am beginning to worry. There isn't much time left to prepare for the season."

"I think I may have someone for you. Do you remember Larry Hanson?"

- -

"Sure, he used to work for you. I thought he was in jail for robbing a quick stop. He took a shot at a trooper, as I recall."

"That's him. He called me a couple of days ago. He is out of jail and looking for a job." Ivan knew Larry Hanson had the special qualifications his brother was looking for in a deckhand.

"How soon can I put him to work?" Josef asked.

"He was in Fairbanks when he was released from jail. He said he could be here by this weekend. I haven't seen him in three years, for obvious reasons, but he was a good hand and is willing to do anything if the pay is right. On top of that, he's dependable. Ne never missed a day when he worked for me. I think he is just what you are looking for." Once again, Ivan nearly smiled.

"Have him call me when he gets to town. Let me know what time you will be in Ninilchik for the graduation, and Ella and I will meet you." Josef stood and walked to the front door. He slipped on his shoes and said good-bye to his brother. It had been a worthwhile trip to see him.

- -

CHAPTER 5

Wednesday was graduation day for the seniors of Ninilchik High School. Will Trippet had driven his private vehicle to the home of Sean Adams in the early afternoon. He was treated to a light meal of barbequed salmon, coleslaw and baked beans. The meal was delicious. While Sean's wife cleaned up the dinner table, Will and Sean sat on the back porch drinking an excellent glass of iced tea. Sean's two children were in the living room playing video games and talking about the graduation dance to be held after the official ceremony. Sean's son, Randy, was also graduating that night.

"Have you talked to Vlad Resnic since you were here?" Sean asked Will.

"No, but I plan to see him and congratulate him tonight at the ceremony," Will replied. "The school principal called me and told me he would recommend Vlad for a scholarship if I would write him a letter of recommendation. It's a special scholarship for children with no parents, provided by a government grant. I wrote the letter and e-mailed it to him. It looks like Vlad can get a full scholarship if he is willing to go to the University of Alaska at Fairbanks. It would get him a criminal justice degree without costing him much. As I understand it, he would have to pay for his room and food. Everything else would be paid by the grant.

"Wow!" Have you told him about it?"

"No. The principal said he would get confirmation and the two of us can tell him tonight after graduation."

"If he's interested in college, it will be a great opportunity for him." Sean secretly wished his own son could get such a helping hand with his education. He knew it was going to take everything his boy could earn as well as everything Sean could provide.

"What time do we have to be at the auditorium?" Will inquired.

"The program starts at 7:00, but I have to deliver Stan to the school before 6:00. He has to get his cap and gown on and be inspected by everyone. Our school isn't very large, but we do things in a proper manner," Sean said while laughing.

"I'll ride with you, if you don't mind. It will save a parking space at the school. I need to meet with Principal Penbrook anyway."

Will Trippet felt good about the offer of a scholarship. Penbrook had said he felt sorry for Vlad. The boy was a good student and the locals knew he never indulged in his father's poaching activities. Will was aware that, in fairness to Victor Resnic, he had never allowed his son to be involved in any illegal activities. It appeared he was adamant about it, in fact.

Will rode in the front seat of the mini-van while Sylvia and the children piled into the backseat. Stan and Stella, Sean's children, were both excited about the dance. Sean and Sylvia would chaperone. Sean had already warned his wife to be discreet and to allow the kids some latitude. It was something her Pennsylvania Dutch background would not easily allow.

As the small group found seats close to the stage, Will noted that Josef Resnic was in the audience. He appeared to be carrying on a conversation with a large man seated next to him.

Will elbowed Sean, "Who is it Josef Resnic is talking with?"

Sean looked until he spotted Josef Resnic. "You might want to be on guard later. That's Ivan Resnic. Like I said before, he is a large man with a reputation of being mean. I doubt he will be violent with all these people around, but you can never tell. Maybe the two of us should stay close together tonight."

"You could be right, but I seem to remember Josef said his own son was to graduate tonight along with Vlad. I doubt either of them will do anything here."

Ivan Resnic was speaking to his brother. "I brought Larry Hanson with me. He is waiting over at the Inlet View Bar. I told him we would meet him there after your son's graduation. I want you to check him out tonight and let me know if he will do the job for you. I already told him there was to be no drugs on the boat. He didn't drink much when he worked for me, but that was a few years ago. You will have to decide if you can work with him. Like

I said before, he did a good job for me and he keeps his mouth shut about what goes on."

"I'll talk to him and get a feel for his personality. If he is all you say, he can start tomorrow. I have to get the boat ready and I need the help." Josef looked up to the stage as the students began to assemble. "Have you told him what I am willing to pay?" he asked his brother.

"No, you can take that up with him. After all, he will be working for you."

>>>>>>>

The faculty filed in and took seats on stage, along with a bearded sea-captain-looking man who was wearing a Greek fisherman's hat.

"The guy with the hat is our local state senator. He is giving the address to the students this evening," Sean informed his friend, though Will had already recognized the man.

The class was impressive in their dark green robes and caps. They filed in and took the stage in a predetermined order. Vlad was in the last row while Stan Adams stood in the front row. Will guessed this was due to the order in which they would receive their diplomas—alphabetically.

When everyone was in place, the lights dimmed and from somewhere in the hall outside the auditorium, the school band began to play the school song. When they finished, Mr. Penbrook stood and walked to the podium where he made only a few short remarks and introduced Senator Seaton of Homer.

Senator Seaton was a handsome and articulate man. A commercial fisherman by trade, he looked the part even when on the floor of the senate chamber. His address to the audience and the graduating class lasted almost an hour. It was a poignant and moving speech intended to be remembered by each graduate. Once the Senator sat down, Mr. Penbrook once again took the stage and thanked everyone for attending. With the formalities out of the way, he began to hand out the graduation certificates and shake the hand of each student. Stanley Aaron Adams was student number four to receive his diploma from the principal, beaming and proud, as he should have been.

Sean Adams could not hold back his pride as his son took his diploma. The boy was grinning broadly while his father clapped his hands together and whistled loudly. Silvia Adams was embarrassed by her husband's outburst and elbowed him in the ribs.

The line passed quickly and when they had returned to their original places, the band once more played a lively and loud song. When it ended, the students moved the tassels to the opposite side of their caps. Mr. Penbrook said, "Congratulations, students." Then, all caps were sent flying into the air. The auditorium became extremely noisy as everyone in the room began to talk at once. Sean and his family made their way to the stage to hug their son. Will went with them but at the stage, he climbed the stairs to shake hands with Vladimir Resnic. He congratulated the boy and led him to where Mr. Penbrook was standing. The noise in the room made it difficult to be heard, but the school principal informed the new graduate of the scholarship available to him. Vlad seemed overwhelmed and kept asking, "Is it true? A scholarship? For me?"

"Your uncles are here, Vlad, and they will want to see you. I'll come to Ninilchik in a couple of days and we can talk about your future. Have some fun at the dance tonight. Always remember this night. It is a time to remember and a time for which you can be proud." Will saw the two uncles coming up on the stage and chose that moment to depart. They had seen him, but to their credit chose not to make a scene.

Sean, Sylvia and Will walked outside for some fresh air. The majority of the students in the graduating class did the same. In front of the school, they gathered in small groups and laughed and talked. To the world, they were graduates and adults, but they were still schoolchildren in their own eyes. Individuals moved from one small group to another, saying congratulations and promising to stay in touch for the rest of their lives. The excited gathering began to break up and boys looked for their dance dates. Everyone in the graduating class was dressed for the dance. Boys retrieved the flowers they had left with their parents and pinned them on their dates. It was a joyous time filled with anticipation and hope.

The appointed chaperones made their way to the gym where the dance was to take place. Sean had seen a couple of bottles being passed around the in the parking lot but decided to ignore it for now. There was plenty of time for the students to be sober and responsible as the dance progressed. Inside, they listened to the band warming up and then found seats near the exit where they could keep an eye on the attendees. Will planned to stay until the dance was over before returning to Soldotna. Watching the kids reminded him of his own graduation night, and he smiled at his own memories.

The Resnic brothers had found their pickup and driven the short quarter mile to the Inlet View Bar and Restaurant where they found Larry Hanson. He was seated at a corner table in the bar drinking a cup of coffee and waved to Ivan Resnic as the two brothers entered. Ivan went directly to the table while Josef stopped at the bar and ordered a beer for himself and a double vodka martini for his brother. He set the drinks on the table and shook hands with Hanson.

Hanson was pale, though his handshake was strong. He looked to be about five feet ten or eleven with stringy, blond hair. His jacket was on the back of his chair, leaving his arms uncovered by his Salty Dawg tee shirt. Two new jailhouse tattoos adorned his upper arms. He didn't speak, only nodded in recognition when the two Resnic brothers sat.

"You remember my brother Josef, don't you, Larry?" Ivan asked in a pleasant voice.

"Sure, but it's been a long time. Good to see you again, Josef." Hanson's voice had a harsh, gravely tone to it.

"Good to see you again, Larry. Ivan tells me you are looking for work." Josef paused and sipped his mug of beer. "I'm looking for a deckhand and Ivan recommended you. If you want the job, we can talk terms." Josef took another sip.

"Yes," Larry began, "I am looking for work. I used to work for Ivan and he treated me good. I think we might work it out. Is this is the same kind of operation Ivan had a couple of years ago?"

"It might be. Do you have a problem with it?"

"No, I just wanted to know what I might be doing. I'm good with it."

Josef looked squarely into Larry's eyes before speaking. "Ivan says you keep your mouth shut and work hard. If that is the case, I can use you. I don't come to the beach every night. I sometimes fish at night. And sometimes it's a long run to the tender to unload our catch. I'll pay 15% of the fish tickets to you. That's a lot of money, but you will have to earn it. I want to put provisions on board by tomorrow afternoon. You can fuel the boat and clean it tomorrow. There will be a lot of work to do in the next three days. Are you interested?"

"It sounds good to me. I will have to have some time tomorrow to find a place to live. I don't have much gear, but I need a place on shore to keep my stuff and live when we are on the beach."

"Well, I guess you have a job. I have a small cabin on my property. If you want it, I will throw it in on the deal. There will be one other thing," Josef said sternly. "No drinking on the boat. It's too dangerous. And no drugs on the boat or at the cabin. I don't want to draw any attention to our operation. Drugs always draw attention. People you buy from and people you sell to will talk to avoid being arrested. I don't need that headache." Josef sipped the last of his beer and watched Larry's face. "Are we clear on that point?"

Larry looked into his coffee cup for a moment before answering. "I went away for three years for dealing drugs. I'm done with that. I haven't done anything since I went to jail. The dope nearly killed me and I will never go to jail again for any reason. You don't have to worry about me."

"Ivan, would you drive him to the house. I have to get the family from the school. Show him the cabin. I'll be there later to help you get squared away. I should be home in about an hour."

Josef said his good byes and walked to the school where his own truck was parked. Ella was sitting in the cab listening to the FM radio when he opened the door.

"Let's just sit here and wait for the dance to end," she said.

They sat, holding hands, until the music in the gym stopped and the graduates were leaving for the night. Josef hoped his son would go to college, but they had never spoken about it.

CHAPTER 6

Three days later Josef Resnic and Larry Hanson were driving to the Homer boat harbor where the Volga was moored. The back of the pickup driven by Josef was filled with fresh meat and vegetables. They had food and provisions for a least a month. It took most of the morning to carry and stow the goods on the large fishing boat. Traditionally, a drift gillnet boat is 32 feet in length. Though other drift fishermen laughed at Josef for building a "super boat," inwardly they envied the extra room it provided. It was, without a doubt, the most comfortable boat in the fleet. It was also better riding in the choppy Cook Inlet waters where the shorter and lighter boats were pounded hard by the waves and forced to slow their speed when the waves began to build. This boat had proved its merit in 20-foot seas and 40-miles-per-hour winds. It had been expensive, but it was safe and allowed him to fish when others were finding a safe anchorage to wait out storms. All this utility was wrapped in one of the most beautiful hulls on the water.

The engine was warming up and the gear had been stowed when Larry Hanson entered the cabin. "Everything looks ready to sail except the gillnet reel. The axels aren't tight and the hydraulic lines haven't been hooked up. Do you want me to start on that job?"

"No," Josef answered. "We're going out to the Galaxy to do some work. Before we go out, I guess I should tell you how this will work. You must have had some idea about how we operate when you signed on. You are about to lean how we do it. If you have any doubts about the job, leave the boat now." He looked at Hanson with stern, hard eyes. "Are you in or out?"

Hanson met the steely glare with a broad grin and a certain amount of excitement. "I guess you are finally going to tell me what we are doing out here, though I think I have guessed most of it. And I like it."

"OK, here's how it goes. We go out to the Galaxy and pull off the gillnet reel. We replace it with a smaller reel for pulling halibut gear. You and I go out behind Chisik Island and fish halibut for a few days. That gives us a chance to shake down the boat and get used to fishing together. We stay out there until the fish-hold is full. Then, we go back to the Galaxy and unload the halibut. We fillet all the fish and pack them in ice. Ivan takes the fillets aboard the Galaxy and freezes them. He keeps them on his boat until the end of August when he sails back to Seattle. During salmon season, we fish legally in closed waters, mostly at night. The legal catch is sold to the cannery in Homer or Kenai. The other is held on the Galaxy until Ivan returns to Seattle. We have a wholesale fish company in Washington and we sell all that fish through that company. We have been successful with this method for a long time. Your take is the same for both kinds of fish sale; however, you will have to wait longer to be paid for the fish we take to Washington. "

As Josef finished explaining, his icy stare was back. "Are you still in?"

"So, that's how you do it," Larry chuckled. "I like it. If it's as good as it sounds, you can count me in for next year, too."

"Glad to hear it. Be prepared for a lot of hard work, but you can also count on a good payday at the end." Josef made a short walk around the deck surveying everything in sight. "OK, cast off. Ivan moved the Galaxy to the other side of the inlet and we have to meet him over there. We will change reels and load ice when we get there. Welcome aboard, Larry. Let's get to work."

Josef maneuvered the Volga away from the mooring and slowly idled toward the opening from the harbor. The sea was nearly flat in Kachemak Bay and the forecast was for ten-knot winds and two-foot seas in the inlet. Once outside the harbor, Josef pushed the throttles ahead slightly. There was no real hurry to get there. Josef loved the sound of the twin Caterpillar diesel engines below his feet. All the gauges were reading normal. Larry had completed his chores on deck and entered the cabin.

"I have only been on the water for ten minutes and already I love this boat," Larry commented, a wide grin pasted to his fact.

Josef slipped from the captain's seat, holding the wheel in his left hand. "Climb into the seat and get used to the Volga. If you like her now, you'll want to marry her when we get to the other side.

Larry climbed into the seat vacated by the captain of the boat. He scanned the gauges to make sure everything was in the green or normal operating area. "She sure sounds nice."

"Kick her up a little if you like." Josef wanted his new deck hand to get used to the big boat. "Once we get out past the buoy and clear of local boat traffic, you can kick her up a little more and make some turns to see how she handles. I think you'll be pleasantly surprised."

For the next hour, Larry Hanson enjoyed himself at the helm of the Volga. Josef had been right—the boat was impressive in every respect. It also had some impressive equipment. One nice addition was the bow thrusters. These allowed for precise maneuvering at the dock and, Larry reasoned, made it easy to hold next to the big fish tender they would be using.

They were passing St. Augustine Island when Josef put the coffee on the stove. He fried up some hamburgers and served potato salad from the fridge. "I hope you like my cooking. And I hope I learn to like yours." He handed Larry a plastic plate filled with a huge lunch. "Here, I'll show you how to set the autopilot." After Larry took the plate, Josef punched a few buttons on the GPS display and the boat began to hold a pre-set course by electronic means. "Black magic," Josef said to his deck hand, grinning. It pleased him to be able to show off the gadgets on the Volga.

During lunch, the boat continued toward Ursus Cove where the Galaxy was anchored and waiting. Josef called the Galaxy on the marine radio to let them know they were approaching and wanting to tie up alongside. They were given permission. Josef let Larry make the tie-up. He needed to get used to the boat and especially the thrusters, which were a new thing for him. All went smoothly and, by the time the lines were secured, Ivan was leaning on the rail above them.

"Come on aboard, Josef, and bring your crew."

Josef nodded and waved a reply. Minutes later, the two were in the wheelhouse of the Galaxy being met by Ivan.

"How is the new boss?" Ivan asked as he shook hands with Larry.

"We're getting along fine, and I love his boat."

Ivan turned to Josef. "I have your gear on deck ready to install. Two of my men can help. You will need the small davit to lift the equipment and position it for you to bolt it in. We've been here three days and haven't seen another boat, so there shouldn't be any unwanted eyes watching us. We did the job in two hours last year and it should be easier this year."

"There's no hurry. We have enough daylight to get the job finished. I think we will stay tied up here until late this afternoon and pull out just before dark. I want to run up to Tuxedni Bay and lay out my first set. We will need a little time for Larry to get used to the equipment."

Installing the specialized equipment was no small task. First, a special reel loaded with halibut long-line gear was installed and attached to the hydraulics of the gillnet reel. This reel was much smaller than the one used for nets. Then, a fancy roof was fitted over the reel. It really wasn't a roof at all—it was a ramp. When the pins were removed, the ramp allowed the reel to pull the fish on the weighted long-line up and over the transom of the boat. Hooks were removed and the fish slid into the fish hold. They were taken out the next morning and filleted, packed in iced plastic totes and, when they were full, delivered back to the Galaxy to be re-packed and flash frozen.

Larry thought this was an overly elaborate system for catching a few illegal halibut, but he changed his mind after the first night of fishing. By morning, the two men had caught and filleted more than 200 halibut, yielding an estimated 3,000 pounds of fillets. The sun was up and Larry slept while Josef pilots the Volga back to Ursus Cover to be unloaded. Once the cargo had been transferred, the two men went below for a well-deserved rest. The process would be repeated that night and for several nights to follow. Results improved as Larry became more proficient with the process.

The end of May was nearing and the nightly catch of halibut was getting less each night. Josef wanted to change to gillnet gear and return to Homer for fuel and fresh provisions. He was pleased with the performance of his new deckhand. He worked hard and learned quickly. His experience at sea on fishing vessels was evident. The last night he told Larry his plan to go to port.

"I like the way you work, Larry, but I have to know. Are you going to have a dope or drinking problem when we get to Homer?"

"Nah, I'm over all that. Three years in the slammer took that all out of me. I just want to buy some fresh duds and rest up for salmon season. I could use a few dollars, though, so I can buy myself some clothes."

"That's why I asked. I want to advance you some cash when we get to Homer, but I don't want to have to send a search party to find you when we go out again. I don't have a problem if you want to have a few beers, but I can't have you going off on a three-day runner. Understand?"

"Yeah, I understand. A few years ago, that might have been a problem, but not anymore. I'll go back to your place and stay in the cabin tonight. Tomorrow I'll catch a ride to Soldotna and do some shopping for personals."

"I guess I can trust you to do that." Josef was quiet for a moment and then asked, "Do you have a current driver's license, Larry?"

"Yeah, that's the first thing I did when I got out."

"There is an old pickup at the house. You can use that to get around for the few days we will be on the beach. The insurance is in my name and I don't want the rates to go up, so try not to have any mishaps, OK?"

"Thanks, Cap'n. I appreciate it. I won't let you down. If there is anything you want from town when I go just let me know and I'll get it for you." Larry was beginning to like his new boss; the man had heart.

CHAPTER 7

For several days, Will Trippet was busy with routine assignments, mostly paperwork and hours of computer entries. The river level was still very low and few guides were fishing. Each day the numbers climbed a little, but the catch ratio was declining. The fish had not hit the river in appreciable numbers. Sports fishermen were doing well south of the Ninilchik River, but the run had not yet reached the Kenai River. Some said the river was too low, while others said the water was too cold. Fish and Game biologists were using test nets to judge the numbers of Chinooks entering the river, but their catch numbers were also very low. All this made it less imperative for Will to be on the river checking licenses and catch numbers.

Trippet leaned back in his office chair, stretching his back and relieving kinks. He was bored and needed a break from this routine. Checking his wristwatch, he noted the time was nearly noon. He lifted the receiver from its cradle and dialed Gordon Ponset.

"Ranger Ponset speaking. How may I help you?"

"Gordy, Will Trippet. You could help by buying my lunch."

"You sweet talking devil! Where have you been keeping yourself? I haven't heard from you since the brown bear roundup. I thought you had been fired or something."

"Thanks for your concern, Gordy." Will knew that every conversation with Ponset started this way. "I came across something you might be interested in. I have been on desk duty most of the past two weeks. A couple of days ago, I came across a file from 1972. I opened it to see why it was still in the file cabinet and it turned out to be a case file on a bear attack in September of '72. A man and his wife were camping up Funny River when they were attacked, before dawn, by a huge brown bear. The guy was a Fish and Wildlife Protection Officer. Have you ever heard about this case?"

"I think I have. What was the officer's name?" Ponset asked.

"Uh, his name was Al Thompson. Does that ring a bell with you?"

"Yeah, it sure does. If you bring the file for me to read, I'll buy lunch. People around here still talk about this one. See you at Froso's in twenty minutes." Gordy sounded excited.

"Good, I'll bring the file. You bring your wallet." With that, Will began to tidy his desk before leaving the office. A few minutes later, he was waiting outside the restaurant in his truck. He used the few minutes to give the file a quick perusal. He made a mental note to locate Officer Thompson and get the story firsthand.

When Gordy arrived, the two men went inside and found a booth near the front windows. Both men ordered iced tea with lemon. The waitress came with their drinks, but the two men had been talking and not reading the menu. Consequently, they were not ready to order. She stood patiently while they made up their minds. Finally, Will ordered the lasagna and garlic toast, and Gordy ordered a BLT with fried. She thanked them and left the table.

"Can I see the file?" Ponset asked.

Will handed it to him and said, "I don't want you to get so excited you forget to pay for lunch."

"It will be worth it if you will let me make a copy of the file." Ponset was looking through the forms and cover pages looking for the narrative statement. He found it and closed the file.

"You have heard me speak about a retired biologist by the name of Ted Spraker?" Gordy asked.

"Yes, I remember the name," Will commented.

"He and Al Thompson were friends in those days. I think he would like to see this."

"Come by my office after lunch and I will make you a copy. If you are this happy about the official report, then I suppose you mail soil your shorts when you hear I have a statement made by Joyce Thompson, the officer's wife. She was with him during the attack." Will noted the surprised look on his old friend's face. Gordy's jaw had actually dropped and his mouth was agape. "By the look on your face, I would guess you want to see that, too." Will was chuckling now.

Ponset regained his composure before remarking, "Would it be too much to ask you to get your lunch to go?" Now he was chuckling with Will. "Of course, I want to see that rep-ort, but don't expect to get another free meal out of the deal."

After finishing their lunch, the two men drove to Will's office where he made a copy of the file and another of the separate statement by Joyce Thompson.

Ponset hurried back to his own office to read the files. He scanned the original case file and read the victim's statement before turning to the additional statement written by the victim's wife. Once he started reading, Ponset couldn't put it down.

WILDERNESS NIGHTMARE
As witnessed by Joyce Thompson

My story is a true one of our experience when my husband and I backpacked 15 miles into Alaska's wilderness to hunt trophy moose with a bow. The beautiful trip turned into a nightmare and a fight for our lives when a brown bear attacked us in our sleeping bags three hours before dawn.

It was September of 1972 that we planned our backpacking trip into the Kenai National Moose Range on the Kenai Peninsula, an area mostly closed to aircraft or track vehicles. We planned to catch last ten days of moose season, which closed the end of September. Arrangements were made for horses to pack out a moose in the event we were successful in getting one. Al was going to hunt with a bow; but if time ran out and he had not gotten one, I would shoot one with my rifle, as we only wanted to take one moose.

The night before leaving, we gathered our gear together in one spot, double-checking to see if we had missed anything and eliminating any items we could get along without. Al was taking his 65# bow and glass arrows tipped with razor sharp black diamond delta heads. He would carry his 44 mag. revolver, and I would take my 30.06 rifle. We finished by stuffing our gear into two very full packs.

The next morning, we had a friend drop us off at a horse trail where we could start our hike so our truck would not be parked along the road for 10 days. We adjusted our packs and started down the trail. It was a beautiful day, warm and sunny. The leaves were golden and the smell of fall was in the air. I recalled the previous year about this same time in September when I had dropped Al and our friend Dick off at this same trail. It was the same kind of day. As I had watched them walk out of sight, I had fought back the desire to call out, "Wait for me! I'm coming, too." Fighting back my disappointment at being left behind, I had driven home. Now, I was following down the trail, happy and feeling like a million dollars.

It took 8 ½ hours of steady hiking to reach the area where we wanted to camp. Every muscle in my body ached and my feet were sore. As it was almost dark, we made a hurried camp, fixed something to eat and turned in for the night. The next day we developed our camp into a very comfortable one. We built a lean-to out of logs and plastic, placing boughs on the ground for a mattress and covering them with plastic flooring. The front of the lean-to had a plastic flap to close out the cold night air. Al built a makeshift table from a piece of wood we found. We gathered an abundant supply of firewood and picked up paper and pieces of litter left behind by prior campers.

That evening we went for a walk. The cold frosty nights had brought about the start of the "rut" season for the moose. I spotted a cow. We sat quietly watching her, concealing ourselves in the thick brush. She turned her head watching behind her, as we heard a bull grunt. His antlers measured about 50". I waited for Al to bring up his bow, but he passed up the shot, confident of finding a larger bull. We heard another bull that turned out to be smaller, so we headed back to camp.

Our third day started at daybreak. Al, being the first to get up, built a small fire and made coffee for me, and tea for himself. We packed a lunch of jerky, raisins, juice and candy bars, and stuffed them in a daypack and headed out.

We had not been walking very long when we heard a bull grunt in the distance. By walking slowly and quietly, we were able to get close enough to see two bulls. Their antlers were at least 60". The bulls called their challenge to each other. Al was unable to get close enough to either one of them for a good shot with his bow, and we did not see them again that day.

How exciting it was to watch a ritual that goes on every year when the fall air is crisp and the leaves turn golden. During the summer and early fall, the bulls in mountain areas are usually above timberline while the cows and their calves prefer the dense cover at the lower elevations. As the "rut" season approaches in late September, the bulls start moving down. Several times as we walked, we noticed a pungent odor. The source was an area about 20-30 inches in diameter where a bull had pawed the area clear and filled it with urine. This would be the area to which he would return from time to time hoping to find some feminine company.

We noted there appeared to be plenty of browse in the area. The small trees where moose fed heavily were stunted, misshapen and very bushy—not at all like the beautiful trees they should have been. However, at the same time, when a moose nips off a branch, the following year several branches replace it, making more food for the moose. By mid-day, we had reached the farthest point Al wanted to go. We sat on a sunny slope, ate our lunch and rested before starting back to camp.

We walked about eight miles. The day had been sunny and warm, but the warmth disappeared with the setting sun. After eating our evening meal and cleaning up the camp, we sat by the campfire talking and enjoying that magic quality a campfire has. The setting sun was replaced with a full moon, which bathed our camp in moonlight. The campfire glowed and the crackling of the fire was the only sound on this still evening. I placed more logs on the fire, put on a pair of long underwear and crawled into my sleeping bag.

Before crawling into his bag, Al located matches and a light, and placed his .44 magnum revolver on a piece of yellow paper towel for easier spotting and laid my 30.06 rifle by his side with the safety off and a shell in the chamber. Unlike me, he left his sleeping bag partially unzipped for quick access to a weapon. The combination of a warm sleeping bag, a tired body and the crackling of the fire soon had me drifting off to sleep.

I was awakened about 4:00 a.m. by Al's whispering in my ear. He had sensed something and whispered to me not to move as something might be out there in camp. I listened, straining to hear a sound that might locate an animal. As I kept watching into the moonlight, I saw the silhouette of a brown bear move along side of me. Al did not see the bear from his position. The animal was only inches from me, with just the plastic between us and didn't make a sound. It seemed to be moving away, when all of a sudden the bear was on top of me. He had plunged through the top of the lean-to with a bellowing roar. This was Al's first sight of the bear. He grabbed the rifle; but with the impact of the bear, the rifle flew from his grip. For a fraction of a second, the bear appeared confused as the logs broke and the plastic tore, and he stood on his hind legs, towering over us. His head was huge and round and he appeared to be the color of gray driftwood in the moonlight. He came back down onto us, trying to tear me out of my bag. A scream passed from my lips, which was never heard above the noise of the raging animal. I knew it would be a sudden death, with his strong claws ripping through my flesh; or perhaps those powerful paws would break my neck first. I could see no way of coming out of this alive and was sure I was going to die.

There was no time for Al to locate the .44 revolver. He knew the only way to save me was to distract the bear immediately. He also reasoned that if he would turn his head in search of the revolver, the bear might instinctively go for his neck, thus killing both of us. Al grabbed the bear's head with his left hand and slugged him with his right. The bear grabbed Al's left forearm in his jaws and, by standing up, pulled Al out of his sleeping bag, tossing him through the air. Al landed at the foot of the lean-to. Like a flash, the animal was over him. The claws ripped through Al's right side, almost penetrating a lung, and pinned Al to his chest. His teeth raked along Al's skull and managed to grip the scalp with his teeth. The bear ran on three legs with Al pinned to his chest. He stood straight up, shaking his head violently as a cat with a mouse. Al's feet never touched the ground. After running a distance of approximately 25 yards, a large portion of scalp tore loose from Al's head, causing the bear to momentarily lose his grip.

Realizing that the heavy weight of the animal and the horrible noise were gone, I rose up. Al's sleeping bag was lying beside mine empty. I had not seen Al's struggle with the beast because my head was covered, and I was baffled as to where he and the bear had gone.

I stood up in my sleeping bag, pulled the bag down and stepped out of it. Searching for a weapon, I saw the .44 revolver lying on the yellow piece of paper towel. The rifle was not in sight. Where was Al? Where was the bear? Even though it was not completely dark, I could not see any movement or forms nor hear any sound. However, the bear was only about 25 yards from me and I strongly sensed danger. My first impulse was to run, to get away from the area. My common sense told me my best chance was to stay in this clearing and in camp because the bear would overtake me if I ran, and he would have the advantage away from camp. My next thought was to stick the revolver in my waistband and try to climb a tree. Unlike black bear, brown bear do not climb trees unless they pull themselves up by using tree limbs. Dressed completely in white, including socks, I must have been very visible as I moved in the moonlight. The trees were large and had no low limbs for me to reach. Dismissing any chance of escape, I cried, "God, please help us," and braced myself while holding the revolver in both hands. I may not be able to kill the charging bear before he got me, but I would not give up my life without a fight.

As Al was being carried by the bear, he thought, "What a hell of a way to die," then he thought of me faced with the shock of having a dead husband, miles from anywhere or anyone, and having to hike out of there alone. He became angry and a strong fight for survival overcame him. A brown bear is capable of dragging off a full-grown moose. His strong claws can move boulders and huge hunks of earth. A blow from his paws can break the neck of a moose or another bear. No man could come close to matching his strength. Al realized his only chance was to convince the bear he was dead.

When his scalp had torn off and the bear had momentarily lost his grip, Al had fallen onto a hump of peat moss. He grasped the hump with his right arm, holding his face and stomach down to keep from being ripped open, took a deep breath and held perfectly still. The bear cuffed at him, leaving horrible claw marks along his side and shoulders. He bit into Al's back twice while standing over him, looking for signs of life. There was none. To accomplish this and remain conscious displayed remarkable self-discipline as the pain must have been excruciating.

I heard the bear. He was moving away from me, heading toward cover in the direction of a little lake in the area. As I stood listening to locate the bear, I heard Al call to me. He was running toward me. Moving closer to him, I could see his knit shirt was torn and he was covered with blood. "I'm hurt bad, but I'm going to live," he said. In the next breath, he ordered, "Find the rifle, quick."

"Where do you think it is?" I asked.

"Look at the end of the lean-to. It may have landed there," he answered.

Only moments had passed since the attack, but it seemed much longer. As Al wiped the blood from his eyes, he held the revolver while I searched for the rifle. I had to feel around for it in the darkness. I found it and a shirt for Al to hold on his head as blood was pouring down over his eyes.

Our minds were working fast, lining out immediate things to do. A fire! Got to get a big fire going! This was quickly accomplished thanks to the dry wood, kindling and paper we had collected on our cleanup. In a few seconds, the flames were high and the wood was starting to ignite. Al slumped on the sleep bag. He was cold and starting to shake. The temperature was about 25 degrees. He must have lost a great deal of blood and was possibly going into shock. "I've got to get him warm and look at his wounds," I thought as I pulled our sleeping bags close to the fire for him.

We started to check his wounds. He had been badly mauled. I looked for spurting blood, which would indicate bleeding from an artery. His legs were uninjured; he had a large hole in his side under his arm from the bear's claws. This required a large compress, which we had included in our first aid kit. I had sewn large game bags from unbleached muslin for this hunt. The material was new and clean. I tore it into long strips to use for bandages. Al's head was very bloody. Half of the skin on his forehead was missing, taking the bottom half of his left eyebrow and extending into his hairline. Due to all the blood and poor light, I did not notice part of the scalp was gone but thought it had been torn back and was still attached. I wrapped his head around several times with bandages, which were quickly soaked with blood. His left arm was badly chewed and the pain was severe. Al instructed me to take my knife and cut off the shredded piece of flesh that was hanging from the largest wound. There appeared to be a great deal of muscle and nerve damage. All I could do was squeeze a tube of first aid cream on the wounds as far as it would go and wrap up his arm. I made some strong tea on the fire and gave it to Al to drink, along with some aspirin. During the process of bandaging, we watched and listened for any sign of the bear's return.

We still had three hours to wait for daylight. The night air was cold, causing the water to freeze in our plastic water jug. Up until now, I hadn't noticed the cold even though I didn't have shoes on. I found my shoes and clothes and quickly pulled them on. This was the longest three hours of my life. I talked loudly, often repeating myself just to be making noise. Al laid resting and drinking strong tea. I circled the fire, listening for any noise in the brush and watching for any moving shadows. I used a large share of the wood we had gathered to keep the fire bright until daylight.

Gordy Ponset read the statement in disbelief. It went on for several more pages that outlined how the two had walked the 15 miles to the road for help. It told how troopers went back to the site to recover the warden's scalp and take it to the hospital to be re-attached. This was an incredible story of courage, strength and woodman-ship. Surviving the initial attack had been miraculous, but having the presence of mind and the skills to stop the bleeding and to make the injured man able to trek to safety is the stuff of which Alaska legends are made. He read both the case file and the witness report again.

He dialed the number for Will Trippet. When the Wildlife Trooper answered, he said, "I owe you another lunch."

CHAPTER 8

T wo days later the two officers were in the same booth at Froso's restaurant. Will Trippet could see the excitement in the eyes of his old friend, Gordy Ponset. Will, too, was bathed in excitement and wanting to talk about the bear mauling case, but tried to control his emotions.

"That is the most exciting report I have ever read," Gordy told his old school mate. "I don't know many men who could have demonstrated the presence of mind or courage or even the physical strength these two individuals showed. I thought at first it might have been a fairy tale, but Ted Spraker assured me it was the gospel. It's just an amazing story."

"I feel the same way," Will admitted. "I have talked with some of the old-time locals and some of them remember the case. They also remember some of the old F&WP officers from that era. There were several remarkable officers in those days, but two stand out. Al Thompson and Dan France enforced the game laws in this area back then. Those names still strike fear in the hearts of poachers on the Kenai Peninsula." Trippet paused in his conversation, looking at the table, composing his thoughts. "I hate to admit this, even to myself, but I could use some of that old-time knowledge and initiative. I have been getting reports of a major commercial poacher. He is working the commercial fishery out of Homer. For the life of me, I can't figure a way to go about catching this guy besides catching him in the act. Reading this old case file makes me want it even more."

"I thought I let my enthusiasm run away, but it looks like you caught the same bug," Gordy snickered. "What are you planning to do about your poacher? You know I can't help you much with a commercial fish case, but I'll give you any help I can, just ask."

"Thanks Gordy, but I have to work this out by myself. I think I am going to drive down that was this afternoon and nose around. An idea may come to me while I'm down there in the salt air. Glad you liked the old file. And, by the way, thanks for the lunch—again."

When the two men left the restaurant, Wildlife Trooper Trippet pondered his problem while driving south. He picked up the radio and called for Sean Adams to ask for a meeting when he reached Ninilchik in just a few minutes. At a paved parking area on the inlet side of the Sterling Highway, the two men parked and spoke through open driver side windows.

"Howdy, Will. What brings you down south today?"

"I'm on my way to Homer. I thought I would nose around the harbor and see if I could pick up any information about our Ninilchik friend. Nothing has come to light so far. Either this guy is very crafty or very lucky. There must be someone down this way mad enough at the guy to give me some kind of a break. His gillnet season opening is less than a week away and I still don't know how to go about catching him. It sure is frustrating." Will was shaking his head and grinning at Sean.

"When you get to the Harbor, look around for a scruffy-looking geek with a long beard and wearing Hilly Hanson rain gear. He has stringy blond hair and hangs out at the dock hitting on folks coming off halibut charters. He asks to clean and filet their fish. He uses the public cleaning station on the dock. He actually does a pretty good job. Resnic once threw him off his gillnetter. I don't know this fellow's name, but he goes by the name of "Hey-Boy." I can't say he knows anything, but if anyone will talk it will be him." Adams turned in the seat to answer his radio. "Gotta go," he said, putting his car in gear and turning on the overhead lights. He sped north, waving out the side window as he drove off.

Trippet drove to the Homer Spit and parked his patrol car near the Seafarers' Memorial. The air was cool, but his armored vest was warm and stopped the cool breeze. He reported his location to dispatch and exited the car. At the top of the ramp leading to the docks, he stopped and surveyed the entire harbor. A few yards up the first dock, he saw "Hey-Boy" cleaning fish at the public cleaning station. Three fishermen were standing nearby watching his work. Trippet strolled down the ramp and slowly sauntered up the dock to where the fish were being cleaned. When he neared the cleaning table, he stopped and leaned against a boat in the first slip. Trippet stayed there until Hey-Boy finished his business with the fishermen. The aged hippy was hosing down the cleaning station when Will approached.

"Hello there," Will said as he approached. "How's business?"

"Pretty slow," the man answered said and continued to wash down the cleaning table.

"When you finish cleaning up, can I talk with you a few minutes?"

"I s'pose. Who are you anyway?"

"My name is Wilson Trippet. I'm an Alaska Wildlife Trooper. Folks call me Will." Will saw the uncomfortable body language. "Don't be alarmed, this has nothing to do with you or your fish cleaning business. I just have some questions about a commercial fisherman and someone told me you were acquainted with the man."

"OK. So, I'm not in any trouble?" Hey-Boy asked, seeming to relax a little.

"Not for anything I know about. Say, you have been working hard and must be cold. How about I buy you a cup of coffee?"

"That sounds good. I'll be finished in a second." He hosed more slime and blood from the dock. "Who are you interested in, anyway?"

Trippet looked around to see if anyone was listening, then continued. "I need some Information about a man by the name of Resnic, Josef Resnic. He runs a boat called the Volga. Are you familiar with the man or the boat?"

"Oh, yeah." Hey-boy was chuckling. "You can see the boat for yourself if you walk to the end of this dock. It's parked across on the dike side. It's the big white one with the roof over the net reel. Strange piece of equipment if you ask me." He pointed to the other end of the dock. "Walk down there and take a look. I'll wait here."

Will nodded and walked the 150 feet to the end of the floating dock. At the end he saw the Volga. It was indeed impressive. It was very clean and tidy for a fishing vessel. No one seemed to be aboard the boat. He made note of the vessel numbers and planned to ask the harbormaster when it had arrived and how long it planned to stay. After closing his notebook, he walked back to where Hey-Boy waited.

"How about that coffee now?" Trippet asked.

"I'm done here, let's go."

"I'm just curious, how did you ever get a name like "Hey-Boy"? Trippet inquired.

Again Hey-Boy was chuckling. I'll tell you, but you have to keep it a secret." He stared at Will for confirmation. Will nodded and the fish cleaner continued. "I'm from New York. My dad is retired now, but my family is rich. I went to college and have two master's degrees, one in business and one in philosophy. While I was in college, I did a lot of dope—bad stuff: cocaine,

LSD, heroine, weed, anything to get high. I was born Heywood Boynton. In my drug days, my friends took to calling me Hey-Boy. It stuck with me. I kind of like the name."

"I would guess most people would remember it." They were at the restaurant door. "I'll buy you lunch if you want it." Trippet pulled the door open and followed him inside. They found a table near the back of the room where they could talk quietly.

The waitress came with menus and asked what they wanted to drink. They both ordered coffee. When she had delivered their coffee, taken their order and left the table, Will asked, "How do you know Josef Resnic?"

"I worked for him once. He didn't have a regular deckhand. He used his brother, Victor. Victor got sick and had to have his appendix taken out. It was right during red salmon season and Josef needed a deckhand real bad. I heard about it and got the job. Josef is a good fisherman and the boat is a dream to work on, but we fished all-day, fished hard. Then at night, he wanted to motor to a closed area and set his nets. I didn't feel good about it an' told him so. He went off like a rocket. He said do it or he would cut me up and use me for crab bait. He said he had tied an anchor on a guy once and dumped him in 450 feet of water because he didn't want to fish like that. I don't know if he really did that, but I believed he would. I fished the way he wanted until we came to port and I quit. He said if I ever said anything about how he fished, he would take care of me for good. He scared the hell out of me and I never said anything about it to anyone." Hey-Boy heaved a big sigh and stirred his coffee.

Trippet was writing as fast as he could, taking notes during the conversation. He still had no proof, but he was getting more specific information about Resnic. "Weren't you afraid to stay in Homer?"

"I thought about leaving, but I didn't know where to go. I just kept to myself and, until now, never said a word about it. I'm still scared of him."

"I don't blame you for that," Will sympathized. "Do you think he is still doing the same illegal fishing?"

"Oh, yeah. I hear rumors now and then." He looked into the eyes of the trooper. "Are you going to try to catch him at it?"

"That's my goal. If he is fishing illegally, I want to put a stop to it. Have you got any ideas about how to go about catching him?"

"No, I don't, but don't ask me to help you. I s'pose you know he is in cahoots with his older brother, Ivan. He runs that big tender, the Galaxy. It's a big boat and he takes a load of fish with him when he goes back to the

Seattle area in the winter. Josef is bad, but his brother is worse. If you intend to confront these boys, you had better have someone watching your back. You could join that other guy, trying to swim to shore with an anchor tied to your back." Hey-boy was becoming very nervous and kept eyeing the door.

"Heywood, you have been a big help. I thank you for the information. I would appreciate it if you would give me a call if you learn anything I could use to catch the men." Trippet glanced around the room and saw no one suspicious. "I think you had better leave now and I will get the lunch." Will gave Hey-Boy his card.

"I hope you nail this bunch, Trooper. They are dangerous and ruthless men and, if you take them out, I will be able to sleep at night. And, yeah, I will call you if I hear anything new. Good luck and good hunting." Hey-Boy walked to the door, turned and gave a small wave of his hand.

CHAPTER 9

Will Trippet had been kept busy in the office with normal daily duties and patrols. The first new moose calves were beginning to show up around the Peninsula. Usually sightings begin in mid-May, but they seem to be a little later this year. On May 28, the first reports of a new calf came in. It was June 3 when the first call came in about a calf moose hit by a car. That call was in town in a residential area. Will was called to pick up the dead moose and dispose of the carcass. He had been called out several nights in a row to answer calls about road-hit moose, both cows and calves. He had not had time to follow up on the F/V Volga case.

King salmon fishing was picking up in the Kenai River, and the four rivers in the south portion of the Kenai Peninsula opened for fishing on Memorial Day weekend. Huge crowds of fishermen migrated from all parts of the state for the event. Every parking space on the lower Peninsula was filled with RVs, campers, tents, cars and trucks. Thousands of fishermen invaded the Anchor River, Stariski Creek and Ninilchik River. Each of these streams is small and shallow, but large numbers of Chinook (also called king salmon) migrate to them each year to propagate. Chinook are the largest of the four species of salmon in Alaska waters. Most weigh in at 20 to 45 pounds and, in the Kenai River, they have been known to reach more than 95 pounds. These trophy fish are the prize fueling the crowds of fishermen for the four weeks these small streams are open to salmon angling.

All the Wildlife Troopers were busy during this time and Will Trippet had little time to pursue anything else. Memorial Day weekend signaled the beginning of long hours with little sleep and frequent nightly call-outs to answer complaints by the public. Most fishermen believe in following the statutes, but some will do anything to catch fish. Snagging fish elsewhere than in the mouth is illegal. One fish per day is the limit with the freshwater catch limited to two fish per year. In salt water, depending on where you are fishing, you can keep up to five fish per year. Nighttime brings out the worst in some fishermen. Heavy drinking usually accompanies someone catching salmon with a gill net in fresh water, but it is a common violation.

Another common violation is someone catching his one salmon, going to the camper with his fish, changing his clothing and returning to the river for another attempt. The numbers of fishermen and the scarcity of officers make it difficult to watch everyone all the time. These four weekends, beginning with Memorial Day, present a challenge for enforcement officers. Most officers enjoy the frantic pace. It is a wild time on the Kenai Peninsula.

By the end of June, it all comes to an abrupt halt when the fishery in these rivers closes for the year. By this time, the commercial fleet is in the salt water laying their nets for sockeye or red salmon. This is the money crop in Cook Inlet waters. Millions of dollars are netted each year beginning in June when the fish return. There are boundaries to be observed. Wildlife Troopers have patrol vessels watching the fleet as well as aircraft flying overhead to watch for boats straying outside the prescribed fishing areas.

Trippet had passed the word to the pilots to be on the lookout for the Volga, emphasizing it may be fishing in closed waters and after prescribed hours. The fleet is not allowed to fish every day, which means enforcement patrols by aircraft were few during closed periods.

In the office late Tuesday evening, Will was completing his daily paperwork when Sergeant Donavan Fleer came into the office. He unloaded his survival vest on his desk and headed to the coffee pot. Back in the squad room, he took a healthy gulp of the strong brew. He took off his duty belt and placed the twenty-two pound belt with his gun, radio, taser, handcuffs, keys and several other required items on the desk with his survival vest. He took another long drink from the cup and stretched his back. He was stiff from several hours of flying the Cessna 185 on floats doing airborne fisheries patrol. He reached into his desk to find his pilot's logbook. Finally, he sat at his desk, finished his coffee and gave out a big sigh.

Until now, he had not said a word, but once settled into his desk chair he spoke to Will who occupied a desk on the other side of the room.

"I saw your boat out there today, Will. He was inside the lines and had all his numbers displayed properly. I like that boat, the Volga. She seems like a big boat for a drift fisher, but it seemed to handle OK for them."

"Yeah, I looked it over the other day when I was in Homer. I thought it looked too big, too." Trippet commented. "Did you see any sign of the big tender, the Galaxy?"

"No, but there were lots of boats in the inlet today. I only went down the inlet as far as Kalgin Island. All the east side set nets were in the water and I spent most of the day alternating between checking gillnetters and set netters." Set net sites were where gillnetters worked from the beach. On the east side of Cook Inlet, there are hundreds of these sites where they normally fish the same periods as the drift gillnetters.

"When you go out again, I'd like to go along as a spotter. Would it be alright with you?"

"Ask the Captain. It's OK with me if he says you can go along." Fleer stood and stretched his back again. "You might want to reconsider, though. It makes for a long day."

"Thanks, I'll ask him." Will had flown as observer on fisheries patrol before and knew what to expect. "I'm done for the day, Don. Is there anything I can help you with before I leave?"

"Thanks anyway, Will. I'm only going to catch up my logbook and make some entries in my daily activity log. It's been a long day and I'm going home and get some sleep."

Will was about to climb into his truck when he had a call on the radio attached to his lapel. It was dispatch. A cow moose with a new calf had attacked an elderly man who was injured badly in the attack. The address was only a mile east of Soldotna near the Sterling Highway. Dispatch advised that an ambulance was on the way.

With lights and siren operating, he drove through the heavy summertime traffic to the home where the attack occurred. It was near the golf course in a very nice neighborhood. The ambulance had not arrived when Will got to the home. Several people were crowded around the victim on the front lawn. An elderly woman met him, sobbing.

"Oh, Trooper, help him please. He isn't moving and won't answer me," the woman pleaded.

"Yes, Ma'am, I will. Are you alright?" Will asked.

"Yes, I'm fine. I was in the house when it happened." She continued her sobbing as the ambulance pulled into the drive.

Will called to one of the ladies standing near the injured man to have her take the lady back into the house until the medics had finished. He said he would come in and tell the ladies what was happening.

The medics went to work immediately. Two medics tended the victim while Will and another medic backed the bystanders away to give them room to work. While they examined the victim, Trooper Trippet asked one of the onlookers where the moose had gone.

The man explained, pointing to the next house. "I live over there. I was in the yard watching the cow moose and her new calf when Fred came out of his garage. I don't think he saw the moose standing there eating his shrubs. When Fred came around the corner and the moose saw him, it spun around and began stomping him. It quit once and went over to the calf, then came back and stomped poor old Fred some more. I ran down here yelling and waving my arms trying to frighten the moose away, but it just looked at me. For a second there I thought it was going to come after me, but it didn't. It went over to the calf and nudged it along and they both went around the garage and out the back of the house into the trees. Is Fred going to be OK?"

"I don't know. I hope so. He looks pretty beat up. The medics will check him over, get him stabilized and probably transport him to the hospital. We will just have to wait and see. In the meantime, I need to have your ID for my records. Is there someone here who can stay with the wife for a while?"

"Yes, my wife is in the house with Nora. She will stay as long as she is needed. I hope Fred is OK. We have been neighbors for a lot of years." He rubbed his hands together, worried. "We have moose here all the time. They bring their new calves to the neighborhood every year. Nothing like this has ever happened before."

Will handed the man's driver license back to him. "Well, Mr. Petrie, moose are wild animals and sometimes people and animals have a conflict. It doesn't sound like Fred did anything to incite the encounter; it just happens sometimes. If you will excuse me a moment I want to check with the medics."

The medical personnel were loading the victim into the ambulance as Will walked up. "How is he, Terry?"

"It doesn't look good," the paramedic whispered. "Can you drive the wife to the hospital? We need to get there as soon as possible."

"You bet. I'll be right behind you."

The ambulance, lights and siren going, screamed out of the drive, turning left toward Soldotna. Trippet walked to the house to speak with the wife.

"Mrs. Duncan, would you please get your purse and come with me to the hospital?" He turned to the other lady. "Mrs. Petrie, I would appreciate it if you and your husband would follow us to the hospital to be with Mrs. Duncan."

"Certainly, my husband and I will be right there. Is he going to be all right?"

"I don't know. He is hurt badly. Please just follow us in."

Trooper Trippet parked near the pedestrian entrance to the emergency room at Central Peninsula General Hospital. He helped Mrs. Duncan inside where a nurse met them at the door. She quietly announced the doctors had pronounced Fred Duncan dead when he arrived.

"Oh, no!" she cried and clung to the trooper. Just inside the automatic doors is a small exam room. The nurse escorted Will and the sobbing wife into the small room. "What am I going to do without Fred?" The nurse provided Kleenex tissues.

"A Mrs. Petrie will be here in a minute. Will you bring her here?" Will needed to get into the emergency room and see the medics and the doctor. In the midst of all the sadness, he still had to take notes and get vital information for his report.

It was almost midnight when Will left the emergency room. It was still daylight when he climbed into his truck. "I hope I don't have any more days like this for a while," he thought as he drove away.

CHAPTER 10

Red salmon season was off to a slow start this year for Josef Resnic and his one-man crew. The run of fish in the area he normally fished seemed to be coming in late, but they were doing much better this week and prospects for a good season were improving. Larry Hanson could now handle the boat nearly as well as his skipper Josef could. There had been no mechanical problems with the boat; however, Hanson was having trouble converting the sunroof over the net reel to its down position as a ramp for pulling illegally caught halibut over the transom of the boat. The trouble was with the engineering of the tilting arms. When the pins were pulled and the roof lowered to form a ramp, it took both men to jerk and wiggle the arms into place. The roof was heavy and cumbersome, making it nearly impossible for one man to set up properly. Hanson had spent many hours studying the problem and thought he had figured out a solution.

"I think I know how to fix the problem with the ramp, Josef," Hanson said to his boss.

"It's a pain in the neck, Larry. If you can fix it, get at it." It was late in the day and the nets had been pulled for the end of the fishing period. The men on board the Volga were motoring toward the fish tender Galaxy anchored a few miles to the south. "What kind of solution are we talking about? Will we need to use the welders on the Galaxy?"

"No, I don't think so." Larry explained, "I think the problem lies with the way the lower pins are placed. If we put some washers on the hinge bolts on the inside of the support arms, we can spread the bottom enough to allow free clearance of the main supports when we rotate them up and down. The way it's built, we have to pull the pins and rotate the roof to the down position while we are lowering the support arms. During that operation there is too little support for the main arms and they twist and hang up on the reel. I think if we spread the base at the fulcrum point, it will allow more room for the twisting motion. All the side pins are spring-loaded and once they are pulled one man can let the roof down to the ramp position with a rope. When everything is let down into place, the springs will snap the pins into place and lock. Raising it back to the roof position should work the same way in reverse."

"I see what you mean. It might work." Josef seemed to be thinking about the problem then asked, "All we need is some washers for the axels and a couple of strong hands to help hold things in place while we put in the spacers? I'll talk to Ivan and we will get a couple of his crew to help us after we unload."

The two men secured the Volga to the side of the Galaxy and began unloading their catch. The fish were weighed and counted by one of Ivan's crew and a receipt or fish ticket was issued for the amount. Ivan stood on the upper deck watching his crew take the fish aboard. When it looked as if the transfer was about complete, he walked down a metal stairway to the deck below. He arrived as Josef and Larry were climbing up onto the main deck of the Galaxy.

"Welcome aboard the Galaxy," Ivan called to the men. "We are having steaks in the galley tonight. Would you care to join us for dinner?"

"You bet, thanks for asking, Ivan. I think Larry must be tired of peanut butter and jelly by now." Josef and his brother both laughed.

Ivan sat with the two men at dinner. Josef asked if Ivan could provide some large washers and a couple of men to help install them. Ivan agreed and asked if there was anything else he could do for the crew of the Volga. Josef said that was all they would need this night and thanked his brother.

After dinner, two men helped Larry find the proper washers to be used as spacers and came aboard the Volga to help with the maintenance. Once the new parts were in place, the men released the pins and rotated the roof to a ramp and back again. They did this four or five times to make sure it would work as planned. Everything seemed to function properly now and they thanked the men for helping them. It had been a long and strenuous day so Josef opted to motor back to his fishing area and anchor for the night. Both men would sleep well tonight.

The sun was high and bright the next morning. The sea was flat and it looked like a good day for fishing. Larry had cooked pancakes and sausage for breakfast. Both men relaxed and drank coffee awaiting the opening time.

They were sitting quietly in the cabin relaxing when a distress call came over the marine radio.

"Mayday! Mayday! This is the fishing vessel Daydreamer. I broke a drive-shaft and it ripped a hole in the hull. I am taking on water and sinking. We are one mile south of Kalgin Island. We are leaving the Daydreamer and boarding our Zodiak lifeboat. We have survival suits on and will have an EPRB in the lifeboat."

"This is Coast Guard aircraft monitoring your channel. We will come to your location and circle. We will notify the cutter, but he is south of Homer and cannot arrive in less than three hours. Is there another vessel in the area able to help this crew?"

Josef snatched the microphone from its clip and spoke. "Daydreamer, this is the Volga. We are at anchor four miles south of you. We are on our way. Coast Guard, do you copy the Volga?"

"Affirmative, Volga. Thank you for the assist. We will be in the area, on this frequency, if you need assistance. Coast Guard standing by."

Larry had already started the engines and was warming them up while idling ahead and winding in the anchor line with the electric winch in the bow. By the time the anchor was in its nest, the oil temperature was beginning to come up. He pointed the bow north and shoved the throttles to the stops. The big boat nearly leaped ahead. Within minutes, they could see the sinking vessel and the small rubber boat with three men in red survival suits floating nearby. Larry expertly came alongside the lifeboat and stopped.

"Is anyone injured?" Josef called to the men.

"No, just scared," came the reply.

Larry was dropping the anchor while Josef helped the three men board the Volga. Josef and Larry used the small electric davit to hoist the Zodiak lifeboat to the rear deck of the Volga. The men pulled off their survival suits and thanked their rescuers. They were given coffee and Josef reported to the Coast Guard about the sinking boat and its crewmembers. The Coast Guard said the ETA for the cutter was now two hours.

Josef turned to Larry, "We have time to make a good set before they arrive, Larry. Head out to our fishing area and I will run the net out on the first set. Keep your eye on the GPS; we don't want to get a ticket."

"Can me and my men help you make this set, Captain?" asked the rescued Daydreamer skipper.

"No, we have a system and it's pretty easy. You can help pick the net later if you are still on board," Josef spoke as he continued to go about his chores.

"Help yourself to more coffee in the cabin. Listen for a call from the cutter. They probably won't call for another hour, though."

Everything went smoothly and the net had been pulled when the cutter called. There were a large number of fish in the net and the Daydreamer crew helped pick the net as it came aboard.

When the cutter arrived, it sent a launch to the Volga with two seamen and one officer. They spoke to the Daydreamer crew and said they would take them aboard. They had marked the site of the sinking and called for a spill response team to come check the sunken boat for fuel and oil leaks. The officer took Josef and Larry's information and thanked them for their assistance. They assured Josef he would be getting a commendation letter for his efforts. With that they all saluted, boarded the launch and motored back to the cutter.

Josef watched them board the cutter. "Let's get back to work. We've lost too much time already."

CHAPTER 11

Sergeant Donavan Fleer had called Wildlife Trooper Will Trippet late Wednesday evening. He told the trooper he would be flying a long day on Thursday. After some discussion, the two men agreed to meet at the Soldotna airport in the early afternoon. They made a sketchy plan for the flight. Don Fleer said he had a tip that someone on the west side was fishing after hours and outside the designated boundaries set for the fishing period. Fleer warned his passenger not to drink too much coffee before the flight as there was no way to know how long they would be in the air.

The Cessna 185 was fitted with amphibious floats, meaning there were landing gears inside the floats that could be lowered to allow for landing on a paved runway or retracted to land on water. These floats are made of a composite material and nearly oblivious to the effects of salt water. Will met Don Fleer and received his briefing before the flight. The two men had studied a map of Cook Inlet and decided on a couple of areas where someone could think their activities might be overlooked. The two men boarded the plane and taxied to the end of the runway. Both men wore noise-canceling headsets that allowed them to hear and talk with each other.

Fleer looked at Will then down at his seatbelt making sure it was tight. "Are you ready?" he asked.

"I'm ready. Let's do it," Will replied.

It always amazed Will how short the takeoff roll could be before the Cessna 185 lifted off. The air was smooth and clear. They had taken off to the west and proceeded to climb while heading straight away from the runway. Donavan maintained a steady climb rate to 5000 feet before leveling off. They flew a little to the north until they approached the West Forelands and turned south at the mouth of the Kustatan River.

"I plan to stay at this altitude for a while. We can't see any bears or seals from up here, but if anyone is being sneaky, they won't get suspicious. The Volga has been working about 25 miles south of here. She's easy to spot from the air. It's a big boat, much larger than most of the fleet. She is also stark white and very clean. The other thing that makes her stand out is that awning or roof over the fish reel. Never saw one like that before. Probably makes it nice to work under, but it has to be unhandy when pulling nets. They seem to do all right with it, though." Fleer was changing course frequently to look at fishing vessels and check his GPS for position of the vessels.

"Did you see the Volga on your morning flight?"

"Yes, they were down near the south end of Chisik Island. I went over them a couple of times, but they were legal when I saw them. I suspect they will stay legal until the rest of the fleet heads in at closing time, that's six o'clock today. Some leave a little early to beat the rush to the cannery dock, but the Volga sells her catch to the tender Galaxy. Galaxy comes up as far as Tuxedni Bay to buy fish." Fleer was trying to explain what he had been seeing so far this season.

"Josef Resnic runs the Volga and his brother Ivan owns and skippers the Galaxy." He grinned at Fleer. "Handy, huh?"

The two men patrolled the entire inlet, swooping down on two boats fishing outside the lines. Trippet copied their ADF&G numbers that are required on the side of the boat. While Will wrote down the numbers, Don Fleer marked their positions on the Global Positioning System. This mark would be accurately recorded in the GPS equipment and later written in his report. Will manned a digital camera and photographed the boats for evidence. The digital photos had the date and time printed on them. As 6:00 approached, the men flew over the fleet to be sure there were no nets out past the closing time. When it looked like all was proper with the fleet as it headed to Kenai and the cannery, Sergeant Fleer spoke to his passenger.

"I'm going to land up in Tuxedni Bay. We can get rid of some old coffee and drink some new. I have some sandwiches in a small ice chest on the back seat." Will nodded ascent. Donavan smoothly banked the Cessna toward the bay at the foot of Mount Redoubt. Dropping down to an altitude of 100 feet, they skimmed the bay causing thousands of puffins and other sea birds to scoot out of the path. At the upper reaches of the bay, there were brown bears everywhere. From the glacier to the last stream, bears wandered everywhere searching for and finding fish to eat.

There was little wind at the head of the bay and the plane did not drift much. The two men stepped out onto the floats and watched the animals, relieved themselves and stretched. Fleer passed a sandwich and a cup of steaming black coffee across the seats to his fellow officer. Will was glad for the stop and a chance to get out of the plane for a while. He marveled at the beauty of the setting, taking in the clean, fresh, salty air.

"A day like this could make me want to finish my commercial pilot rating," Will commented.

"It would suit me if all the days of air patrol were this nice," Fleer said as he took another bite of his roast beef sandwich and a long drink of hot coffee. "If the Volga is going to do anything illegal, I think they'll wait until everyone has gone home. If he had a good day and his fish hold is full, he might go to the tender and unload before going back to fishing. How long do you want to wait before we check on him again?"

"I don't want to waste your time, but as long as we are out here I'd like to do whatever it takes to give him time to do his after-hours fishing. I'll leave it up to you," Will offered.

Fleer thought a moment and said, "I'll throw out an anchor and we can take a nap for a couple of hours before we take off again. We don't have enough fuel to do too much patrol, but it looks like he operates in this area and I can fly about an hour before going home for fuel. Is that alright with you?"

"That's more than I expected. Thanks, Don. I owe you." Will reached through the cabin of the plane to shake hands with the sergeant.

They both climbed back inside, pushed the seats back as far as they would go, leaned back and slept the sleep of the innocent. When they awoke it was after nine o'clock, but the sun was still high in the sky. A little breeze had kicked up and the plane was bobbing at the end of its anchor line. Both men stepped out onto the floats once more before preparing to take off again.

As they lifted off and the sergeant raised the flaps, he leveled the plane at 1,000 feet.

"Where do you think they will be at this time of night, Don?"

"I'm not sure, but my guess is that they will be near the mouth of some spawning stream. I think they will set out a net on the south side on one of those rivers or creeks. The tide is coming in and the fish will be south of the stream right now."

"OK, I guess we just go look," Will said with a small amount of excitement in his voice.

They flew outside of Chisik Island and south toward Silver Salmon Creek, Johnson River and Chinitna Bay. Fleer had said that would use up about all their spare fuel.

They saw the Volga drifting just to the south of Silver Salmon Creek. It appeared to be fishing, but no net was visible in the water. As they approached the fishing boat, they saw a blond-headed man dressed in water repellent clothing on the back deck. He seemed to be shouting something to the man in the cabin. As the Cessna circled the vessel, they saw it stop its forward speed and drop anchor.

"They spotted us for what we are. They dropped anchor. I think they were fishing and we caught them after they picked the net. Bad timing. Too bad, Will. Ten minutes sooner and we would have had them. This Resnic guy is crafty and seems to always to be on the lookout. We didn't get them this time, but now we know what they are up to." Fleer spoke as he circled, looking out the left side window.

"Yup, you're right, Don." Will, too, was disappointed. "I think we might as well head home. They won't make another set while we are in the area." Trippet blew out a huge sigh before muttering, "We will have to be a lot smarter to catch this bird."

Donavan Fleer waved through the side window at the men on the deck of the Volga. The blond man gave an obscene gesture. With that Fleer leveled his wings and pointed the nose skyward and east toward Soldotna.

CHAPTER 12

Will Trippet was at his desk the following morning catching up on his reports and computer entries when his desk phone rang. He was attempting to correct an error in his entry and the phone ringing startled him momentarily.

"Wildlife Trooper Trippet," he answered.

"Hello, Trooper, this is Vladimir Resnic. I'm getting ready to go to Fairbanks. That friend of yours called and gave me a job. I just called to thank you for everything you did for me. I don't know how I will ever be able to thank you enough."

"I'm glad to hear from you, Vlad. How have you been?"

"I'm doing fine. I've been working at the mercantile and trying to keep the place cleaned up. I have been really busy. I really miss my dad." There was a touch of sadness in Vlad's voice.

"I understand, Vlad, but it will get easier as time goes by. I know you loved your father and that alone makes it difficult, but it will get better." Will didn't really know how to console the young man. "How soon will you be leaving for Fairbanks?"

"I'm leaving tomorrow. Mr. Dennison, your friend, has an apartment over his garage and he said I could stay there. I won't have to pay rent until after I get paid from my job. I'll be working in the office at his freight company doing billing and filing for the company. They are paying me a full-time salary and when I interviewed for the job they said I passed all the tests with flying colors. Mr. Dennison said he usually didn't hire inexperienced people, but he told me, you said I could handle the job. I really thank you for the recommendation, Trooper Trippet."

"Vlad, if we're going to be friends, I think you should call me Will. You've earned the right."

"Thank you, Will." His voice was more cheerful now. "Is it all right if I call you from time to time and let you know how I am doing at school?"

"I'd be disappointed if you didn't, Vlad. Just remember I'm here if you ever need anything. Good luck with the job and with school. Stay in touch, young man." Will felt a certain amount of pride in helping the boy.

"Thanks again, Will. I'll call you again in a couple of weeks. School registration starts next month and I'll probably be busy after that. Thanks again, for everything."

As Will walked to the coffee pot, he couldn't help thinking how much the boy had matured in the weeks since his father's death. He had chosen responsibility over despair. There was little doubt in Will's mind the young man would be a success. That thought made him feel good.

Back at his desk, he finished his computer entries and reviewed the reports he had written. He was about to leave the office to go to Russian River to check bag limits and licenses when Marcy Winston buzzed the intercom.

"Someone is calling about an abandoned moose calf, Will. Will you take the call?"

He punched the button for line 2, "Wildlife Trooper Trippet, how can I help you"

"Hello, Officer. This is George Klingmeister. I live at Mile 12 Funny River Road. I've had a cow and a new calf in my yard the past couple of days, but the calf came here alone this morning. I walked out back to see where the cow had gone and didn't see her, so I looked around the back and in the trees behind my property and found a cow, dead. Looks like a wolf or dog kill to me. In any event, I have a week-old calf hanging around. Do you want me to do something for it?"

"If the calf is only a week old it probably won't survive, Mr. Klingmeister. I can come out, but I think I will notify Fish and Game to come look at it. Sometimes they take a new calf to the moose pens at Swanson River. If you have lived here for any length of time, you know that's a research station where they study moose. Give me your phone number and I will have them contact you right away. Thank you for calling."

"I'll be here."

Will notified Fish and Game, which is the biology division, although they do have enforcement powers. What he had told the caller was sad, but they were the cold, hard facts, the young calf would likely not make it.

He stopped at the reception desk on his way out and told Marcy about the phone call and that he had called Fish and Game. He said he would be on the radio going to Russian River. He started his truck and thought how good it was to get out of the office. He had decided not to take the Sterling Highway route, but to turn and patrol Skilak Lake Loop Road. In the old days, this had been the highway, but now it was just a scenic by-pass. There were several campgrounds and lakes on this route and he would stop to check them out as he went by. It would make his time more relaxed before entering the combat fishing zone of Russian River.

Will reached Russian River campground shortly after 2:00 p.m., checked in with the parks ranger and walked down the trail to the stream. In spite of the number of times he had made this hike, he marveled at the beauty of the area. Even with thousands of fishermen in the area, it was a wild place. Ferns and tall grass lined the trail. Tall spruce trees provided shade on these hot and sunny afternoons. The air smelled fresh and clean, except for the occasional whiff of cigarette smoke he encountered along the stream. He checked the licenses of each fisherman he encountered. Will walked to the falls, about four miles, before starting back toward the campground. He had written two citations for no fishing licenses and four for over limit. He was now carrying a bag with several seized Sockeye Salmon. As he walked back down the trail, he stopped to watch an oriental man fighting a fish. The man landed the fish and immediately clubbed it to death, unhooked it and placed it on his stringer. Will had seen the fish hook in the dorsal fin. As he approached the Asian man, Will introduced himself as a game warden. He asked the man for his fishing license which the fisherman calmly produced. Will wrote the license information on a citation.

"I am going to cite you for failure to release a fish hooked elsewhere than in the mouth." Will continued to write. "I will also be taking the fish with me as evidence of snagging. Do you understand what this ticket is for?"

"Why you give me a ticket? I do nothing wrong," the man stated.

"You can argue that point with the judge. When I came down the trail, you were fighting a fish. I watched you club it to death and put it on the stringer. I also saw you take the hook out of the fish's back. That is an illegal act by Alaska Statutes. Do you understand now?"

"I did not do those things you say. Why you say that?" He had raised his voice slightly and was overheard by the next fisherman downriver who walked up to see what was happening. He, too, was Asian and, as it turned out, was a fishing partner of the first man.

The second man asked the first something in what Will assumed was the Japanese language. The first man answered him in the same language. The second man then asked Will, "Why you say my friend taking fish not legal?"

"I have explained to him that I witnessed him keep a fish hooked elsewhere than in the mouth. That is why I will take his fish and issue him a citation for snagging," Will said, trying to explain it to the second man.

"My friend says he did not do this thing. Why do you accuse him? Do you not like Japanese?"

"Sir, I am not going to debate this with you. I have written the citation for doing an act I witnessed. You have the right to plead not guilty and to tell your story to the judge when you appear in court. Until now I have allowed your friend to continue fishing, but if you wish to protest any further, I will have to ask you both to leave." Will had heard it all before and bent down to take the snagged fish off the stringer.

The two men had another conversation in Japanese before the first man spoke again to Will. "I thank you for being so kind. I did not understand at first. Thank you, officer." The second man spoke to the first in Japanese again. The first man again spoke to Will, "What day do we go to the court, officer?"

"I have written the date on the ticket." Will pointed to the date with his pencil. "If that date is not convenient for you, you can call the court and ask to have the date changed. Are there any other questions?"

"You have been patient, officer, thank you. Can we continue to fish?"

"As long as you do it in a legal manner," Will answered. "I'm not here to be hard on you, but I am charged with the welfare of the fish that return here to spawn. I am only looking out for the fish." Will twisted the top of the bag closed and said, "Have a nice day," before walking down the trail.

As he drove back to Soldotna, the sun was high even though it was nearly 9:00 p.m. Will still had to tag the fish taken as evidence, place them in the freezer and write reports to file with the citations. It was close to midnight when he left the office to go home.

CHAPTER 13

It was after midnight when Will reached his home. He was tired but not ready to go to bed and sleep. He was wound too tightly, too many things occupying his mind. He went to his computer and sat down, opening a can of Coke in the process. He took a long drink of the caffeinated drink while waiting for the computer to light up. When it did, he pressed the buttons for e-mails and saw the first one on the list was from Captain Tom Olson. It read, "Trooper Trippet, I have changed your schedule. You will not need to come in this weekend. I talked with Donavan Fleer and decided you now have enough information to justify letting you work this full time. Be in my office on Monday at 9:00 a.m. for a briefing. I plan to send you out on one of the enforcement boats to work the commercial fishing opening. We will discuss it further on Monday. Have a good weekend."

Will read it a second time. This was good news. He turned off the computer and went to his desk to prepare a plan for catching the Volga. It would be difficult. He had thought of little else in the past weeks and still had not formed a definite plan. Working on the patrol boat would add another dimension to the investigation. If he could coordinate his efforts on the boat with Don Fleer's aerial surveillance, they might just get enough to make a case against Resnic. Now he was excited and knew he could not sleep.

After a restless night, he awoke and fixed some breakfast and coffee. It was another sunny day, but clouds over the mountains to the west were an omen of changing weather. He ate his scrambled eggs and bacon, and then took his coffee to the back deck to relax. It was difficult for him to grasp the speed with which the summer was passing. But today was his to spend as he liked and he planned to wash his own vehicle, a Jeep Laredo Grand Cherokee, and relax.

He mowed the grass, poisoned dandelions and washed the car. As he stepped out of the shower, the phone was ringing. It was Gordy Ponset according to the caller ID.

"Hi there, Gordy," Will answered. "You must be working today. You usually don't call on your own time."

"Very funny, old buddy. Did I interrupt something between you and your girlfriend?" he chided his friend, knowing Will wasn't going with anyone on a regular basis.

"The girls are all in the front yard fighting. What's on your mind? I'm standing here dripping from the shower."

"Sorry, Pardner. I just took a chance calling you at home. Are you going to be home for a while? I have someone I would like you to meet."

"Sure, Gordy, come on over. I'll be dressed by the time you get here. And stop at the Dairy Queen and bring me a Peanut Buster Parfait, would you? I've been doing yard chores and I'm hot."

"See you in 20 minutes. I'm bringing a retired game warden with me. I think you will be interested in his story."

Gordy introduced the big man he had brought with him as Dick Dykema. He had blond hair, broad shoulders and a calm manner. It was immediately apparent he was a jokester when he asked Will if he was going to share his ice cream treat. "Being retired I can't afford those kind of treats," he said in a serious tone.

Will shook his hand and invited the two men to the back deck where they all sat in the sunshine. "Would either of you like some coffee or a Coke?" Will asked.

The two men each asked for Cokes and waited. Will returned with the drinks and glasses of ice. "What's on your minds?" Will inquired, digging into his ice cream and spilling peanuts down his clean shirt.

"You remember that story about the warden that was mauled by the bear?" Gordy asked.

"Oh, yeah, I would sure like to meet that guy, uh, wasn't his name Al Thompson?"

"That's him, Will," Gordy continued. "Dick was mentioned as the friend who hunted in the same area with Thompson the year before his attack. He is also one of the men sent out to find and kill the bear after it attacked Al."

Will turned to Dykema, "I'm really pleased to meet you. There can't be too many people around with first-hand knowledge about the incident."

"There are a lot of versions of this story around, but the one you have is the best one. Al's wife, Joyce, wrote it and details the facts very well. She and Al and I have been friends since we were young. Al and I hunted together back in Michigan before coming to Alaska."

"You were with Fish and Wildlife Protection?" Will asked.

"Yeah, I was stationed in Homer, King Salmon and Soldotna, and worked all over the state. Mostly I flew around patrolling the Alaska Peninsula, working out of King Salmon. This entire thing with Al took place before I transferred over here," Dykema explained.

"Just out of curiosity, I would like to hear your story, if you have time," Will said as he finished his Peanut Buster Parfait. He put the empty container under his chair to keep the wind from blowing it into the yard.

"The week after Al was released from the hospital I was sent out to find the bear and destroy it. Al didn't ask, he just said he was coming along, bandages still covering his head." Dykema told how they hiked up the Funny River horse trail in near 0-degree temperatures. After being chewed up by the bear, Al should have been weak and in bed, recovering, but he insisted on going. The trip froze part of his skin graft and caused some problems with his healing. In the days that followed, there were people sent to find the bear and they claimed they found it. The bear they killed was a black bear and not the brown bear that attacked Al and Joyce. Dykema continued his narration to its completion. At the end, he looked down at his feet and said, "I should never have allowed Al to go along. It caused him to suffer and I think his only motive for the trip was revenge. He's a good friend and I hated seeing him suffer like that."

Will and Gordy had listened to the story for almost an hour without saying a word. This first person account was priceless. Gordy was the first to speak.

"I told Dick's wife I would have him home before 2:00, so I had better take him back. I don't want Lynn mad at me."

Will stood to see the men out. "I want you to know how much I appreciate hearing this from you. I know the memories must be painful. Thank you." He reached out to shake the hand of the retired officer. "The Department isn't the same as when you were doing the job and there isn't much I can teach a man of your experience, but if there is ever anything I can do for you, just ask." Will gave him his card and watched as he and Gordy climbed into Gordy's truck. He waved and returned to the back deck to pick up trash and think about how he would go about dealing with Resnic.

Will decided he could make his time worthwhile by doing regular fishery patrol and at the same time have Don Fleer keep him posted on the whereabouts of the Volga. He was sure Resnic was attempting to look legal during fishing hours and doing his illegal practices after hours when enforcement officers were following the fleet to the canneries. If Don could spot Resnic doing any illegal fishing and he was nearby on the enforcement boat, they might be able to get him red-handed. It wasn't much of a plan, but it was all he could come up with.

CHAPTER 14

An anxious Will Trippet was in his office early on Monday morning. His first order of business was to call Fish and Game and attempt to get a handle on how the fishing periods were to be allocated for the coming week. He was told there would be the regular opening on Tuesday, but that the run of sockeye was building and it was likely there would be extra hours and even the possibility of an extra period on Wednesday. He asked how the average catch numbers were adding up and was told by the director of the commercial fishing allocations that early catches, on average, were down about 15% from predicted numbers. He also said the cannery managers were complaining about the low fish numbers. Those cannery fish managers were urging continuous openings to bring up the catch numbers. They also said if something wasn't done the canneries would be forced to lay off workers.

Will knew that in the past such threats from the cannery operators influenced the decision about fishing hours and periods. Will also knew those decisions had harmed fish stocks and caused low returns. Everyone had an opinion. Commercial fishermen would fish 24 hours a day if they were allowed. Sport fishermen would stop commercial fishing entirely if they had a vote. Subsistence fishermen, who, in theory, were all Alaska residents and fished for a food supply, feared the commercial fishing fleet would catch too many fish and authorities would close the subsistence and dip-net personal use fishery. That fishery represents thousands of residents.

These decisions are based on predicted fish return numbers, escapement numbers or the number of fish to actually reach the spawning beds and the likelihood that minimum numbers of fish would survive the trip up river. Will had watched this tightrope act play year after year, and each year someone was angry at the results. It did have an effect on Will and his job as a Wildlife Trooper because he felt a responsibility to protect the fish and wildlife stocks. It seemed to him that greed was the motivation on every side of the argument and no one was looking out for the welfare of the fish. Fish catch limits in Alaska are very generous and with a minimum amount of skill, a fisherman can fill his freezer either by sport fishing or subsistence catches. It worried Will when minimum numbers of fish on the spawning beds dropped below optimum numbers for reproduction. He knew he could not fix the entire problem, but he would do his best to stop those who were fishing outside the law—that was his job.

His phone call led him to believe this job would last three and possibly four days. This would be a good opportunity to catch Resnic at his shenanigans. Will packed a knapsack with everything he thought he would need on the boat. Luckily he was not prone to seasickness.

Captain Olson poked his head into the office and said good morning. "Give me fifteen minutes, then come in and we will discuss your assignment."

Will had a yellow legal pad in one hand and a cup of coffee in the other when he arrived in the Captain's office. "Are you ready for me?" He asked.

The Captain looked up from his desk. "Yes, come in, Will. I was just finishing up some notes."

Will took a seat in front of the supervisor's desk and asked, "Am I still on for tomorrow?"

"I just got off the phone with Dean Steadman in Homer. He will expect you to be on the boat, ready for work at 4:00 tomorrow morning. He and I talked about how to go about this and we agree that most of the day will be spent on regular patrol. I will expect you to dedicate your time and energy to any task called for by Steadman. He will help you and Donavan Fleer chase down your boat if it is determined he is in violation. Is that clear?"

"Yes sir, I understand, Captain. I thought about this all weekend and I think we would be spinning our wheels to spend all day trying to catch the Volga doing something wrong. Resnic is cagey and he has been at this a long time without being caught. I don't think he will do anything during the day with other boats around. It's my guess he will fish legally all day and when everyone heads home to the cannery, he will find some secluded spot to lay out his nets. That's what he was doing when Fleer and I flew over him the other day. I think he will go to the Galaxy late in the evening and off-load his catch. It seems logical that he and his brother Ivan are doctoring the fish tickets to cover up their extra catch. Everything seems to point in that direction."

"I would like to see you nab this bird. If your suspicions are accurate, he is taking a large number of illegal fish. It's possible he is taking more than just sockeye, too." Captain Olson pulled a file from his desk drawer. "I've had Steadman look at the cannery fish tickets to see how many fish were sold by Ivan Resnic and the Galaxy. The cannery manager is a friend of Steadman's and remarked that the Galaxy is riding lower in the water each time she comes to port. That would seem to indicate your theory is correct and he is filling the hold with fish for the trip south the end of August. His fish tickets do add up correctly, though, and he appears to be operating in a prescribed manner."

"Thanks, Cap. I was going to try to make that inquiry today myself." Will made a note on his yellow pad. "I am going to call Dean when I get back to my office. We will have a few things to arrange, but I'm ready."

"Do what you need to do and take the day off. The period opens at 6:00 o'clock in the morning and you have to be out on the water when they drop their nets," Olson advised his officer.

In his office, Will called Dean Steadman. "I hear you are my boss for the next couple of days. Does this mean I have to call you SIR, Sir?"

"You should always call me Sir." Both men laughed. They had worked together many times. "We will be going out on the Enforcer tomorrow. She's a bigger boat, but fast. The trouble with it is that everyone knows the boat and can see us coming five miles away. It has one positive effect in that when they see us coming they play nice. I was briefed on what you are trying to do. It's going to be tough catching this guy in the act from the deck of the Enforcer, but we can give it a try." Steadman paused a moment. "Has the Captain filled you in on the schedule?"

"Yes, he said I was to be on board at four. It's been a long time since I had a chance to be on the Inlet. I'm looking forward to it. Do I need to bring anything special?"

"Nope, we're provisioned up and have soda and coffee and lots of junk food. We'll have dinner on the boat and T-bone steak is on the menu. You haven't gone vegan, have you?"

"If you can cook it, I can eat it. See you in the morning."

The summer sun was shining when Will Tripper walked down the dock in the Homer harbor. The sea air smelled good and Will was looking forward to his day on the water. The boat was idling, warming the engines when he arrived. Through the side glass, he saw Steadman in the cabin. Two men were on the back deck stowing some gear and checking equipment. Steadman saw Will and stuck his head out of the cabin.

"Good morning. You know Eric and Dave, don't you Will?" he asked.

"Sure do. Hi, guys. Where is Loco? Have you fed him to the crabs?"

"Not yet," Dean answered. "We tried, but the crabs spit him out; said he was too greasy." Everyone laughed. "He's in the engine room and will be up in a minute. Come on in and store your gear. Just find an empty bunk up forward and leave your stuff on it." He looked at his wristwatch. "OK, guys. Cast off. Time to go." Dean returned to the cabin, dimmed the overhead lights and took the wheel.

CHAPTER 15

The Enforcer is a great boat for patrol. Originally built to patrol rivers in Viet Nam, it and three others were given to the island of Kodiak by the U.S. Government. Kodiak decided they couldn't use the boats and sold them to the State of Alaska. The State made a deal with a marine repair company and gave them one of the four boats and a sum of cash to make them usable as patrol boats for the Fish and Wildlife Department. The boats work well as patrol vessels, even though the rear deck is small so when a a commercial crab pot is seized there is no room left for working. The boats are fast and stable with enough room to make the crew comfortable when on long patrols of a week or more.

Dean Steadman piloted the 65-foot Enforcer out of the small harbor and into the open water of Kachemak Bay. The crew was kept busy stowing gear and making ready for the business of the day. The engines were humming smoothly when the sound became loud as Loco opened the hatch and came out of the engine compartment.

He climbed out of the hold and spotted Will right away. He walked over and thrust out a greasy hand to shake with trooper. "What did you do to get banished to this slave ship?" He asked Will, a pleasant smile on his face. "I thought you were a landlubber."

"As a rule I am, but special circumstances make for special solutions. I suppose your skipper has filled you in on why I am on board, but I'm here to help you do your job, too. Just remember, Loco, I don't do windows," Will laughed with the crew.

Steadman spoke to the entire crew while he had them inside. "You all know Will Trippet. He will be assisting us in our regular duties today. Will knows his way around a boat and he knows how we operate. It will take us less than an hour to get to the lower boundary of this fishing period. Get your visiting done and be ready to work when we arrive on site. Keep your eyes open for nets in the water early or nets south of the line. We will start on the south end and work our way up the inlet. The majority of the drift boats will be just south of the Kasilof River. Someone is bound to try to crowd the mouth of the river. You guys know what we're looking for. Stay alert and let me know if you see anything." His basic instructions were simple and clear. They crew knew their jobs. Next, he turned to Will, "Do you want to take a hand at driving the boat?"

"Sure. I've never run a boat this size before. Anything I need to know?" Will asked.

"Just follow the front of the boat and don't let it get under the water." He slid out of the seat and gave Will a one-minute course on the throttles and gauges. "I'm going topside and glass the area. Keep her on this heading. They aren't supposed to have nets in the water for another half hour, but sometimes they get anxious and drop one in early." He picked up a plastic insulated cup with a lid and walked out of the cabin.

The morning was uneventful and only a small number of vessels were fishing the southern extreme of the open area. The Enforcer moved north, checking boat registration numbers and crew licenses. The fishermen were friendly toward the officers and some had questions about the reported emergency opening for tomorrow.

"There must be a school of fish over there," Steadman pointed toward the middle of the inlet directly off the Kasilof River. "Loco, take the wheel and let's check them out." He was talking about a small knot of boats clustered together in a small area of water. Loco slowed the boat before reaching the small fleet to keep from interfering with the fishing. The men watched as the boats pulled nets and picked fish, then circled around laying out the net again. Boat captains were shouting at one and another about someone "corking off," which happens when one boat circles around and lays a net close to another and intercepts the fish. Another regular complaint is boats getting too close to one another and sometimes colliding, usually with little damage done, but tempers can become raw.

As the fish moved, so too, did the fishermen. As each boat left the area, the Enforcer stopped it and its permits were checked. This routine was repeated throughout the day. Steadman and his crew had only written a couple of citations for crewmembers without proper licenses. It was well afternoon when the crew let the boat drift and stopped their work to eat some lunch. They were a friendly bunch and Will admired the way they went about their work.

Late in the afternoon, the Enforcer had worked its way near the northern boundary. Only one boat was that far north. As they motored south again, there was a call from Donavan Fleer flying his Cessna near Chinitna Bay to the south.

"I saw the Galaxy. She is back in Ursus Cove. Some local boats have been using her to sell their fish. Some were loading ice. It seems like a pretty slow day out here," Donavan reported. "Dean, pass on to Will that his friend is working down this way. It looks like he has caught some fish and I think he will be going to the Galaxy in a short while. I'll try to keep checking on him this afternoon. I'll talk with you later."

"Thanks for the report, Donavan." Dean turned in the seat to look at Will. "You heard him, Will. We are going to stay in the northern sector until after the period closes and the boats go in to unload. There is always someone who breaks down or runs out of fuel and we have to tow them in."

Eric was on the top deck glassing the area when he called to Dean. "Skipper, there is a boat on the west side and I think he has a net out in the mouth of the Kustatan. He's too far away and I can't read his numbers."

Dean Steadman spun the wheel and headed toward the possible violator. As they got closer to the Kustatan River, he could see the boat. Eric called again to report the boat was pulling a net. Dean increased the throttles and the Enforcer lurched forward. Eric had a video camera going, recording the location and the crew franticly reeling in the net. The offender had spotted the Enforcer coming and wanted to be gone when the boat reached their fishing spot. There was no chance; the Enforcer was very fast. By the time the crew of the Blooper had picked up their net, the patrol boat was alongside.

Will was laughing, "They haven't even picked the net. They wound the net on the reel with the fish still in it."

"Eric, keep filming. Dave, you and Loco put the fenders over the side. We'll tie them up to us." He then turned to Will. "We'll be here awhile. We're going to have to pick the net and count the fish. We'll have to check permits and licenses. You can help with that. Be careful, they are sometimes armed and angry. It should be okay, though, I know this skipper. We've cited him before, right here in this same spot, in fact. The Blooper is a pile of junk. I don't know how it stays afloat. OK, let's go to work."

When the crew had secured the Blooper to the side of the Enforcer, Will went over the side to the fishing vessel. He came to the deck right in front of the skipper of the Blooper.

"Who the hell are you?" the skipper asked.

"I am Wildlife Trooper Wilson Trippet. And, who are you?"

"I own this boat. I am Dmetrie Kristov. The two crewmembers are my sons Thomas, the tall one, and Gregory, over there by the reel." Now came the bluster of innocence. "I want to know why you Gestapo Troopers came aboard my boat. I am fishing an open period and this is my fishing district. You can't just come aboard whenever you want. I'll sue you for this."

"Captain Kristov, I assure you we are not here to harass you, but I will have to see your permits and crew licenses. If everything is in order, we will allow you to get back to work," Will explained to the Captain.

"Hrumph," the Captain uttered as he turned to enter the cabin. He returned a moment later with a handful of papers in a plastic folder. "Here, read them and get off my boat."

"That's not very friendly, Captain." Will looked through the papers in the folder and found the captain and his boat and crew were licensed for this sector. "Everything seems to be in order, Captain Kristov, except for one little thing."

"And what would that be?" Kristov inquired.

"The most important thing is that you are not licensed nor allowed to fish within one mile of the mouth of the river. I judge your distance to be about 150 yards. It looks to me as if you were netting off the entire mouth of the river," Will calmly described the issue. "How do you explain that?"

"We drifted in here after we picked up the net, you know the tide and all." Kristov was beginning to stammer.

"I see that all the fish visible in the net are Coho salmon. You must understand that Coho are allowed as incidental catch only. When you fish here you must know you are only going to catch Coho."

"Those are incidental fish. We were in the rip and had to reel the net in with fish in it. The reds are deeper in the net." Kristov was very nervous now.

"Well, Captain Kristov, I am informing you that I am going to cite you for fishing a closed area and I'll be seizing the fish in your net. The number of fish will be noted and if you go to court and convince the judge of your innocence, he will likely return the fish or see that you are paid for them. Do you understand all this?"

"Oh, I understand alright. You Gestapo Troopers just like to use your authority to rob us poor fishermen. Everybody knows I work hard and never break the law." Kristov was barking into the wind.

"I am going to have my crew come aboard and pick the fish out of the net. It will make things easier if you cooperate and help us. You can count the fish taken by us. It will be much easier if you allow us to put the net, after it is picked, back into the water. It will also do less damage to the webbing. Is that okay by you, Captain?"

"You might as well. If I say no, you will probably shoot me." The Captain's bluster was more nervous now. His sons had yet to say a word. Will surmised the boys had advised their father against setting the net too close to the river mouth, but stood silently behind him.

Will looked up at the deck of the Enforcer. "Dave, Loco, bring a couple of totes down here and help me pick the fish from the net."

Dave grinned at Loco and said, "I'll go down there. You can run the davit and lower the totes. Try to miss me when you drop them." He was laughing when he stepped off the Enforcer.

The skipper had dropped the Enforcer's anchor and was sitting calmly in the water with the fishing vessel tied to its side. He kept the engines idling, but left the cabin to watch from the back deck. Eric continued his filming chore as the men sorted the net and picked the catch. Each fish was identified by species; all the fish were Coho salmon. A count of the catch was made and verified by the captain and crew of the Blooper. Captain Kristov was advised of the fact that his entire operation had been filmed by the crew of the Enforcer. An hour later, the count was complete and the totes were hoisted to the deck of the Enforcer to be iced down. Dave, Loco and then Will climbed back aboard the Enforcer and untied the Blooper. The boat fenders were pulled back on board as the boats drifted apart. In a final gesture, Will saluted Captain Kristov. In return, the skipper displayed an obscene gesture.

It was late now and the fishing period was officially closed. The crew tied down their cargo and met in the cabin for coffee. The tide was changing and the wind had picked up to about fifteen miles per hour. Will asked permission to use the trooper radio to call Donavan Fleer.

CHAPTER 16

Donavan Fleer had pulled his Cessna up to the beach near Fitz Creek in Chinitna Bay. The fishing period had ended and he intended to conserve fuel by waiting for a call from Will Trippet. The sockeye season was on the downturn and fewer fishermen were fishing this period. He had seen no violations while flying over the fishery, not meaning none occurred. He sat on the sand finishing his lunch and watching the seabirds. A small group of Beluga whales was chasing Coho salmon near the mouth of Clearwater River. Donavan could count five brown bears near the mouth of the Clearwater River with the 100 or so seals keeping a wary eye on the animals.

He was finishing his can of Mountain Dew when Will called on the assigned channel.

"Donavan, where are you?" he asked the pilot.

"I'm on the beach in Chinitna Bay. The wind is picking up and it looks like we are going to get some weather. Where are you?"

"We just finished and are headed south toward you. Have you seen our friends?"

"The last time I checked on them, they were tied to the Galaxy, unloading their catch. That was in Ursus Cove about an hour and a half back. They are probably headed this way by now. I saw two large schools of Coho swimming just off the beach heading toward Chinitna Bay. It's my guess that, because it's close, they will target those fish tonight. What's your ETA to this area?"

There was a short pause before Will answered. "Dean said if the water is not too bad we will be off the Spring Point in 45 minutes, but if the water builds it will be a little longer."

"OK, I'll wait another 30 minutes before I take off again. The Volga is easy to spot from the air, so I will stay at altitude until you get close by. If they are fishing down here, I will drop down and try to distract them while you get closer. I'll call you if you need to come at high speed."

"Sounds like a plan. Dean is nodding approval. See you in a few minutes." Will Trippet was excited. This might be the break they needed. As they passed Johnson River, he noted the water was beginning to stand up a little. The Enforcer was taking it well. The wind was out of the south, directly on her nose.

"It's building pretty fast. I think if Resnic is going to lay out nets, he will do it on the lee side of Chinitna Bay, right inside the bay itself. I think the water is going to get sloppy real fast and he will get inside Seal Spit before he goes to work. At least that's what I would do-if I were a poacher." Dean Steadman winked at Will and grinned. They held steady for several minutes and could see Spring Point when Donavan called.

"It's getting really bumpy up here. The Volga just came around Seal Spit and is headed up the bay. I can see the deckhand standing near the reel and it looks like he is going to let it out. They haven't slowed, so I think they want to get to calmer water before they fish." Donavan let out a huge "OOF" before releasing the mike button. "I'm going to move out over the inlet away from these mountains. Perhaps the air will be a little nicer."

"Do you think they have seen you?" Will asked the pilot.

"I don't think they have. It looks like they are taking care of their own problems without looking for me."

"Stay safe, Don. We just came around Spring Point. Eric says he can see the Volga on the other side of the bay. We're stopping and will wait to see if they drop their net."

"Roger that. I just flew past the entry to Ursus Cove and the Galaxy is in there, all lit up. The crew must be working late. I'm going to the center of the inlet. Let me know if you need me. I'm in my last hour of fuel and I need half that to get home. Keep me informed."

At that moment Eric, who was on the upper deck with binoculars, called the skipper. "The Volga is laying out net, Boss. I have them on video, but we're a long way out."

"Thanks, Eric. Hang on and I will motor slowly in their direction. If they spot us, we will make a run at them. Get their picture and hang on." Dean knew how quickly these waters could build and was both warning and instructing his crewman.

Will was watching from the cabin with his own set of binoculars. "I can see the net in the water. It's choppy and I can't tell if the corks are bobbing from fish or waves."

"It looks as if they are so wrapped up in their work that we'll be able to get right in on them without being spotted," Dean said, sitting upright in the seat. "Take a look, Will. Are both men on the back deck?"

Will brought up the binoculars again. "Holy smokes, you're right. They aren't paying attention to us at all."

"I'll stay off their bow. With both men on the rear deck, we might get to them before they can see us." The Enforcer moved ever closer to the Volga.

Eric remained on the upper deck filming the approach while enduring a biting cold wind and sea spray.

They had pulled to within two hundred yards of the Volga when Steadman pulled back on the power. He slowly moved the big boat alongside the Volga's left rail. The fishermen were startled by the bow of the big boat passing so closely to their boat. Before they could fully realize what was happening, uniformed men appeared on the deck of the Enforcer. They were even more startled when Will Trippet called out Josef's name from the rear deck of the trooper vessel.

"Mr. Resnic, stop what you are doing, please, and come to the rail."

Loco turned a bank of large lights on the deck temporarily blinding Resnic and his deckhand. Dave was dropping huge rubber fenders over the side when Loco came to help. Dave then hooked and held the Volga in place with a long-handled boat hook.

"Turn those damned lights off," Resnic shouted. "It's light enough to see without them." Larry Hanson was now at the rail with Josef, shielding his eyes from the bright lights.

Will shouted again to the men. "Throw us a line and we'll tie you off to the cleat on your deck. We will be coming aboard to inspect your permits and licenses." Hanson threw two lines to the Enforcer. "Step back from the rail and I will come aboard."

In the cabin of the Enforcer, Dean answered the call on the radio. It was Donavan Fleer. "It looks like you have it handled, Dean. If you don't need me, I am going to head back. I'm getting low on fuel."

"We have it now, Donavan, thanks for the help. See you tomorrow." With that Fleer flashed his landing lights and turned toward Soldotna.

On the deck of the Volga, Will Trippet asked both crewmen for identification. He wrote the information on his notebook and handed the items back to them.

He turned to Resnic, "I will need to see your permits and boat registration as well as yours and Mr. Hanson's commercial licenses." Hanson went into the cabin to retrieve the papers. "Mr. Resnic," Will continued, "didn't you realize you were fishing after closing hours for this fishing period?"

"I guess I lost track of the time. It's been a long day." Resnic was not admitting to anything.

Hanson came back with the folders containing the official papers for the boat and crew. Will turned, reaching up to give the papers to Dave on the deck above him. When the lights on the Enforcer went out, Will could see Eric, still on the upper deck with his video camera in hand.

"Mr. Resnic, I shouldn't have to inform you that this area is closed to driftnet fishing. This is to protect the spawning Coho salmon that are returning to the small rivers at the head of the bay. Our crew will assist you in retrieving your net and picking the fish. We will take these fish as evidence. If the court finds you not guilty, the fish will be returned or you will receive payment for your catch. Do you understand this?"

"Yes, I understand, just get on with it and get off my boat." Resnic was clearly unhappy with his circumstance. "Larry, help them with their totes and run the reel while they pick the net. We want to be helpful to these—officers."

"Whatever you say, Skipper. Do you want me to serve them tea and cookies, too?" the angry Hanson remarked.

"Thank you, Mr. Resnic. And while we are about it, I would appreciate it if you would show me your fish tickets for this period," Will requested.

"I haven't taken any fish to the cannery this period," a surly Resnic replied.

"I understand, Mr. Resnic, but we know you have sold fish to the fish tender in Ursus Cove. That's your brother's boat as I recall. Isn't that the Galaxy parked over there?" Will was enjoying this too much.

"OK, OK, I'll get them," he said, muttering his disgust as he went to the cabin.

Dave and Loco were shaking fish out of the net as it came over the transom. Will saw only Cohoes in the net while he watched the men. Hanson was skillful in operating the net reel. At first Trippet feared the deckhand might attempt to catch one of his men in the net and cause him injury, but allayed that fear as he watched.

Resnic returned with a bank bag full of fish tickets. "Write down the numbers and amounts. I won't let you take those off this boat."

"Mr. Resnic! You sound as if you don't trust me. I'm hurt." Will was having some fun at the expense of Josef Resnic. "But, if it makes you feel better, I will write the information down and return the fish tickets to you. I do appreciate your cooperation, sir."

By the time Will had recorded all the fish tickets, his crew had finished picking the net. Loco gave him the tally on the fish, which nearly filled one large tote. Dave stayed on the Volga to attach the lines to the davit on the Enforcer and get it lifted to the deck above and then he too climbed aboard the patrol boat.

When Will had finished writing down the numbers, he handed the bank bag to Resnic. "We will leave you now, Mr. Resnic. Do you have any questions before we leave your boat?" Will tore a citation from his book and handed it to the captain.

"No, I ain't got no questions. Now get off my vessel. You have already cost me a day's work."

"I must advise you, Captain, that you must leave this area. It is closed to drift gillnet fishing and you have committed a serious violation. I am warning you that if you are caught again in these waters I will seize not only your catch, but also your vessel. Is that clear to you?"

"Of course it's clear. I'm not an idiot. Besides the weather is getting bad and we will have to hole up tonight. Now, if you are through badgering me, get off my boat." An angry Resnic turned and entered the cabin of the Volga.

Trippet climbed aboard the Enforcer and watched as the crew loosed the lines from the Volga and secured their cargo. Will returned to the cabin to speak with Dean Steadman.

"I hate to admit this, but I really enjoyed that," Will commented quietly. "It's been a long time in the making, but we got him."

"I know it's late and the weather is kicking up, but with those fish totes on the back deck we need to head in to the cannery. Homer is closer and the water may not be as bumpy as trying to get to Kenai. We will be going out again for tomorrow's opening, so we won't get much sleep. You can stay on the boat with us, Will. Eric can fix us some dinner as we head back to port." Dean watched Will a few seconds and then added, "You did a great job today, Will. Do you want a transfer to the Enforcer permanently?"

Will Tripper smiled, "Nah, you guys work too hard."

CHAPTER 17

Dean Steadman had slept only an hour in the cabin of the Enforcer tied to the dock in the Homer boat harbor when he awakened at 3:00 a.m. and began his day. Turning on dim cabin lights and starting a pot of coffee, he stepped out on the rear deck to check the weather. It was late July, but the days had begun to lose daylight. Especially on this cloudy night, the sky was almost black. He noted the wind had abated some and there was no rain.

Eric heard his skipper moving around the cabin and was up when Dean started the engines to warm them. He met the boat captain when he returned to the inside of the cabin. The rest of the crew was asleep in their bunks. Old salts seem to like the hum of the engines and the gentle motion of the boat; it helped them sleep peacefully. Eric had poured two cups of coffee by the time Dean returned.

Eric greeted the skipper with a fresh cup of hot coffee and a short, "Mornin'."

Dean returned the greeting and set about making logbook entries while sipping his coffee, giving a satisfied sigh from time to time. Eric had busied himself with making coffee and filling thermos bottles for the morning. At exactly 4:00 a.m., Steadman ordered Eric to cast off the lines and watch for boat traffic. This was a daily ritual and each man knew what the other would do. Eric finished his chores and stepped onto the forward deck, while Dean slowly moved away from the dock and motored out of the harbor, into the dark night and into the slightly choppy waters of Kachemak Bay.

Once out of the harbor and past the marker buoy, Eric returned to the cabin. Below decks, Dave and Lobo slept like babies as the boat bobbed gently in the morning waves. The weather was predicted to be gentle with seas of less than two feet. The boat movement was strange to Will Trippet and awakened him. He went into the head, shaved, washed and combed his hair. He wore the same uniform he had worn the day before, but, though it had lost its sharp creases, it was reasonably clean. His body ached from the unfamiliar activities of the previous day, but he felt good despite the lack of a good night's sleep. Dean Steadman was in the pilot chair when Will came up from below. Eric was sitting at the table, reading a newspaper that had miraculously appeared during the night.

"Good morning," Will quietly announced as he climbed into the cabin.

"Mornin'," came two replies. Eric poured him a cup of coffee and offered him the newspaper, which he refused with a wave of his hand.

"Sleep well?" Steadman asked without taking his eyes off the water in front of him.

"I sure did, Cap. It must have been the sea air," Will replied.

"It's pretty dark this morning so I'm not traveling very fast. The big halibut party boats are moving out this time of day and they don't move very fast. I guess it's not good to have all those hangovers hanging over the rail first thing in the morning. The six-pack boats will be faster and going out later. There is only a fourteen-foot tide change this morning and in this area, it will be high just after 8:00. I plan to go straight across and up the west side of the inlet. I was thinking it might be interesting to see where the Volga is at this hour, although, I don't expect him to be committing any violations today."

"I checked my messages and the office told me the fleet would be allowed to fish today and tomorrow, but only for twelve-hour periods. It looks like you will have to put up with me one more day."

"We can put up with you for that long, but remember we treated you like a rookie yesterday. Today you're one of the regulars. No mercy today." Steadman looked at Trippet with a broad grin, "Now pour the Captain a cup of coffee."

"Aye, aye, Captain," was the response. Will poured the captain more coffee and delivered it to him. "What is the plan for today, Dean? Anything special on the docket?"

"No, I think we will just patrol up the west side this morning and the middle rip and east side this afternoon. The sockeye run is dying off quickly. The drifters are catching as many silvers as reds right now. The reds are worth more at the cannery, but the silvers are larger, so I guess it averages out."

Once on the west side, they cruised into Ursus Cove and could see the Volga tied to the side of the Galaxy. There were no other boats in the area and Steadman moved his boat to the north toward Chinitna Bay. At 6:00 a.m., the drift fleet, at least those boats within sight, had nets in the water. The Enforcer moved northward, stopping to check random vessels for permits and licenses. Everyone seemed to be operating within the law. The Enforcer was large and visible, making it the equivalent of a black and white patrol car on a city street. Word had spread throughout the drift fleet that they were patrolling in the upper inlet.

"This big boat makes a good deterrent, but it's easy for people to know where we are operating. We probably won't drive up on any violations today," Steadman noted.

They turned east once past Three Mile Creek and moved to the middle of the inlet. There was a huge, debris filled, rip in the center. Schools of fish like to follow this wild water because it is filled with feed, both large and small. Sockeye salmon are plankton feeders, whereas Coho salmon are bait-fish feeders. Both varieties find food along the rip in the center of the inlet. One of the problems with fishing this area is the amount of flotsam tangled in the nets.

At twelve minutes past noon, the Enforcer got a Mayday call from a fishing vessel with a net tangled in the rip. The net was so heavy there was a danger of it taking the boat down with it. The location was nearly 20 miles south of their location and Steadman gave an ETA of fifty minutes. That time seemed optimistic to Will, but Steadman knew what he was doing.

"I'll bet this guy has a net full of fish and doesn't want to cut it loose," Dean said, speeding ahead and watching for floating logs.

"Does that happen a lot?" he asked.

"Enough. It's not unusual to find a boat with the hold full of fish and dragging a full net behind it attempting to make it to the cannery. Sometimes they even make it. When they don't, they call us."

"Why would they endanger themselves, their crew and their boat like that?" Will asked the skipper.

"The only answer I have is greed," replied Steadman. "Some men can't resist making 'just one more set.' We see this almost every year. It has to be greed." Eric, Dave and Loco readied boat hooks and lines. Every hand kept an eye out for the distressed vessel.

"Giant Killer, Giant Killer, this is the Enforcer. We have you in sight. We are two miles north of your position, ETA five minutes."

"Enforcer, this is Giant Killer. I think you will need to swing around and point your ship north, like us. Our net is drifting to the east side of the boat. I recommend you come up on the west side of our boat."

"Roger that, Giant Killer. Are you taking on any water?"

"Only waves over the rear deck. Nothing in the hull, but I am afraid to move the boat out of the rip. We are too unstable."

"OK, Giant Killer. We are coming up on your port side. Be ready with a line."

Will went to the rear deck to lend a hand. He could see the three-man crew scurrying around the deck of the smaller boat. The rear deck was under water, being drug downward by the weight of a drift gillnet full of fish and debris. Both crews worked to tie the Giant Killer to the side of the Enforcer. Once that was accomplished, both crews began the task of pulling in the net. Slowly and carefully, they inched the net onto the net reel, picking out fish and debris as they retrieved the net. It was riddled with holes from the sticks and limbs that had tangled in the webbing. There were a large number of fish in the net and the crew pulled the fish and dropped them into the fish hold. The sticks, logs and trash were tossed back into the murky brown waters of Cook Inlet.

It took more than an hour to reel in the net and make the boat float, as it should. Will and Dean asked the skipper for his permits and licenses. They checked the ID of every man aboard and verbally warned them of unsafe practices.

Will was in the cabin of the Enforcer when the boats parted and they continued patrolling. "That is the most bazaar thing I have ever witnessed. Those guys towed that net right into the rip. They must have seen the school of fish and completely disregarded personal safety to get at them." Will was shaking his head.

"Like I said, greed," Dean commented as he turned the nose of the big boat to the west. "Let's go into Tuxedni Bay and drop an anchor. The crew needs some food and some rest. We can slip out of there this afternoon and see if anyone is fishing after hours. If Donavan is flying, he can check on your friends on the Volga."

"Sounds good to me, Dean." Will hated to admit he was getting weary. Tired men have accidents, he remembered someone telling him once.

CHAPTER 18

The entire crew welcomed the break and each of them slept soundly. Will slept like a log on a sandy beach. They had only slept about an hour and a half, but Will Trippet awoke refreshed. To his surprise, the crew was already up and moving around the boat, tending to minor chores, like coiling lines and stowing boathooks. Will poured a cup of hot coffee and walked to the back deck where the others were busy. The afternoon sky was beginning to brighten as the weather improved.

"What can I do to help?" Will asked.

They all looked toward him, but it was Dean who answered. "Hey there, Sleeping Beauty. We were about to come see if you were still alive. We're done out here. Dave made a pot of soup and there is a kettle of it on the stove. Go in and get some and we will be right in to join you."

Trippet saluted with his coffee cup and turned to reenter the cabin. Inside he found the pot of hamburger soup that smelled delicious. There was warm bread on the cupboard beside the stove and bowls beside the sink. He ladled two scoops into his bowl and buttered a thick piece of bread. He was wiping his mouth with a paper napkin when the rest of the crew entered.

"That was good stuff. Which of you made it?"

"Dave made the soup and the bread," said Loco. "I washed the dishes."

"If you eat like this all the time, I am going to ask for a transfer. Thanks."

"There was a phone call from your boss, but he said not to wake you. He asked to have you call when you got up," Dean reported.

"Thanks," Will said as he reached for his cell phone, amazed that there was reception on this side of the inlet. Looking at his watch, he wondered if the captain would be in the office this late but dialed anyway.

"Captain Olson, Wildlife Troopers," he answered. Marcy had left the office for the day.

"Hello, Captain. Will Trippet. Dean said you wanted me to call."

"Oh, Will. How is it going out there? I talked with Donavan and he said you had some luck on your personal project."

"Yeah, we are heading out now to try again. What did you need, Cap?"

"Bad news for you, I'm afraid. I am running out of personnel. The dip net fishery, the Russian River and the personal use fishery have used up my resources. I am going to have to ask you to come back tonight and be in the office tomorrow. I have three big game cases with no one to handle them." Captain Olson explained.

"I have no idea what time we will get to the dock tonight, but I will be there in the morning. What are the big game cases?"

"There are two DLP cases and a double moose poaching. One of the Defense of Life and Property cases is a bear in Sterling and the other is a cow moose on Feuding Lane. The animals have been taken care of, but there is nobody here to do the reports. I need you, Will, otherwise I wouldn't have called."

"We are heading out of Tuxedni Bay now to finish our patrol. See you in the morning."

Will explained the situation to Dean Steadman. Dean understood the need for his newest crewman to return to headquarters, but liked having Wilson Trippet on board the Enforcer. They discussed it while they moved the boat out of the bay and around Chisik Island. The only boats visible north of the island were traveling fast toward the canneries so Dean pointed the bow south along the same beach they had followed the previous day. The wind had let up and the water was much calmer than it had been when they approached the Volga the day before.

The little intercom blinked and Steadman answered as they passed Spring Point. "You ain't going to believe this, Skipper," Eric reported. "The Volga is in the same spot with a net out." Eric was on the upper deck with his binoculars and video camera.

"Are you sure it's the Volga?" asked a startled Steadman.

"It sure looks like it from here," Eric replied.

Dean was looking through the windshield with his own binoculars. "Sure enough, Will. It's him. I don't believe it. He will spot us if we go straight across the bay. I am going out into the inlet and approach from his bow. He will probably see us anyway, but if he is busy, like he was yesterday, we might just get up on him before he sees us." Dean was laughing aloud. "Do you want to drive his boat back to the Homer Harbor, Will?"

Will was excited and apprehensive; what could Resnic be thinking? "Whatever it takes, Dean."

Steadman swung the Enforcer to the left, pointing it directly across the inlet toward Kachemak Bay. He hoped to deceive any lookout on the violator. The boat maintained course and a medium speed for several minutes while they angled away from and across the mouth of Chinitna Bay. As they cruised out of sight, hidden by the point of land, Steadman wheeled the nose of the boat toward the bay and increased the speed to nearly maximum. The waves were insignificant here and the boat was moving fast without taking much of a pounding. As they passed Seal Spit, they were able to see the Volga. Travelling at high speed, the Enforcer closed the distance in a short amount of time. Dean backed off the throttles as he approached, allowing his wake to pass his boat and rock the fishing vessel. Two men appeared at the rail of the smaller boat as the bow of the Enforcer made its way down the side of the Volga. The distance between the boats now was only a matter of a few feet. The men disappeared behind the wheelhouse of the Volga. Momentarily, an armed man returned to the rail.

"Gun," Eric shouted from above.

Dean instantly flipped the switch for the loud speaker on deck. "Put your weapon down, Resnic," the voice boomed through the speaker.

"Get the hell away from my boat or I'll shoot," Resnic shouted from his deck.

Again through the speaker Steadman ordered, "Don't make things worse for yourself, Resnic. Put down your weapon. Tell your crewman to step to the rail beside you."

Larry Hanson came out of the cabin to talk with Resnic. Resnic shoved him away and again pointed the rifle at the Enforcer. Hanson backed away from his skipper with his hands high. Josef Resnic, his face red with rage, pointed the gun in the air and fired. "Get away from my boat," he shouted again.

While Eric and Dean continued to confront Resnic, Loco and Will walked to the back deck of the Enforcer, which was now only about eight feet away from the Volga. Loco used a boathook to snag the front rail of the fishing vessel while Will jumped to the smaller Volga. He worked his way down the side of the cabin to where he could see Hanson. Trippet motioned for Hanson to move toward the fish reel and continued toward the rear deck, while on the Enforcer Dean continued to challenge Josef Resnic. Now Resnics voice was a high-pitched squeal and he was making little sense in his rage.

When he was astern of the cabin, Will quietly stepped over the rail onto the deck. Once he had solid footing, he lunged at Resnic, ripping the rifle from his hands and dropping it over the side. A surprised Resnic was slow to respond and Will had him in a headlock, forcing him to the deck. Both Eric and Loco scrambled to get on the Volga to assist him. Resnic was a big, well-muscled man, strong and mean, now face down on the deck with one arm behind him. Eric was the first to arrive and assist Trippet, whose knee was in the middle of the prone fisherman's back. Eric assisted in snapping the handcuffs to the irate and nearly incoherent fisherman. Loco was holding Hanson away from the action, though he was making no move to join in the fracas.

Will and Eric lifted Resnic to his feet and helped him sit on the lid of the fish hold.

"Thanks for the assist, Eric," Will said in a strained voice, holding his hands on his knees, catching his breath.

"I would have been here quicker if I had known you were doing your Errol Flynn act. Great job, Will. I was sure I would be the first one shot when he opened fire." He moved closer to Trippet, "I think I got that whole episode on video," he muttered quietly.

Will slapped Eric on the shoulder and moved to talk with Hanson. "Staying out of it was a wise move on your part," he said to the deckhand. "Did you know he was going to pull a gun on us?"

"He said he would, but I didn't think he would really do it. I just got out on a three-year stretch and I don't want to go back to jail. All I want to do is make some money fishing. I knew we weren't supposed to be fishing, but when the skipper says fish, I fish. That's all, I just fish."

"Are you willing to testify about your illegal fishing?" Will asked Hanson.

"Not a chance, Man. Josef and his brother Ivan are both ruthless men. I wouldn't last a day if I testified against them. I'll take the heat for my part, but that's as far as I am willing to go."

"Are you saying you think they would do you harm if you testified?"

"I don't think so, Trooper, I know so. It's happened before."

"OK, Larry, if that's the way you want it. I have a lot of paperwork to do. We'll take Josef aboard the Enforcer. It might help your case of you helped Dave and Loco pick the net and count the fish. We will be seizing the Volga and its catch."

"Yeah, I'll run the gear for them. Thanks for the offer, Trooper. Sorry I can't help you more."

It was very late and very dark when the two vessels entered the harbor at Homer. Will had worked on the arrest report during the entire trip. Dean had radioed for assistance at the dock and they found Sean Adams waiting on the dock when they tied up. Adams took Resnic into custody and hauled him to the Homer jail for booking.

Dean and Will had a final cup of coffee while discussing the voyage. The men had worked well together with the effort paying great dividends. They shook hands and Will walked up the hill to his truck. It would be a long drive to Soldotna.

CHAPTER 19

Early Friday morning, Will drove from the office toward Sterling. There were two cases of animals shot in defense of life and property, both in the Sterling area. In the case of the bear, Will knew the shooter. The man, who was a Kenai River guide, and his family, lived near the river in a huge, log home. His business name was Lotsaluck Fishing Charters. The owner's name was Tom Pasternak. His father was an old-time homesteader in the Sterling area. Tom was a short, square-built young man who stayed fit by rowing a drift boat five days a week. His wife, a cute little blond named Patty, booked his charters and kept the books. She also drove the shuttle to carry the clients back to the starting point at Moose River where they had parked their cars. Tom was on the river with clients this morning, but Patty was home with the kids.

When Will pulled into the yard, the two children, ages nine and twelve, ran out to greet him. Patty had heard his vehicle and stepped out onto the front porch, drying her hands, and waved at Will as he stepped out of his truck. The children were excited and both wanted to show Will the hide of the bear their dad had shot. Will waved back at Patty and followed the kids to the back yard where there was a large bloody spot on the ground only a few feet from the back steps. The boy, the younger of the two, tugged at Will's hand pulling him to the woodshed where the bear hide was stretched out on the floor. Both children chattered all the while, not giving Will a chance to say anything.

When the little group came out of the woodshed, Patty was on the back deck, waiting to talk with the trooper. "OK, kids, leave the trooper alone. I'll tell him what happened. Now go play."

Both children said, "OK, Mom," and ran to the front yard again.

"Come on in, Will. I have fresh coffee and a hot apple pie, just out of the oven. We can talk in the kitchen."

"That sounds wonderful, Patty. I've been on the boat for a couple of days and could do with a piece of that pie."

Inside the kitchen, Patty seated him at the table and brought a large piece of American Apple Pie. "Do you want a little ice cream with that?" she asked.

"No, thanks. I'm trying to watch my weight." The coffee was hot and he sipped it carefully. "How many clients are staying with you?" Will asked out of curiosity.

"Only three, the other one has relatives here and is staying with them. As poor as the economy has been, I'm surprised anyone can afford to come up to Alaska to fish. Tom and I are lucky, though, we have been really busy all year."

Trippet took the notebook from his pocket and placed it on the table to take notes while he ate his pie. "Tell me what happened here yesterday, Patty."

"It was kind of funny, actually. We were all here in the kitchen having breakfast, Tom, the three clients and me. The kids were still in bed. One of the clients picked up his coffee cup and stepped over to the back door. It was open, but the screen was closed. All of a sudden, he started stuttering and stammering and pointing at the screen with his coffee cup. He was spilling coffee everywhere. I got kinda mad at him for a second. Then we all saw the bear coming up the steps onto the porch. Tom yelled at the clients to get back from the door and went to the living room closet for his shotgun. By the time he came back, the bear was at the door, sniffing and looking. The clients were backing up into the living room, scared to death. Tom jacked a shell into the shotgun and started yelling at the bear. Tom walked right up to the back door, yelling and yelling. The bear stopped and turned around. Then it walked off the deck and down into the yard. Tom opened the screen and walked outside, still yelling at the bear. The bear went out about twenty feet and we thought it was leaving, but then it turned around and came running back. Tom fired two shots and the bear fell by the foot of the stairs. We were all frightened. Tom checked the bear, but it was dead.

We called your office and asked for you, but they said you weren't in the office. They sent another man out and he helped Tom skin the thing. They put the hide in the woodshed and he said there would be someone here today to make the report. The clients were impressed with it all; they have all booked for next year. They are all on a full-day charter with Tom now." Patty sat down at the table. "Would you like some more pie or coffee, Will?"

"No, thank you. It sure was delicious. Thanks, Patty." Will was making notes and asking questions about the incident. He looked at Patty, "Are you afraid for your kids, for their safety, I mean."

"No, not really. We've lived out here all our lives and we see bears quite often. They usually don't try to come inside, though." Patty seemed resigned to bears as a part of life.

"I think that's all I will need for my report, Patty. I have another call on Feuding Lane and I have to leave. I'll have to roll the hide and take it to town with me, sorry you can't keep it, but it will be auctioned and Tom can bid on it when it comes up. It sounds to me as if this is a genuine self-defense shooting and I don't anticipate any further contact will be necessary about the incident."

Minutes later, with the bear hide tied up and rolled in a tarp, Will drove away hoping his next contact would be as pleasant.

Feuding Lane is a dusty track about four miles in length stretching from the Sterling Highway to the Kenai River. Short side roads travel to either side off the main road, mostly old seismic trails converted to roads by homesteaders. One such road led to the home of Charlie Canter. It was a small, log house with a front yard cluttered with old trucks and cars, none of which would ever run again. The condition of the place mirrored the cluttered mind of Charlie Canter. He was harmless enough, but most folks just thought he was eccentric, and he was. Charlie came out the front door when he heard the trooper vehicle pull into the yard. He waved to Will when he stopped the truck.

"'Bout time you got here," Charlie said as he turned and stepped back up on his broken porch.

"Good morning to you, too, Charlie." Will followed the old-timer to his porch. "I heard you shot a cow moose here yesterday. Do you want to tell me about it?"

"That officer that was here yesterday said someone was coming to talk with me about it. Glad it was you." Charlie was never what might be called cordial. "What do you want to know? The old bag had a calf and when I came out of the house, she kicked me. Damn near broke my ribs, too."

"Are you OK now, Charlie?"

"I'm a little sore, but I'll be all right."

"Glad to hear it. Where were you when she kicked you?"

"Right out there in the front yard." He was pointing to an old green shape in the yard. "See that old Studebaker pickup? Right in front of that. I saw the calf, but I didn't see her until she came at me with her ears back and doing a hunnert miles an hour. I tried to jump out of the way when she kicked, but she got me anyhow. I grabbed that ice-chipping bar and whacked her upside the head. She spun around and run off. Then she shook her head and came at me again. This time I saw her coming and sidestepped her. As she went by, I stuck her in the chest with the bar. Killed the old heifer."

"Where is the calf now, Charlie?"

"I don't know, Trooper. It ran off into the spruce trees and never came back. I figured she would come back to check on her mamma, but I never seen her again."

"I want you to wait here, Charlie. I'm going to walk around and see if I can find it. A calf that young usually doesn't make it, though."

"Go ahead, I'll be right here."

Will Trippet had done this many times before and had always come up with a bad ending. He walked into the trees and circled the homestead, then circled back around again a little farther out. On the third pass, he came upon the calf, dead, half eaten and the remainder covered with leaves and grass. It was obvious a bear had killed the little guy. To Will it was a sad sight. He snapped some pictures and walked back to the house.

"Find it?" Charlie called when Trippet came back into the yard.

"Yes, Charlie, I found it. A bear got to it first. I think the bear is still in the area, so be careful." I need to see your driver license, Charlie. It has your ID numbers and address. I just need to write them down. I would like you to come into the office and sign a statement for me sometime next week. Will you do that for me?"

"Sure, Will." He had a serious look on his grizzled face. "That moose meat, do you think I could get some of that? I could sure use it."

"I'll see what I can do, Charlie. Thanks for your help. I have to go to North Kenai on another call, but I'll see you next week." As he climbed into his truck, he looked back at the old man and admired him for his tenacity to life. Quick thinking and fast response had probably saved his life, but the old homesteader seemed to look at it as just another day on the old place.

It was a long drive to Nikiski and Will considered stopping for lunch, but he remembered the piece of apple pie and decided to skip lunch. It took a while to locate the complainant on Halibouty Road. Carol Beeson lived alone in a secluded house trailer. The timber surrounding her house was thick and lush. There was plenty of browse for moose. It had been a long time since Will had heard as many songbirds chirping in the trees. He stepped up to the door, standing on the small deck and wondered why anyone would live here. He knocked on the door.

"Who is it?" a voice on the inside asked.

"Wildlife Trooper, Ma'am. Wilson Trippet," he called back.

The door opened revealing a short, chunky woman of about 50 dressed in a bathrobe and with hair that had not seen a comb in a very long time. The odor escaping through the open door nearly made Trippet wretch.

"Would you mind stepping out here, Ma'am?" Will asked.

The woman cautiously stepped out. "Are you Carol Beeson?" he asked.

"Yes, that's me. Is this about the dead moose I called in about?"

"Yes, it is. The officer who responded had other calls and I am here to do the report. Do you mind speaking with me?"

"No, it's OK. I don't know much about it except I took a walk around my place yesterday and over there," she pointed toward the woods on the west side of the driveway, "I smelled something bad and went to look. There are two moose over there in the trees. It looked like they had been shot."

"Have you heard any shots recently, Ms. Beason?"

"No, but I am hard of hearing and when the TV is on I have it pretty loud."

"Have you seen any suspicious vehicles in the area recently?" Will asked her as many questions as he could think of without gaining any useful information. He wrote down her name, address and other information before telling her he was going to look at the moose and would be at the scene for a while. Taking a metal detector from the toolbox in the back of his truck, he walked out of view and into the woods. The animals were easy to find. The odor was bad and the animals were bloated. He found bullet holes in both animals. Neither displayed any signs of being butchered. This was a clear case of someone shooting the moose for pleasure. He began at the bullet hole and scanned the carcasses for bullets that could remain inside. He found none and surmised they had been shot with a large caliber rifle and the bullets had gone completely through the animals. He searched the surrounding area for any evidence left behind by the shooter, but he found none. He tried to find where the shooter had entered the woods, but no trail could be found. With nothing to go on, he returned to his truck to make notes about the scene. It was unlikely anyone would ever be arrested for this poaching.

On the way back to the office, he checked the time and it surprised him to realize he had been out on the road the entire shift. He returned to the office and worked late writing the three reports.

CHAPTER 20

It was getting late, but Will decided to call Dean Steadman. He would have been to court with Resnic and Hanson today and wanted to know how it went. He was smiling to himself knowing the Volga crew would not be fishing any more this season.

"Steadman," a sleepy voice answered.

"Dean, Will Trippet. I know it's late, but I just got back to the office and was anxious to hear how it went in court. How did they plead?"

"I hope you're sitting down, Old Buddy. It ain't a pretty sight," Steadman said.

"Why not? What happened?" Will was surprised.

"When we got to court, our regular judge from Kenai wasn't there. We had a substitute from Anchorage and he ripped us," Steadman said in a sour voice.

"You're kidding! Tell me about it."

"Dave and I worked half the night writing the complaints. We charged them with the two counts of fishing closed waters and in a closed period. We also charged Resnic with assaulting an officer and misconduct with a weapon. We told the District Attorney we wanted his catch and his boat because of the multiple offenses, and we wanted Resnic to do time for the gun issue."

"That sounds right. How did they plead?" Will wanted to know.

"The two of them pleaded guilty to the fishing violations and Resnic plead not guilty to the gun charge. He told the judge he should go easy because this was his first offense and didn't want to lose his boat. He said Hanson was just following his orders and he shouldn't even be in court."

"How did the DA answer that?"

"She told the judge she didn't know of any violations prior to this arrest. She didn't even ask for the forfeiture of the catch as part of the fine. It was pitiful. The judge took a long time reading the reports and finally said he was ready to pronounce a sentence."

"You're killing me, Dean. What did he say? How much time did they get?"

"The judge puffed up, looking important, and said what we were asking as punishment and fine was far too harsh. He forfeited the catch on each offense. He said that since this was Resnic's first offense he was going to fine each man $500 with $250 suspended. He did not seize the Volga and he dismissed the gun charge saying Resnic was only protecting himself and his crew. We got nothing, pardner."

"I can't believe it," Will said, disgusted and hurt. He was taking it personally even though he knew that was a bad thing and could cause him to make some bad judgments. He had to relax and get his mind where it belonged.

"I'm with you, pal." Dean, too, was pained by the proceedings. "I guess we'll have to catch him again."

"I'll bet Josef and his brother Ivan are having a beer and laughing their heads off right now." Trippet felt the court had made fools of them and their efforts. "Did the DA say why she didn't object to the sentence? Surely she knew what was going on. "

"Well, if she did, she didn't show it. And worse, she said it would look bad if we targeted his activity and arrested Resnic again." Steadman laughed. "Come to think of it, I'm kinda mad at you for getting me into this mess."

Will Trippet chuckled at Dean, "I don't blame you, in fact I am sort of mad at myself over it." He sighed and became serious again. "I am going to have to cool off before I think about this case and what we are going to do about it. We can't let these guys keep on with what they have been doing. And, by the way, we need to nail Ivan, too. I'm too angry to think about it right now, Dean. I'll call you Monday. In fact, if I can get away I'll drive down and meet with you. See you Monday."

"See you Monday, pardner."

With his enthusiasm dampened and his spirit injured, Trippet closed up his office. As he was leaving, he turned the light on again and walked to the desk to call Gordy Ponset. When Gordy answered, Will didn't even say hello. He just asked, "Want to have a burger and beer?"

"Wow, Will. You must have had a really bad day. I can't remember the last time I saw you drink a beer. What happened?"

"Yeah, you could say it was a bad day. I'm going to the house to change clothes. I'll meet you at Buckets Sports Bar."

"I'll be there in 45 minutes. You're buying," Ponset said.

They met in the parking lot at Buckets. Inside they found a table in the farthest corner where it was unlikely they would be overheard. The place was noisy and television sets glared from every corner of the room. Each table had a speaker with which to listen to any individual television in the room. Hockey and basketball were showing on most of the sets, while a poker tournament was playing on the set over the bar.

A nice looking young woman brought them menus and placemats, along with some Crayolas for doodling on the placemats. The two men ordered Alaska Amber Beer and Bucket Burgers. When she had gone, Ponset asked his friend what had happened to ruin his day.

Will looked around to see if anyone was apt to be listening, and turned to Gordy. "Remember I said I was out to catch that commercial fisherman from Ninilchik?"

Gordy sipped his beer and nodded.

"I was on the Enforcer for two days and we nailed the boat, the Volga, twice. Fishing closed period and closed area. The second time that we caught him he pointed a rifle at us and threatened to shoot. I got over onto his boat and disarmed him. We arrested him and filed a list of charges. He went to court today. The judge gave us his catch and fined him $250 on each fishing charge. He dismissed the weapon charges and gave him back his boat." Will was becoming angry again. "Other than that it was a pretty good day."

"I can't believe it! Who was the judge?"

"Some substitute judge from Anchorage. He must have never dealt with com-fish violations before. The DA was no help either." Will sipped his glass of beer and shook his head. "A lot of man hours and boat fuel along with the aircraft time was wasted. I guess you may have noticed, I'm not happy and I am going to have to cool off before I try to figure out what to do next."

"You need some time off, Buddy. You are getting too personal with this case."

"Yeah, you're right. Want to go fishing tomorrow?" Will asked.

The burgers had arrived and Gordy was chewing on a French fry. "It will have to be in the afternoon. Lori wants me to take her shopping in the morning; it's our day to spend some time together. With her working for the city as a clerk and me at the office until late every day, Saturday morning is our special time to catch up on family gossip. I'll be finished around 2:00, though. Where do you want to go?"

"How about Russian River? There are a lot of people at the confluence on the Kenai River, but we can walk up to the falls and fish our way back to the campground." Will was grinning. "Bring your badge so we can get a place to park."

"Your truck or mine?"

"Meet me at my house when you finish with Lori. I'll make us a lunch and we can take my truck this time." Will knew the Russian River would be a shoulder-to-shoulder fishing challenge, but it was full of sockeye and an experienced angler would have no trouble catching his limit. Most of all it would be a relaxing day with an old friend.

"I'll see you around 2:00." Gordy was munching his burger and fries. Both men scanned the games on the televisions, but never turned on the speakers. Each man had one more beer before ordering black coffee.

It was late and nearly dark when Will returned home. He couldn't tell if it was the beer, the company of a good friend, or the food that had let him relax, but he felt a little better. He still didn't know what he was going to do about Resnic, but he wasn't going to think about it tonight. He went inside and directly to his bedroom without turning on any lights. He was still dressed when he awoke Saturday morning.

CHAPTER 21

At the same time Will and Gordy were leaving on their fishing expedition at Russian River, Ivan and Josef Resnic were having a late lunch at Duncan's Café in Homer. It was the weekend and there were more customers than usual for this late in the day. This was a lunch and strategy meeting for the brothers. Each had ordered the hot beef sandwich and both plates came with mashed potatoes piled high and brown gravy dripping off the side of the plates. The two men ate here regularly when they were in town. The food was great and the price was good, something the frugal Ivan had noted years ago. The waitress, with tattoos adorning both wrists, poured more coffee, left the check on the table and went back to the counter.

"I expected to come into town and find you without a boat. What happened?" Ivan was asking his brother.

"I expected that myself, but I got lucky. The regular judge from Kenai had been called away and they sent one from Anchorage. I don't think he had ever done a fishing hearing. The DA was some young woman, new to the system and we were able to get by pretty easy," Josef related.

"What do you call easy?"

"We pleaded guilty to the two counts of fishing closed waters and closed period. The judge gave us a fine of $500 each for each charge and suspended $250 each on each charge. He threw out the other charges and said we could have our boat back upon payment of the fine. I thanked him very much and paid the clerk of the court the fine. She gave me a memo to take to the harbormaster releasing the Volga to us." Josef shoveled potatoes into his mouth. "You should have seen the look on that Trooper Steadman's face when I got the boat back."

"Don't get too cocky, Josef. This little incident put you on the trooper radar and they will be watching you." Ivan was mopping gravy from his plate with a dinner roll. "I told you not to go out; that they would be watching. You wouldn't listen to me. Now it's cost us $1,000 and put the spotlight right on us. It was stupid, Josef." He poked the soaked up dinner roll into his mouth.

"There is only two weeks left to fish. We are going to have to do something to fill the Galaxy before you go south. What do you suggest?" Josef wasn't exactly asking his older brother for advice.

"That's up to you, but if it were me, I would operate completely legal for the next four periods. Then, when everyone is off the inlet, start fishing the halibut long line at night for a couple of weeks before the weather drives us out." Ivan now had both elbows on the table, sipping his mug of black coffee.

Josef Resnic was smiling at his brother. "Remember how simple it used to be when you had that old wood dory and the two of us fished any time we wanted? It ain't like that anymore, Ivan. We used to row that old dory out of the Ninilchik harbor and start laying out net. We'd fish one direction 'til the tide changed and then fish our way back again. Nowadays we own big boats with lots of power, new nets, and deckhands to do the work, and here we are scheming to make a living. It don't seem right somehow."

"Times change, Josef. Remember how papa used to say, 'times they are a-changin' and we have to change with them'? I don't remember papa having to work so hard to make a living. When he taught us how to fish there weren't many enforcement people out there. And you will remember there were almost no regulations. Things changed when they took out the fish traps. We thought it would be better for drift fishermen, but the way they regulate the fishing periods you can't tell if you are legal or not. Well, Josef, I don't care if we're legal, only that we make money. The set netters don't have to fight as hard and make more money. I guess we should have taken sights on the beach when we had the chance, but we didn't. Papa is gone and so is the way he fished. We have to do what we know how to do, even if we get caught sometimes."

"You're right, Ivan. I'm not blaming you. It's just that, with all the competition out there, we have to take chances sometimes. I don't want them to take my boat again. I don't think papa would like the way we do it, but I'll bet he would be out there with us." Josef now followed the family tradition and had his elbows on the table, sipping his coffee.

Both men relaxed and leaned back in their chairs. Several minutes passed without a word. Finally, Josef sat up straight and emptied his cup. "I guess I need to find Larry and start checking out the boat. It should be OK except for some cleaning and fueling up to shove off Monday. When are you going back out to the Galaxy?"

"I am going to the house and do some work in the office, make some phone calls and head out this evening. We won't pull the anchor until tomorrow morning." Ivan stood. "I hate to keep bringing this up, but we are short of fish and the season is getting short. We can't afford to lose any more time. Call me on the marine radio when you decide what you are going to do and I will tell you where I am located. I still have customers out there who want to sell me fish. Just remember what I said about being on the trooper radar. They aren't going to forget."

"Neither am I, Ivan, neither am I."

Ivan paid the bill and walked to his Chevy Suburban. He sat in the driver seat for a few moments before starting the engine and heading out East End Road.

Josef had another cup of coffee while he sat, thinking. When he had finished he, too, walked to his pickup. Before climbing inside, he took the cell phone from his pocket and dialed Larry Hanson. It was not a friendly voice that answered.

"Hanson," he growled into the phone.

"Larry, it's Josef. I'm going to the boat to fuel up for Monday. Are you ready to come to work?"

"I know you paid my fine and I'm grateful, but with my record I can't afford to be in court. I still owe the state some time and I don't want them to make me come back and do it. This is serious for me, Josef."

"I understand, Larry. Forget the fine. You have done a great job and I like your work. If you come back, I'll see you get a bonus at the end of the season. Meet me at the boat and we will talk about it. I need you, Larry." His remarks were honest. Larry was a good deckhand and knew how to fish. He was able to keep his mouth shut and do what needed to be done. He was also willing to put his efforts into the nighttime fishing being planned.

There was a pause on the other end. "OK, when do you want me there?"

"No hurry, Larry. I'll fuel up and we can clean the boat. When we finish I'll buy your dinner."

"I'll be there in two hours, but we need to talk about this some more. I'm scared, Josef. I don't want to go back to the slammer."

Larry would have to agree to finish the season out, including the night halibut fishing as well as the remaining salmon openers. Ivan needed several thousand pounds more fish to fill his boat and it would take long hours to get the job done. If he stayed, it would be worth the hefty bonus Josef promised.

Josef had finished refueling and was back at his berth when Larry arrived. Josef had cleaned the salt off the exterior windows and was working on the inside when the deckhand came aboard. He only nodded to the skipper before filling a bucket with seawater and dousing the rear deck. For nearly two hours, they worked without conversing. When the chores were finished, Larry came into the cabin and sat in the booth.

"How much bonus?" Larry asked, without preamble.

"It will depend on how we do with halibut. If we do well and fill the Galaxy, I think maybe $4,000."

"If we don't fill the Galaxy, $4,000; if we do I want $5,000."

"Promise to work next year and it's a deal." Josef had expected some negotiating, but this was more than he had anticipated.

"Done, if you buy dinner tonight. I'm going to let you off easy for dinner. It's steak night at the Homer Elks Club. I'm not drinking, but they have a good steak."

Josef was relieved at the quick answer. He had been dreading a debate with Larry.

"The next opener is on Tuesday. I think we will leave Monday, mid-day, and anchor up in Tuxedni Bay. The weather is changing and it looks like rain for the rest of the season. Our August monsoon is coming a little early. And, just so you know, we will be fishing regular periods until the season closes. I don't want the troopers looking at me either. Welcome back, Larry."

CHAPTER 22

In the office very early on Monday, Will Trippet finished his daily reporting and left the office to check on the dip net fishery on the City of Kenai beach. Thousands of Alaska residents use the fishery to provide winter food for themselves and their families. There are always those who attempt to take advantage of the chance to fish for sockeye salmon with a dip net. Some who try are not residents and some are residents taking over-limits or failing to log their catch on the required permit. The sight of a uniformed officer on the beach dampens the illegal activities somewhat.

Will parked as close to the beach as he was able. It was still a healthy walk in soft sand to the beach where the fishermen were working. There were many different techniques and types of net adaptations, but on the whole, the equipment and means were the same. The fisherman will wade into the water, some up to their chin, and walk downstream with the current, attempting to have a sockeye salmon swim into the dip net. It is labor intensive and not very scientific or sporting, but thousands of fish are taken each year using this method. Coolers filled with ice line the water's edge; camp stoves and tents are scattered up and down the beach. It all makes for a wonderful family outing for many people. Some children swim in the icy waters, but those who operate a net dress in rubber wet suits and long underwear.

Will stopped to speak with the city parks official who was paid to watch for people leaving trash or endangering themselves or others. That officer today was Cynthia Dagget, a college student and summer hire for the city. She was a very pretty young woman who worked hard to do her tasks, but she knew little of the state regulations and was not charged with enforcing them.

Cynthia was writing one of the spectators on the beach a notice of violation for littering when Trippet trudged through the loose sand to where she was standing. "Good morning, Cindy," he said when she had finished her business with the teenaged boys she was citing.

She looked up from her notebook to see the trooper, "Oh, good morning, Will. I was so busy I hadn't noticed you."

"I just stopped to check some licenses," Will said. "Not many people on the beach this morning."

She looked up and down the beach. "Not yet, but when the tide begins to change it will be different. Right now, everyone seems to be behaving themselves. An hour from now the crowd will start to assemble. Everyone will be jockeying for the right sport on the beach." She flashed a broad, toothy smile. "How are things with you?"

"I'm fine. You know how summertime is, no days off and lots of hours to work." Will liked the young city parks ranger and admired how she was able to do her job without causing any riots or shoot-outs.

"Say, Will. See the guy in the yellow rain slicker up to his chest in the water, the one with no hat?"

"Yeah, the one with the red cooler on the beach behind him?"

"That's him. I saw him come in this morning and noticed he is driving a Ford F350 pickup with Washington plates," she reported. "He may be driving someone else's truck, but he may not be a resident. He might be worth checking out."

"Thanks, Cindy. I'll check him out." He made a note on his pad. "I have to drive to Homer when I finish, so I won't be here long. Good to see you again."

The trooper walked to the water's edge and checked the license and permit of a fisherman who had come out of the water. Will thanked the man and walked down the beach to where the man in the yellow slicker was fishing. He had stopped walking downstream, but was not coming out of the water. Trippet watched him for several minutes, then walked to the edge of the water and called to the fisherman.

"Excuse me, sir. Wilson Trippet, Wildlife Trooper. Would you come out of the water for a minute so I can check your license and permit?"

The man looked over his shoulder. "Are you talking to me?"

"Yes, sir. I need to check your license and personal use permit. Would you please step out of the water?"

"I'll be up there in a few minutes," the man said, continuing to hold his net in the water.

"I really don't want to get my shoes wet, sir. Come out of the water now."

The man turned and saw the determined look on the face of the trooper. "OK, hold your horses."

As the man waded out of the water, dragging his long-handled net behind him, Will explained his duties. "This is a restricted personal use fishery open only to residents. I have to check your identification, fishing license and permit."

When he had walked several feet up the beach, the fisherman dropped the handle of his net, reached into his shirt pocket and produced a fishing license and permit. Handing the documents to the trooper, he said, "My ID is up in the truck."

"Where is the truck parked, sir?" Will asked.

"Over there, at the end of the road. I got here early and got a good spot."

"Bring your net and we can walk over there and check your identification and you can get back to fishing."

Slowly the man retrieved his dip net and together the two men walked to the road where he claimed his truck was parked. During the walk Will asked, "How long have you lived in Alaska?"

"Longer than I care to remember," he answered.

"Where do you work, sir?"

"I work at maintenance at Elmendorf Air Force Base. My name is Owen, by the way, Owen Padget."

"Pleased to meet you, Mr. Padget. I'm Trooper Wilson Trippet."

Now the two men were at the Ford pickup and the fisherman unlocked the passenger door. Will stepped close behind the man in case he reached for a weapon, but he only picked up the wallet on the seat and opened it. Inside was a military identification card that appeared to be a new issue.

"I will need to see your driver's license, Mr. Padget." Will noted the information on the military ID card in his book. "How long have you been at Elmendorf?" he asked Padget.

The man was fumbling with his wallet and finally came up with a driver's license from Washington State.

"This license says you applied for and got this license two months ago in Washington. I see you have Washington license plates on this truck. Is it your truck?

"Yes, it's my truck. I live in Washington part of the year," Padget admitted.

Will continued to write in his notebook. "Do you vote in Washington?"

"I'm usually in Washington in November, so I vote there."

"You know, Mr. Padget, you cannot be a permanent resident in two states simultaneously."

"I guess I'll have to get an Alaska driver's license," Padget said.

"There is more to becoming an Alaska resident than having a driver's license. You must be a full-time resident for a period of one year. Judging by the dates on your Washington license, you have not met that requirement. I am going to cite you for false application for a resident fishing license and for false application for a personal use permit. This is a mandatory court appearance here in Kenai; the date will be on the ticket. If you wish to have a change of venue, you can contact the court. Do you have any questions, Mr. Padget?"

"No," he said quietly.

"Have you caught any fish today?"

"No, they haven't started yet."

"I'm not going to take your net or cooler, but I will tell you it will be another citation if you are caught fishing again. Do you understand?" Will handed him his copy of the citation. "I am advising you to pick up your equipment and leave the beach."

"Yes, sir. I will."

Padget marched over the sand dune and down to where his net and cooler rested on the beach. Will watched as the man gathered his belongings and returned to his truck. The trooper made more notes in his book before walking down the beach to find Cynthia Dagget.

"Cindy, hold up a minute." Will called as he got close to where she stood.

She turned to see Will striding down the beach, notebook in hand.

As he approached her, he smiled. "That was a good piece of detective work on your part, congratulations."

"What did he have to say when you asked for his ID?"

"He said he had left it in the truck, so we walked up there. You were right; he is from Washington State. I cited him and warned him not to fish anymore. It looks like he is leaving, but if you see him again call my office. I'm on my way to Homer to meet with an officer there and won't be in the office until late today." Will thanked her again, waved and walked back to his truck.

The drive to Homer was uneventful and Will noted that the weather was clouding over and, when he could see the water in the inlet, it was becoming choppy with white caps. Many charter boats dotted the inlet, but many were beginning to move back toward their launch sites because of the rough water. Seasickness is not a pleasant malady and fishing on a 28-foot boat in Cook

Inlet when the sea kicks up will trigger a wretch response in some of the hardiest of landlubbers.

As he approached Homer, he called Dean Steadman. They agreed to meet for lunch at the Caribou Restaurant. They served breakfast all day, which sounded good to Will. A few minutes later, the two men walked into the café together. A nice looking young girl seated them and asked what they would have to drink before leaving to send a waitress.

As she walked away Dean asked, "Well, old buddy, now what are we going to do?"

"I don't know, Dean," Will replied as the waitress arrived with their coffee. Their conversation ceased until she left the table with their order. "Have you got any ideas?"

"No, I sure don't, but the Volga is still in the harbor and Resnic and his deckhand have been getting it ready to go back out fishing. I heard from a friend that Ivan was in town yesterday to meet with Josef. I don't know what they said, but I'd bet it was a strategy meeting." Dean sipped his coffee while the waitress placed the orders on the table. When she had left, he continued. "It's my guess they will lay low for a while. I don't think they will quit illegal fishing, but I'll bet they keep it clean for a while. The season will be over in less than two weeks and they can't afford to miss any more fishing days. My guess is that they will lay low until the season is over and then, when we quit patrolling, finish loading the Galaxy for her trip back south."

"You may be right, but how do we stop them?" a frustrated Will Trippet was asking.

"How do you suppose they are disposing of all that illegal catch?" Dean asked without expecting an answer. "The Galaxy has come to the cannery and sold fish on a regular basis. I have checked the fish tickets and everything seems to be legal. The cannery manager said the same thing; it all appears legitimate. I think they are selling all their legal catch to the cannery and plan to take their illegal catch to Washington and dispose of it through their own fish company. How to catch them is another question and I don't have an answer to that."

Both men ate quietly. There is something sinful about sausage and eggs with hash browns and toast with strawberry jam in the middle of the day. When they had finished, both men leaned back, satisfied, quietly sipping more coffee while taking a few minutes to relax.

"I wonder if Donavan would have time to make some fly-overs after the season closes. He will be out flying the dall sheep areas soon, with sheep season opening on the 10th. Maybe we could talk him into keeping us posted on where the Volga and the Galaxy are working. If they both stick around, it would seem to indicate they are up to no good. Every other fisherman will be putting his boat away and spending his money. These two will want to catch more fish. I think they have all those freezers in the hold and want to fill them before taking the Galaxy south for the winter." Trippet mapped out a likely scenario for Dean to think about.

"You could be right, Will. In any case, I have to get back to the boat. Let me know how you want to go ahead with this. They made me mad and I'll be with you until the end." Dean bought lunch. Will drove back to the Soldotna office, all the while thinking about what to do next.

CHAPTER 23

Life for a Wildlife Trooper stationed at the Soldotna post can be complicated. Salmon run in the Kenai River until it freezes and once upon a
time was open the entire year. The season parameters have changed in recent
years and it now ends near the end of October. The end of salmon season
does not mean the Wildlife Trooper can relax. August 10 is the opening day
for Dall sheep hunting on the Kenai Peninsula. The Dall sheep live in the
tops of the Kenai Mountains surrounded by the glaciers of the Harding Ice
Field, possibly the largest glacier field in the USA. Getting to the hunting
areas without motorized help is for the young and strong. The trek can be
a climb of 4,000 to 6,500 feet, depending on which area you wish to hunt.
Bow hunting for moose opens shortly after, with rifle season to follow in
September. Throw in the fall black and brown bear seasons, road kill moose,
animal attacks and a litany of other daily reports and complaints and you
have a day in the life of a Wildlife Trooper.

Will knew Donavan Fleer would be very busy in coming weeks, but he
wanted to ask a big favor of his time. He pulled a cell phone from his pocket
and keyed the speed dial for Fleer.

"Sergeant Fleer," he answered.

"Donavan, Will Trippet. Where are you?"

"I'm at the Soldotna airport, changing the oil in the Cessna. What do
you need?"

"I need a big favor. Will you be there for a little while? I need to talk
with you."

"I heard about the court hearing and I figured you would be calling." Fleer
had been upset by the court result, too. "I'm at the state hangar. I'll be here,

working on the plane most of the day. If you come, bring me a big Coke, will you?"

Half an hour later, Will stopped in front of the hangar. The Cessna was inside and the door was open. Trippet had stopped at the DQ and bought a 48-ounce Coke for the sergeant. Fleer had heard the truck pull in and stepped out from under the wing, wiping oil off his hands. Will gave the big plastic cup to him and waited for Donavan to stop gulping the drink.

"Ahh! Thanks, Will. That's good and I was really thirsty." He took another big drink. "What's on your mind?" he finally asked.

"I see you're getting ready for hunting season, but I wanted to know if you are going to have a little flying time to help me out." Will was almost pleading with the sergeant.

"Come on over to the desk and let's sit down." The two men walked to the corner of the hangar where some lockers, an old office desk and several old office chairs, in bad condition, were located. Fleer flopped into the chair behind the desk while Trippet remained standing.

"You said you had heard about the Resnic case," Will said in a solemn voice. "It may not be practical, but I still want to nail those two. I have been trying to deal with this calmly and keep my anger out of it, but it's tough. I'm having trouble not taking it personally. I guess I had too much time and energy invested and lost perspective."

"It happens sometimes. Our training says don't let it bother you, but, every now and again, it gets personal." Fleer took another gulp, a smaller one this time. "I have to warn you that with hunting season coming I won't have much time to fly you around. I have to patrol sheep areas here on the penin-sula, then go over to the west side, and patrol the inlet side slopes from the Susitna River south to McNeal River. That's an area larger than some states. In truth, I can't do an adequate job alone and the Feds only send out a plane if their coffee pot is dry. I fly more hours than an airline pilot, most of it close to the ground and in the mountains. I'm not complaining. It's the best part of my job, but I'm just explaining why I can't be of much help to you."

"I knew it was a long shot, but I had to ask," Will said sadly.

"Oh, hell. Don't go getting all weepy on me, Will. I didn't say I wouldn't do it, only that I couldn't spend a lot of time at it." Fleer admired the tenacity of his fellow officer. "What did you have in mind for me to do?"

Trippet gave a big sigh of relief and reached out to shake the hand of the big sergeant. "I noted the part about you patrolling the mountains on the west side and I wondered if, maybe on your return trip, if you could move out over the water and watch for the Volga and the Galaxy. I have thought about it a lot and it seems to me they are going to try to fill their freezers in the Galaxy. We put a crimp in their style when we busted them last week. These guys are shrewd and ruthless men. I think they will fish legally for the rest of the regular season, and that is only a few more days, then, I think, they will go back to work filling the tender. We have heard the Volga fishes for halibut at night. If that's true, I thought you might spot the Volga on your trip home from sheep patrol," Will explained. Then added, "The last thing I want to do is get you into trouble, or worse, cause you to fly more hours than you are already doing. I've been there with you and I know how demanding your job is. But, I really need your eyes out there, Donavan. Can you help me?"

Donavan Fleer stared into his nearly empty cup. Finally, he looked up at Will Trippet. "I won't make you any promises, but, if I get the chance, I'll keep an eye out for the Volga. Believe me, Will, I understand your frustration. In the old days, there wasn't anyone to help out. Yeah, I understand."

"Thank you, Sarge. You have no idea what a relief it is to have your help. I'm going to owe you—big-time."

"Good, you can date my ugly sister," Fleer said, tossing the cup into a wastebasket.

"Thanks again, Donavan," Will said, backing up a step or two. "I'll get out of here and let you get back to work. If there is anything you need, don't hesitate to call me." He gave Fleer a half-hearted salute and walked out to his pickup.

He had just started the engine when his phone rang. It was Cynthia Dagget. "Trooper Trippet," he answered.

"Hi there, Will. This is Cindy, your favorite beach girl."

"Hi, Cindy, what's up?"

"Your friend from Washington State is back. He's driving another car. He's dressed in different clothing, but it's him. He has another man with him and they are both in the water. I've seen them each taking salmon out of their nets, but I didn't count them," she reported. "Are you close enough to come over?"

"I'm just leaving the Soldotna airport. I'll be there in ten minutes, if the traffic will let me. Where do you want to meet?"

"How about at the foot of the hill where you get to the beach?"

"See you there. I might have some trouble with this man now. I think I will have the Kenai Police Department send an officer to back me up. I'll be there in a couple of minutes."

Both Cindy Dagget and the Kenai Police officer were waiting when he arrived. Will said hello and moved to the water's edge. The two city officers waited a short distance up the dunes.

Will walked down the beach behind the fishermen as they floated their nets along. When they reached the end of their planned drift and turned to pull their nets from the surf, they spotted him immediately. Ignoring him, they began to walk back up the beach to start again. Will intercepted them and asked them to drop the nets and produce ID's and permits.

"This is the knot head I told you about. The one who wrote me a ticket this morning," Owen Padget told his friend.

"I see you didn't take my advice, Mr. Padget." Will was accepting the licenses and permit forms from both men. Looking at the two military issue ID cards, Will noticed that one was clearly a copy with the name changed and sealed in new plastic. He turned to the new man. "Your name is Newell Stanley?"

"Yes, sir." The answer came from a nervous man.

"Mr. Stanley, I can't help notice these two ID cards appear to be identical except for the names and birthdates. It looks to me like one of these is a copy that has been altered and resealed. Do you want to tell me which one is the fake?"

"Not mine, officer. I work on the base and use it to go through the gate to get to work every day."

"Let me see your driver license, Mr. Stanley."

The man produced it from his wallet. It was an Alaska issued license. "I see by the date of issue on this that you are probably a legal resident. Why did you help your friend fake an ID?"

Stanley glared at Padget. "I told you this would never work. This could cost me my job."

"Mr. Padget," Will addressed the other man. "This is becoming more serious by the minute. I will have to look it up, but I think falsifying a government identification card is a federal felony. That, in addition to the earlier violation and now this one, clearly indicates you do not intend to obey the laws of this state. I am going to have the City of Kenai Parks Officer bring your net and cooler to my truck where I will tag them for evidence."

Will nodded to Cindy, who was listening nearby. "I am writing you another citation for each of the previous charges. I will note the same court date on the citation to make it easier for you to appear on the charges. I hope you understand I could take you to jail for this, but I won't. When I have finished, you and your friend are free to go. If I see you here again, there will be no mercy. I am also going to report this document forgery to the federal authorities. I'm sure you will be hearing from them. And I'm sure they will want to speak with your friend."

Will ceased his speech and continued writing the citations, as well as making more notes in his book. Half an hour later the two fishermen walked away with one net and one cooler. They were muttering to each other as they climbed the steep grade to where they had parked their truck.

"Good job, Cindy," Will said when the fishermen had gone.

"Thanks, Will. I recognized the first one from this morning; that's why I called you."

Will thanked the Kenai Police Officer for his assistance, loaded his evidence and turned his truck around to drive up the hill. The two fishermen were standing beside a pickup with Alaska license plates, drinking beer. Will slowed and rolled down his side window.

"You should finish those drinks before getting into the vehicle. You don't want to get a ticket for an open container in the vehicle." The men said nothing. Will rolled up his side window and drove to the office.

CHAPTER 24

Tuesday morning had started early for Will. He did an extra mile on his morning run because he had missed a couple of days. Finishing his usual morning ritual with juice, coffee, cold cereal and the newspaper, he showered and donned his uniform with all its attached gear. The belt alone weighed 22 pounds, making it the last thing he put on his body. The drive to the office was a short one and traffic was light. Marcy had beat him to the office and made the coffee. He waited for it to finish brewing before checking with her at the front desk.

"You're in early this morning, Marcy. The coffee is good."

"I see you have your priorities in order this morning, Will. Good morning to you, too." She chided him as he checked his in-box.

Will said nothing, only smiled and waved as he walked to his office.

It seemed everyone in the world had sent him a memo this morning: there were three from the Kenai Court, one from Captain Olson, one from the Colonel's office regarding his promotion status, and one from the City of Kenai regarding the citations he had written the previous day. He read each one carefully and made notes on each one about the response needed. He had finished his coffee and was typing a court complaint on Owen Padget when his desk phone rang.

"Sean Adams for you," Marcy said. "Line 2."

Trippet punched the proper button and answered, "Trooper Trippet."

"Yeah, I know. I recognize your grumpy voice," Adams greeted.

"You would be grumpy, too, if you had a call like this first thing in the morning when everything else was going so well." It seemed trooper humor was always sarcastic. "What's on your mind this morning, Sean?"

"I just had breakfast with an old friend of yours and he wants to see you, discreetly," Adams reported. "Since he is a friend of yours, I bought his breakfast. You owe me for that."

"Who is this old friend I'm buying breakfast for?"

"A scruffy-looking guy by the name of Larry Hanson. He said you would remember him, and thanked you for the ham and eggs."

"He's in Homer?" Will was surprised, not only about him being in town, but even more about Hanson asking for him. "Did he say how I should contact him?"

"He has a cell phone." Adams gave Will the telephone number. "He flew in this morning early and is going back out tonight. The charter plane picked him up at the Galaxy in Ursus Bay. Something has him really spooked, Will. I think you need to talk to him."

"Thanks, Sean. I'll call him right now."

"Let me know what he has to say," Adams said before hanging up.

Checking the number on his pad, Will dialed Hanson. The phone rang six times before the fisherman answered.

"Yeah, whaddya want?" came the gruff reply.

"Is this Larry Hanson?" Will asked.

"Yeah, who's this?"

"This is Wildlife Trooper Trippet. I had word you wanted to talk to me."

"Oh man, I'm glad you called. We have to talk."

"Do you want me to meet with you in Homer?"

"No, the Resnics have too many friends here. I'm scared, Trooper. I think Josef is planning to dump me in the inlet. Can we just talk on the phone for now? I swear, I'll tell you anything you want to know, but I think I'll need some protection from the Resnics." Larry Hanson was speaking quietly and fearfully.

"I'll protect you if you need it, Mr. Hanson, but I'll need information. I think it would be better if I met you in person for this." Will wanted to meet face to face in order to look into Hanson's eyes. He didn't want to be played for a fool.

"I can fly down there and meet you at Beluga Lake. If I can find a pilot, I will be there in an hour." Trippet realized this may be the break he needed.

"The net reel broke down and they got a mechanic and parts sent out by air taxi. I came in to do some business and have to go back when the pilot goes to pick up the mechanic. I don't know what time all that takes place." Hanson sounded completely paranoid.

"Let me call my pilot and make arrangements for a flight and I will call you right back with a time to meet. I'll give you Trooper Adams' number and he will take you to meet us."

"OK, but hurry."

An hour later Donavan Fleer taxied the floatplane to a dock on Beluga Lake. The weather was closing in, so he had to do some scud running to get around the clouds—a dangerous maneuver, but one Fleer enjoyed nonetheless. Feeling his way around the clouds in the plane was exhilarating to the experienced pilot.

Sean Adams' patrol car was waiting at the dock when they arrived. Fleer waited in the plane while Will met Adams and Hanson. The weather was cool but without wind, allowing the men to meet at a small picnic table on the shore near the dock.

Hanson reached out to shake hands with Will as he approached. After shaking hands, they all sat on the benches.

"What is it that has you so frightened, Larry?" Will asked.

"When Josef got his boat back, I didn't want to go out on it again; but he offered me a big bonus to come back. He's fishing legally this week, but when the commercial season ends, he is going to start halibut long line fishing. He and Ivan need more fish to take to Bellingham for their wholesale business. He plans to fish at night to keep out of sight," Hanson explained with a quick overview. "The thing that has me worried is Josef. He ain't going to pay me no bonus. I think he will either cheat me out of it or just dump me in the inlet with an anchor chained to me. I heard he did it before and I know he is crazy enough to do it again. I'm scared, Trooper. I don't know what to do."

"If you're that scared, why would you want to go back to the boat?" Trippet asked.

"If I don't, I won't be able to stay in Alaska. The brothers would get me. And, I might be wrong, he may just pay me, but I don't think so." Hanson seemed resigned to the worst case in his future.

"This is a very dangerous game to be playing, Larry. We will be grateful for any information you can give us, but, if you get back on that boat, we may not be able to get to you in time to save your neck. I want the Resnic brothers in the worst way, but I am not willing to sacrifice you to get them. This isn't a good plan."

"I've thought about it a lot," Larry explained. "They think they have me fooled and they need me until they fill the freezers. I'm guessing that will take about ten days, maybe a little longer if the weather kicks up. I think I'll be safe until then."

"Can you keep your cell phone with you? In case you need to have us come out and rescue you?" Will was asking. "I still don't like it. You realize, of course, how long it would be for us to get a boat or plane to your location for a rescue. By the time we get there you may be crab bait."

"I'm going back out, no matter what you do," Larry said. "Now, we can start by me giving you all the information you need to bust them, or I can go back and catch the plane without giving you anything. How do you want it?"

"Besides staying alive, what do you want out of this?" Adams interjected.

"I really don't want anything except I don't want to go back to jail. I would like to live long enough to spend my bonus." Larry was more relaxed now.

"I hate to be the one to tell you this, Larry, but whether they dump you in the inlet or cheat you out of your money, you will probably not get paid. Sorry, pal."

"Josef has been paying me regularly and I have a little cash in the bank, but I wonder, if after all this shakes out and they sell the Volga and its fish, is it reasonable for me to file a claim against the sale for my wages and bonus?" Even though it had not been determined he would survive, Hanson was scheming to recover his money.

"I don't know, Larry. That is something you should ask a lawyer. If you are bent on going through with this, we are going to have to get a lot of information from you in order to start building a case. We had better get at it." Will placed a fresh notebook on the picnic table and began to take notes: dates, times, incidents and other facts. The men had talked, asked questions and exchanged information for more than an hour when Larry's cell phone rang and the charter company said they were going back to pick up the mechanic, leaving in thirty minutes.

"Ok, Larry. This is a big deal and very dangerous. Keep your phone handy and don't hesitate to call for help." Will was giving last minute instructions. "For whatever it's worth, I appreciate your sticking your neck out for us. Good luck, Larry."

Sean took Larry Hanson back to the charter office, dropping him a block away to avoid having the fisherman spotted getting out of a trooper car.

Back at the floatplane dock, Will climbed into the Cessna wearing a troubled look.

"How did it go, Will?" asked Donavan.

They discussed it all during the flight back to Soldotna. Will was concerned that this could be a terrible mistake.

CHAPTER 25

Five minutes out of Soldotna, Fleer received a radio call telling him an emergency radio beacon was coming from the direction of Tustumena Lake. Tustumena Lake is a huge glacial lake nearly thirty-five miles in length. It sits at the foot of Tustumena Glacier and endures fierce winds, causing waves most Cook Inlet fishing boats refuse to tempt.

"Hang on, Will. We have to go look for this emergency signal." He flipped his secondary aircraft radio channel to the emergency frequency. Immediately he heard a faint beeping signal. "I've got a signal, faint, but I can hear it." He then reported it to the FAA radio in Kenai. "I'll make you a bet about where this signal is coming from."

"Where do you think it's from, Don?" Will asked.

"As you fly up the glacier there is a small lake off to the right, behind a little ridge. It's protected by the mountains, and the winds aren't too bad there. I'll bet some sheep hunters went in there to set up camp and somehow stubbed a toe," Donavan said as he flew up the south shoreline of the lake. "The ceiling is going to be low, but there doesn't seem to be much wind right now. Keep your eyes peeled for any sign of a plane in the water. They're hard to see, so keep looking as we fly over the big lake."

"I see a lot of brown bears near the lake," Will commented into the microphone.

"It's that time of year. These streams are full of Coho salmon right now. Earlier the creeks were running red with sockeye, but most of them have spawned and died by now." Donavan concentrated on his flying while Will scanned the surface of the lake. The end of the lake was in sight as Donavan began to climb. As they passed over the sand beach at the head of the lake,

Will was alarmed to see they were flying directly toward a 2,000-foot vertical rock face. There was a narrow crack in the escarpment with a stream running out of it.

"I don't mean to tell you how to fly, but shouldn't we be turning toward the glacier?"

Fleer chuckled, "I guess I should have warned you. We will be flying through that slit in the rock. The lake is on the other side. The wind us usually down the glacier making this the best approach. Hang on in case it gets bumpy." Fleer quit talking and concentrated on flying the Cessna through the narrow gap. It was only a short distance through, but it required a pilot to pay close attention.

Once between the two mountains in the clear above the beautiful green water of the lake, Will relaxed a little. His eyes were scanning the lake surface when he saw something. "I see a campfire on the end of the lake," he reported. "Hold it, I see something else." He was pointing out the windshield. "There, something in the water."

"I see it," Fleer responded. "It looks like airplane floats." The skilled pilot dropped his altitude and flew alongside the objects. "That's it. Now, see if you can tell what condition the campers are in."

The plane's air speed was now down to seventy miles per hour.

Will assessed the men on the beach as they passed over. "One of them looks OK, but the other appears hurt. They are both in their underwear. They have a tarp for a lean-to with a fire in front."

Fleer was again concentrating on his flying, climbing rapidly to clear the terrain above the lake. He climbed until he flew out over the glacier, then, turned back down the glacier toward Tustumena Lake. Over the lake, he turned again. "I'm going to go through the slot again and land on Green Lake." Before going in he reported what they had found to the FAA and asked for a rescue helicopter to assist.

Flying carefully through the slot, Fleer began to let down flaps and slow the aircraft. He skimmed over the water for more than half the length of the lake before letting the Cessna settle on the water. Finally, he cut the power and drifted to the shore. Fleer had hip boots on and stepped out onto the left float. When it touched the gravel bottom, he jumped off and pulled the plane higher onto the beach. He had taken a rope from cockpit and slipped the end over the cleat on the front of the plastic float. He jumped off and secured the rope to a large bush nearby before turning his attention to the two men.

"Are you both OK?" Fleer asked.

The one standing said, "I am, but Lou is hurt. I think he has a concussion."

"Are you the pilot?"

"No, he was only bringing us to make camp for a sheep hunt. He didn't get out. He's still in the plane. I got Lou out, but I didn't have strength enough to go back for Darrel, our pilot."

"I called for a rescue helicopter before I landed, but it will be a while before they get here. I'm going to try to float back out to the plane and try to get it to shore. If I can get it to shallow water, we might be able to get it right side up and check the pilot. Do you think you are up to helping if we can get a rope on it?"

"I'll do what I can," the survivor said.

"What are your names?"

"I'm Dennis Beaumont; that's Lou Nelson; and the pilot is Darrel Bronson."

Will made notes of the names. "I'm Wildlife Trooper Will Trippet and this is Trooper Donavan Fleer," Will said, speaking for the first time to the men. "I have to say I'm impressed with the shelter and fire. The space blankets are wonderful. You came prepared. Can you tell us what happened, why you wrecked?"

"I'm not a pilot, and I was in the back seat. Darrel was landing, but when we hit the water, the plane bounced. I don't know why, a gust of wind or something. After we bounced, the nose went down and the right wing went down. We hit the water and I kinda lost it for a minute. When I realized what had happened, we were upside down. I got my seatbelt off and I reached to undo Lou's seatbelt. Water was coming inside fast. Like I said, I was in the back seat and I opened the door. It's a big door and the cabin filled with water. I grabbed Lou by the shirt collar and pulled him toward the door. Somehow, I got hold of my fanny pack when I drug Lou out of the plane. I pulled Lou to shore and out of the water and tried to go back for Darrel, but I was so cold I just couldn't do it. I dug out the space blankets and wrapped us both up in them. It was quite a while before I could get his wet clothes off and start a fire. You can see there isn't much firewood here, just small brush and sticks. I had two 6 by 8 tarps in my pack and made a shelter with one. I could only work a few minutes at a time because I was so cold." He looked directly into Will's eyes. "OH, GOD! How am I going to tell Rachael about Darrel?"

Fleer was taking photos of the plane in the water. When he finished he motioned for Will to come to the Cessna. "I'm going to push off and float back to the plane. I'll use the paddle and you get the boathook on your side below the door. When we drift behind the wreck, see if you can hook the tail rope. If you can, I can start the engine and tow the plane to the beach. We might be able to use the tail rope to right the plane and start draining the water out of it."

The slight breeze drifted the Cessna back faster than they wanted, but Will hooked the tail rope on the third drift. Fleer started the engine while Will held the rope. Both men jumped to the beach when the floats touched. Fleer re-tied the Cessna while Will stepped a few yards to the side and began pulling the wreck to shore. With much effort from all three men, the sunken plane stood on its nose. Water drained quickly from the fuselage and the floats again began to lift the plane. They pulled the soggy hulk close to shore. Water poured from the broken plane and as the water drained, the plane rode higher and they were able to pull it closer to shore.

The plane was a Maule, a plane aptly suited for this kind of landing. As it neared shore and close enough to allow him to wade to the pilot's door, Fleer walked out and opened the door. Darrel Bronson was strapped in the seat, his lifeless arms drooping at his side. He made no attempt to remove the body, only closed the door and waded back to shore.

When he waded back to where the other men were getting warm, Will was pouring hot coffee from a thermos. Donavan gathered more sticks for the fire and they all waited for the helicopter to arrive.

Thirty minutes later the big helicopter came and the medics did their work. Pictures were taken and reports written before the helicopter left the scene, taking the injured men and the body with them. Fleer put out the campfire and made sure the Maule was secure enough to leave behind. He took the rifles and backpacks from the plane for safekeeping.

Fleer noted there was hardly a ripple on the surface of Green Lake and decided to take off toward the slot in the mountain. It was getting late and the light would be fading soon. There would be plenty of work for the two troopers when they returned to town.

CHAPTER 26

It had been more than a week since the fateful trip to Homer and much had taken place. The Chinook or king salmon season had ended with fishermen reporting overage catches throughout the season. The crowded personal use fishery had ended and the beaches were deserted, with the throng leaving behind a mountain of trash and debris on the city beaches. The commercial fishing season had also ended in Cook Inlet and the haggling over next year's allocations had begun. Every facet of the industry wanted more of the share: commercial fishermen claimed they were being cheated out of their right to catch fish; personal use fishermen claimed they were not allowed to fish enough days; sport fishermen claimed that commercial and personal use fishermen caught too many fish, not allowing enough fish to get to the spawning grounds; and the sport fish limits were too stingy. No one seemed to want to admit that each of them played a part in the decreased returns. This wrangling would continue until opening day next year.

Will Trippet had his own personal thoughts and opinions on the subject, but seldom spoke of them. He felt he was paid to enforce the law as it existed and not as someone wished it would be. In his office attempting to finish a veritable mountain of forms and reports, he was tiring of office life. He stood to stretch his back when Marcy came in to drop another ream of paper on his desk.

"There's a call for you on line 2," she said as she turned to leave, giving a little wave of her hand as she went.

Will keyed the button and said hello. There was a muffled voice on the other end and he had to listen carefully to hear.

"This is Larry, Larry Hanson. I've got some news for you."

"Larry, I'm glad to hear from you. I have been worried about you. Are you OK?"

"So far, but that may change shortly. I just called to tell you that we are going to fish halibut two more nights and call it a season. The Galaxy wants to head south in a few days to beat the weather. Ivan said he is stopping in Kodiak to pick up some king crab. He asked me to make the trip to Washington with him, but I haven't given him an answer yet."

"Are you still in fear for your life when the season ends?"

"Even more than before. Josef is getting more mean and violent by the day. I think he's crazy. He has been throwing things on the boat and breaking equipment with his tantrums. It's really getting weird. I can't be sure, but I think it has to do with what he is going to do to me. I've been afraid to ask for my money."

"Do you want me to come out and pick you up and take you to Homer?" Will asked.

"Maybe, but not yet. I thought you might be able to sneak out here and arrest him when we're fishing tonight. That way you will have charges against him. You can arrest me too and take me off the boat without any questions from Josef or Ivan." Hanson spoke quietly and nervously.

"I'll make arrangements for the Enforcer to come out tonight. Where will you be fishing?"

"In the fingers," a series of valleys and hills on the inlet floor and a popular charter boat area. "OK, I'm going to call Dean Steadman and make arrangements for tonight. Call me back in an hour and I will let you know what time we will be there."

"Gotcha. One hour." With that, Hanson hung up.

Trippet pushed all the papers to the side of his desk and opened a new notebook. He dialed Steadman and was about to hang up when Dean finally answered.

"Sorry I took so long to answer, Will. We are having a little engine trouble and I was in the engine room. What's up?"

"How bad is the engine problem?"

"We lost an oil pump on the left engine. It caused the engine to heat and we were checking for damage. We're putting it together again now. Why the interest? Do you want to go fishing?" Steadman was laughing.

"I just had a call from our friend Hanson. He said Resnic is winding down his season. He plans to fish the fingers tonight and Hanson thinks today might be the end of his fishing career. I'm telling you, Dean, I've heard from at least two sources that Resnic dumped a deckhand in the inlet one time. I'm afraid for Hanson's life." Will was worried and expressed his concerns to Steadman. "If Hanson says they will quit fishing today or tomorrow, I think we need to make our move. We can get the Volga for illegal halibut fishing, closed season, closed waters and the Lindberg kidnapping. Hanson wants us to arrest him with Resnic to keep suspicion away from him. It sounds like a good idea to me."

Steadman paused a moment before answering. "What time do you want to move?"

"Late, I think. How long will it take to fix the boat?" Will asked.

"Let me check the tide book." A few seconds later Steadman was back. "High tide here in Homer is at 9:00 p.m. Tide at the fingers is about an hour and a half later. If we leave the Homer harbor at 9:00, and move slowly because it will be starting to get dark especially with this cloud cover, we might just catch him pulling a set and be able to run right up on him. There is no wind in the forecast, but we should count on wind."

"You really are an optimist, aren't you, Dean?" Will didn't think it would be that easy.

"We can hope. I guess I had better get back to work or I won't be ready for you."

"I'll be there about 8:00," Will said before hanging up.

While waiting for Hanson to return his call, Will walked to Captain Olson's office. Olson saw him coming and motioned him inside.

"What's on your mind, Will?"

Trippet spent several minutes outlining events for the captain who listened carefully and finally agreed to the late night boating adventure.

Hanson called as he returned to his office. "What time can you get here?" Hanson was again speaking quietly to avoid being overheard.

"We plan to leave Homer at 9:00 and be at your location around 10:00. It will be dark and we may need some time to locate the Volga."

"OK and I will try to turn on the anchor light to make it easy to find us. Josef may catch on to that and tell me to shut it off, though." Hanson was trying to be helpful.

"Keep that phone handy in case we need to come get you earlier. This is dangerous business, Larry," Trippet cautioned the fisherman. He felt a pang of guilt for using Hanson in this situation as it was.

Will checked out of the office, going to Froso's for dinner. He sat in a back booth worrying about what might lie ahead. This whole thing looked bad to Will. In the middle of the inlet at night, attempting to arrest a hostile fisherman and take his boat, all the while keeping the owner from shooting either the officers or Hanson. He ate slowly, pondering the possibilities, none of which were good.

He drove slowly to Homer, but still arrived an hour early. Lights were on in the cabin of the Enforcer and the engines were running. Dean could be seen sitting behind the wheel looking at the gauges. Dave saw him coming and waved him aboard.

"The others are in the cabin. Go inside, I'll be there in a minute," Dave said.

Steadman turned around when Will opened the door. "Ah, Will. I'm glad you're early. We will have to test that new oil pump." He shouted, "Cast off, Dave."

Two minutes later, the Enforcer was moving slowly out of the harbor. It was still light enough to see the channel without lights. As they passed the marker buoy, Dean pushed the throttles ahead a little at a time, watching the oil pressure gauges as he did. He seemed satisfied and pushed them ahead further. Fifteen minutes later, after checking in the engine compartment for oil leaks, Dean seemed to relax.

"I talked with a charter captain from Anchor Point. He said he saw the Volga near the fingers when he came in this evening. It looks like your man gave you good information. Any ideas about how you want to handle this?"

"You're the expert when it comes to an operation like this, I'll leave it up to you. My greatest concern tonight is Larry Hanson. I want to get him out of this alive." Will continued to worry.

"OK, guys. Let's go find the Volga," Steadman said to his crew.

The Enforcer moved slowly up the inlet with Eric on the top deck scanning the inlet for boats. More than 20 miles from Homer, they saw the anchor light on the mast of the Volga.

"Survival suits and bullet proof vests—get them on now," Steadman ordered.

They were moving slowly but steadily toward the Volga. She was anchored now with the tide allowing them to approach from the bow. As they got closer, they saw both men working on the rear deck. Eric was watching through his big binoculars and reported he was seeing halibut being pulled aboard. Without running lights, the Enforcer was able to come alongside without being spotted. Loco hooked the rail of the Volga with a boathook. The rocking motion alerted Resnic who dropped the fish he was working on to run to the cabin. He returned with a large revolver in his hands.

"Put the gun down, Mr. Resnic. This is Alaska State Troopers. We want to come aboard your vessel." Dean's voice was loud and clear through the speaker from the top deck.

"Get away from my boat. I'll shoot any man setting foot on this vessel," Resnic shouted angrily.

Larry said something to Resnic who motioned for him to back off.

"Mr. Resnic, your actions are not helping your case. Threatening an officer is a felony. Put the gun down NOW."

It appeared Resnic mistakenly thought Eric was talking to him. He raised the muzzle of his pistol and sighted on Eric. "I'm not fooling, I'll shoot."

On the top deck, Eric stood up. He was spinning left when the shot sounded. Eric had made a dive for the deck and the .44 Magnum slug missed him by inches.

Will ran to where Loco was holding the other boat, made a leap to the deck of the Volga and moved down the offside as quickly as he could. While Will was making his move, Larry charged Josef Resnic knocking him off balance for an instant. Resnic, in an uncontrolled fit of anger, recovered and swung the pistol in Larry's direction just as Will came around the cabin. He saw the situation and reacted immediately. Stepping over the handrail, Will leaped completely across the rear deck his body striking Resnic in the chest and knocking him to the deck. He rolled the fishing captain over and planted a knee in the middle of his back. Larry Hanson now added his weight to the job while Will pulled handcuffs from his belt. Larry and Will struggled some with the big fisherman, but snapped the cuffs in place. All the while Resnic was screaming and kicking with both feet.

Dave and Eric were now on the Volga to help control the captain.

"I'll kill you. I'll kill you all. Larry, I'll feed you to the crabs. Get off my boat, all of you. Get off my boat." With that, the big man collapsed on the deck, sobbing.

By now, Loco had tied the boats together with rubber fenders between them. The three men, along with Dean Steadman, manhandled Resnic on board the Enforcer. Will was now able to check on Larry Hanson.

"Are you alright, Larry?" Will asked. "Are you injured in any way?"

"I'm OK. Scared as hell, but I'm OK. I have to tell you, Trooper, I've been around a lot of bad stuff in my lifetime, but I ain't ever seen anything like that. He really tried to shoot that trooper on the upper deck. Oh, man, I have to sit down."

"I know this is a lot to ask right now, Larry, but we're going to have to pull in the rest of the long line and salvage the fish. Do you think you are up to helping with that?"

"After tonight, I can do anything. Oh man, I was scared." Hanson's voice quivered as he spoke.

After securing Resnic on the Enforcer, Loco and Dave went back aboard the Volga to help reel in the halibut line. It would have been a successful night for Resnic had he completed his fishing chores. Once the fish were on board, Will and Eric stayed on the Volga with Larry to take the boat to port. Loco and Dave stayed on the Enforcer to help Dean take the boat and the prisoner back to the homeport.

Once again, Dean called upon Sean Adams to transport the prisoner to the Homer jail. It was almost 3:00 a.m. when the two boats entered the harbor and Adams took charge of Resnic. As always, he complained about the late hours and asked for overtime.

"Come back to the Enforcer when you get him booked into jail. We have lots of reports to do. Loco is cooking breakfast. Come back and join us."

Adams poked an arm out the window to wave and drove off toward downtown Homer.

CHAPTER 27

An hour later Josef Resnic had completed the booking process at the Homer jail. He had been up for more than 24 hours and his body ached from fatigue. His anger, still boiling within him, in addition to the stress of the evening's events, had drained all his energy. He felt as limp as a wet mop. His strength was gone and he could not think clearly. Josef was unable to figure out how the troopers could have known where he was fishing. Only two people knew, his brother Ivan and his deckhand Larry Hanson. Ivan was a part of this operation and would never have said anything, even inadvertently, about his plans. Larry was on the Volga and had been arrested with him. In Josef Resnic's mind, it was only bad luck that he had been caught and arrested tonight. In his mind he had been justified in taking a shot at the trooper, but the court would never see it that way.

The jailer was a short, dark haired ex-Fish and Wildlife cop by the name of Mark. Resnic had never heard Mark's last name. Mark, the jailer, had finished the booking and typed the paperwork into the computer. He had taken fingerprints and photos of Resnic and had him change into an orange jumpsuit after being searched. When all this had been done, he asked Resnic if he wanted a cup of coffee. Josef nodded yes. Resnic also asked to make a phone call. "It will be a marine call and will take a little while to complete," he informed the jailer.

Mark put him in a small attorney visiting room where there was a phone and told him he could use it to make his calls. Josef was waiting for his brother to come to the phone on the Galaxy when Mark tapped on the door, opened it and set a cup of steaming black coffee on the desk near the telephone. He closed the door and left Josef to make his call.

A sleepy voice came on the other end of the phone, "Yeah, what is it?" Ivan asked.

"Ivan, it's Josef. I'm in jail in Homer. The troopers got me and Larry tonight. I need you to call the lawyer right away. It's going to be bad. Ivan"

"You didn't do something stupid again, did you, Josef?"

"Well, maybe."

"Oh, no, Josef! What did you do this time?" Ivan was now wide awake and alarmed.

"It was dark and we were busy fishing and the trooper boat came right up alongside the Volga. I hollered at them to back off and when they didn't I got my .44 magnum and took a shot at the trooper."

"Josef, you idiot. I've told you and told you, your temper will get you into trouble." Ivan blew a huge sigh. "OK, when do you go to court?"

"I'll have to go to arraignment today, I think this afternoon. I need a lawyer, Ivan."

"Yeah, I can see that." Ivan thought a few moments, then added, "Here's the deal, get some rest. I'll call my lawyer and have him there as soon as possible. He will be coming out of Anchorage, so it will be a while before he gets there. In the meantime, don't say a word to anyone. I'm calling a plane and coming to Homer." There was another pause. "Have you talked with Larry? Have you told him to keep his mouth shut?"

"I haven't seen him. The troopers had him help pull the long line and get the boat back to Homer. I haven't seen him since, 'cause they brought me in on the Enforcer in chains." Josef's anger was raging again, "I'm going to kill them, Ivan. I swear I'm going to kill 'em!"

"Shut up, Josef. Quit talking like that. You know you can't do that. You have to start using your head. This isn't just a poaching charge; this is an assault charge or worse. Keep your mouth shut and I'll be there as soon as I can get there."

Josef hung up the phone and took a long drink of his hot coffee. As his anger subsided, his strength again left him. He was staring at the floor when there was another tap on the door. It opened and Mark, the jailer came to take him to a cell.

"Larry Hanson, my deckhand, have they brought him in yet?" Josef asked.

"Not yet, but Trooper Adams said he had to help secure the boat and give a statement before they brought him down."

"My brother and a lawyer are coming; would you wake me when they get here?"

"Sure. Breakfast in two hours," Mark said as he closed the cell door.

Ivan was seated in a small visiting room where he waited for Mark to bring Josef out of his cell. Josef was a pitiful sight, dressed in the orange jumpsuit and his eyes swollen and red from lack of sleep. "You look terrible, Josef. Sit down. Have you seen Larry?"

"No, I don't think they have brought him to jail yet."

"Alright, I had a short talk with the lawyer. We are going to bail you out when you are through with court today. He said you would be arraigned this afternoon, be read the charges and asked to plead to them. He'll explain when he gets here, but plead not guilty to everything. Let the lawyer take it from there. Once they have you charged, the lawyer and I will decide what to do. He said this would probably be a felony charge of assaulting a police officer. You really did it this time, Josef." Ivan stood to leave, tapping on the door to notify the jailer. "Stay cool and keep your mouth shut. If you fly off the handle, it will only make things worse."

Josef nodded and thanked his brother. Mark took him back to his cell and fed him breakfast. After eating, Josef washed his face and combed his hair in an effort to look more normal. He flooded his eyes with cool water to help with the redness and swelling. It helped some, but he was still tired and depressed. He found an old magazine on the bunk and opened it to have something to do until Mark came back to tell him the lawyer had arrived.

In the small attorney visiting room once again, Josef sat across the table from the lawyer. "I'm Calvin Stroud. Your brother, Ivan, has hired me to represent you in court today." He opened a new yellow legal pad. "Now, I need to have you tell me exactly what took place tonight. I want it all, the good, the bad and the ugly. This is only between you and me, attorney/client privileged information. I have to know it all. I can't defend you if I don't know what happened. Ivan said you shot at the trooper. Is that correct?"

Josef hung his head, stared at the floor and quietly said, "Yeah, that's right, I guess."

"You guess? Don't you know how serious this is? If I can't make this look justifiable, you will be going to jail for a very long time. Now sit up here and start talking to me." Stroud wasn't fooling around.

"It's just that they surprised me and they made me angry. I wanted to defend myself. I was busy pulling a halibut skate and they came right up on our port side before I saw them." Again Josef was looking at the floor.

Stroud finished making his note, "So, you were fishing illegally and when they came alongside you didn't know who they were. Is that correct?"

"Yeah, that's right," Josef lied.

"I don't know what the troopers are charging you with, but I'm leaving here and will be at the court when it opens this morning. As soon as I find out, I'll be back to talk with you. You will be allowed to wear your own clothes to go to court. Be presentable. I want you to look as much like a businessman as possible when we get before the judge. I'll advise you later on what to plead, but unless I tell you different, don't say anything to anyone. Do you understand?" Calvin Stroud tapped on the door to alert the jailer. When it opened he told Mark to let Josef take a shower and shave before court time.

Stroud returned to the jail a little before noon. A new officer met him at the door. He showed Stroud into the attorney visiting room and moments later returned with Resnic.

"The troopers have charged you with illegal fishing for halibut, unsafe operation of a vessel, possession of illegal fishing gear, assaulting an officer, attempted murder of an officer and assaulting your deckhand." Calvin Stroud touched Josef's arm, "Do you understand how serious these charges are?"

"Yeah, I know."

"I don't think you do. The fishing charges are misdemeanor charges and we can work with them, but the assault charges are Class A felonies. Even if I can get them to drop some of the charges or reduce them, you are looking at a long, long time in prison. I don't even know if I can get you out on bail today. Now listen closely. Here is what is going to happen in court today." Step by step, Stroud outlined the arraignment procedure. Again, step by step and charge by charge the lawyer instructed him as to what he should and should not say. The two men talked until the jailer came to take Josef back to dress for court.

A trooper came to transport Resnic to his court hearing. Because of the felony charges and assault charges, he was manacled hands and feet. Once in the courtroom the handcuffs were taken off.

His was the only case in this court today. The clerk read the charges, which were lengthy.

"Do you understand the charges as they have been read to you?" asked the judge.

Stroud signaled for Resnic to answer the "yes" the two had rehearsed.

"On Count One;" he summarized the charge, "how do you plead?" the judge inquired for the record.

"Not guilty, Your Honor," Resnic replied.

And so it went through all the charges. When this was finished, Stroud stood and asked the judge to set bail.

The judge asked the District Attorney for his position on bail. The DA claimed the defendant was a flight risk and asked that bail be denied.

The judge thought a moment and made a note on the form attached to the file. "I will allow bail in the amount of $100,000. I will set a trial date and will leave the vessel Volga in the custody of the State of Alaska until trial. The catch will be sold to the cannery and the proceeds held by the court until the outcome of the trial. See the clerk of the court on the matter of bail." With that the judge stood, gathered his papers and both he and the court clerk left the courtroom.

The trooper returned to take Resnic back to the Homer Jail. Stroud had told him to keep quiet and to wait until he had arranged bail. When that was done, Stroud returned to the jail with release papers and picked up Josef and drove him to Ivan's home.

CHAPTER 28

Will Trippet and Dean Steadman were both in the back of the courtroom during the arraignment. They sat silently during the proceeding, but when it ended, both men breathed a sigh of relief. The regular judge and DA had heard this case and the charges were read, they were already ahead of the last hearing. Both men were satisfied with the outcome and after a short conversation outside the courthouse, they were back on duty. Will had told Larry Hanson he would give him a ride back to Ninilchik and his rented cabin when court was over. Larry was waiting at the harbor when Trippet returned.

"I want to thank you for helping me out, Trooper. One trip to the big house was enough for me. I never want to go back," Hanson said as he rode along. "Josef is getting crazier by the day. I really was afraid he would throw me in the inlet. I guess if he ever finds out I had anything to do with him getting arrested and losing his boat I could still wind up in the water."

"Are you sure you'll be alright when I let you out? Resnic is going to be coming home sometime today after he makes bail. The lawyer seemed sure he would. I think Ivan will put up the money for bail and get him out." Will knew Hanson rented his cabin from Josef. "You can tell Resnic you stayed on the Volga last night, which is true, and you can tell him the reason we gave you for not going to jail with him was that your citations were only fishing violations. All of which is true, so he will believe it. He doesn't have to know how you helped us out."

"Thanks for that, too. I'm only going to stay at his place until I can find another place to rent. Right now, I think I will be lucky to get my wages, let alone the bonus he promised. As soon as I get my money, I'm moving. I guess

I only have myself to blame. I knew he was doing illegal stuff, but I needed a job bad and this one paid good. It was away from drugs and criminal stuff and I thought it wasn't that bad. I sure was wrong about that, wasn't I?"

Most of the rest of the drive was done in silence. When they reached the cabin in Ninilchik, Will gave him a business card. "That has my cell phone number on it and you can reach me at any time at that number. When your court date comes up, I'll put a word in for you with the DA. Call me if you need anything."

Hanson climbed out of the truck, waved and went inside. Will couldn't help but wonder if Resnic was going to buy into this story. He had a lot to do when he returned to the office and spent the rest of the drive concentrating on his list. As he neared Soldotna, he was suddenly hungry but didn't want lunch. He dialed Gordy.

"I'll buy you a donut at the Moose Is Loose," he told his friend.

"Be there in ten minutes," Gordy replied.

The Moose Is Loose is the finest pastry shop on the Kenai Peninsula. Fresh pastries handcrafted on the premises and a staff of counter clerks that made stopping a pleasant event. As he walked to the counter, a young clerk with an array of stars tattooed on the back of her neck stepped up to wait on him. Trippet knew her and was familiar with her broad smile, razor sharp wit and acid tongue.

"How are you today, Trooper Trippet?" she asked, showing a set of perfect teeth and a happy sparkle in her eye.

"Hello, Miss Emma. I'm doing well, thank you, and yourself?"

"I'm good. I'd be better if I had a boyfriend, though." She wiped her hands on a towel and smiled again.

Will chuckled and said, "All the boys around here know you and are afraid of you."

"You aren't afraid of me, are you, Trooper?"

"No, I'm not, Miss Emma, but, of course, I carry a gun and can protect myself."

"Oh, you are just so mean," she replied. "What can I get for you?"

Just then, Gordy came through the door. "I'm just ordering, Gordy. What do you want?"

"I'll have a plain cake donut and apple juice," he told the girl.

At the table in the back room, the two men wasted no time digging into the pastries. They discussed the arrest of Resnic and Hanson as well as the outcome of the arraignment. At that point the conversation drifted to other subjects to have a friendly, off-duty, chat like two good friends will have.

Will left the coffee break relaxed and tired. He went to the office to start his day, again.

>>>>>>>

After his release from the Homer jail, Josef Resnic rode with Calvin Stroud to the hillside home of Ivan Resnic. It was early in the day, but Ivan poured each of them a tall single malt scotch. Ivan seldom drank, but this occasion called for it. They were all seated in the living room looking across the cloud covered bay to the mountains on the other side.

Calvin Stroud finished his drink and set the empty glass on the coffee table. "I'm not staying long, Ivan, but I feel I have to give you my opinion of what is taking place in this case. I'm afraid I can't offer either of you much encouragement. I could have worked out a deal if the charges were only for fishing, but Josef made it impossible by assaulting and shooting at a trooper. I might have even been able to do something about it if it weren't for the last fishing violation when he was also charged with assaulting a police officer. I know that charge was dismissed, but the DA will surely bring up the continued violent behavior on Josef's part. This isn't simply going to go away."

"I have warned Josef time and again about getting angry, but he continues to ignore me. That being said, what do you think his chances are?"

Stroud shuffled his feet, not wanting to say the answer. "I don't know any other way to tell you, Ivan. I think Josef is going to jail for a long, long time. I'll represent him and do the best I can, but it's way past being able to make a deal or getting the charges reduced. This is going to trial as a felony. The troopers have videos and recordings of the incident. There just isn't a good way to defeat that argument." He stood. "I'll leave your car here and take a taxi back to the airport. I've called for a charter to take me back to Anchorage. I'll call if there are any changes, but don't get your hopes up." With that, he gathered his briefcase and coat and let himself out.

Ivan sat a long time thinking about the whole case before saying anything. To him it all came down to "how can I minimize the costs?" After several minutes of silence, he looked at Josef.

"What do you think we should do, Josef?" he asked.

"I think we should take on the state and beat the case." Josef was still angry.

"You heard Calvin. He doesn't think you can beat this. I don't think you can either. I think we have already lost the Volga. That is a loss of more than $400,000. We have lost whatever fish you would have caught in the next ten days. The troopers are not going to let this stop here; they are going to bring it to my doorstep and when they begin to check the fish in my freezers against the fish tickets in my office our whole operation is likely to fail. If they take the Galaxy and the fish in her hold, we will be bankrupt. That makes this an expensive temper tantrum, Josef." Ivan was speaking calmly and quietly, "How do you think we should deal with it?"

"I'm sorry, Ivan. I never thought about all this leading back to you. Do you think it will really cost us everything?"

"Yes, I do." Ivan was massaging his chin. "I might have a plan, but I don't think you will like it."

For the next several minutes, the two men discussed the plan. Ivan had been right—Josef didn't like it.

CHAPTER 29

Having been desk-bound for three days completing the reports and complaints in addition to catching up on the accumulated memos and requests in his in-box, Will Trippet was feeling confined and wanted to get out of the office and into the field. He had thought long and hard about the Resnic case and worried that some technicality could blow it out of the water as happened with the last time Josef Resnic was arrested. He was sure there was a way to seal the fate of the Resnic brothers, but couldn't quite solidify a plan. On the third afternoon, he called Dean Steadman.

The two had talked about the case for several minutes when Steadman asked, "There must be a way to assure a conviction. We spent too much time to lose it all now."

"I've thought about that every minute since I left Homer. I think I have a plan, but there is no guarantee it will be successful."

"Let me hear it. At this point I'm open to anything." Steadman was willing to help.

"We have been so wrapped up in trying to get Josef that we have completely ignored Ivan and the Galaxy. We assumed Josef was unloading fish every night when he tied up at the Galaxy. Those fish have to be somewhere. We checked the fish tickets at the cannery and there was no record of illegal catch. Ivan had accounted for all the fish he sold to the cannery. We have no record of him or the Galaxy meeting with some foreign vessel out there. We kept a good eye on both the Volga and the Galaxy. He operated in the open and only came to port for fuel and to sell fish to the cannery." Will was trying to paint a complete picture.

Steadman had been listening carefully and asked, "So, where does that leave us?"

Will was ready with the punch line, "What if the fish are still on the Galaxy. He's nearing the end of the season and our informants have all said he takes the illegal catch to Washington State when he leaves in the fall. He sells those fish through his own wholesale fish outlet in the northwest. My question is do you think we have enough evidence to get a search warrant for the Galaxy? He must have lots of fish on board, probably in his freezers, that aren't accounted for in his fish tickets. He didn't buy these fish from legal fishermen. Even Josef had tickets for his legal fish. Where are all the other fish we know the Volga took all summer long? He fished at night for salmon and he fished at night for halibut. Those fish haven't been accounted for. I think we should try to find them."

"You're right about one thing; we were too concerned about Josef and let Ivan slip away. That's a good follow-up, Will. Give me a little time. I'll drive over to see the DA and ask about a search warrant. I'll try to be as convincing as you were with me." Steadman laughed, "You got me revved up, buddy."

"Thanks, Dean. I plan to be out of the office the rest of the day. If you hear anything, call me on the cell phone."

Trippet gathered his gear and checked out. He had no idea which direction he was headed except away from the office. Bow and arrow season had opened giving him cause to patrol Swanson River Road. It was a popular area for hunters. In the old days, after the forest fires, the first crop to re-grow was willows and deciduous trees. This bumper crop of moose feed led to a bumper crop of moose. Road hunters were able to drive the new oil company road and spot their quarry without leaving their vehicle. Today, fifty years later, the aspen, willow, birch and other leafy plants are overgrown with spruce trees. The vegetation is thick and tall making it difficult to see anything off the road. However, many of the seismic trails leading away from the main road are still passable and provide for easy walking. Bow hunters frequently use them to walk off the main road to small lakes and ponds where a moose may be feeding. It was early evening when Will returned to the Sterling Highway for his drive to the office. His cell phone rang; it was Dean Steadman.

"It took some doing, but I convinced her to ask the judge to issue a search warrant for the Galaxy. Good work, pardner."

"Thanks, Dean, but I'm not counting my chickens just yet," Will commented. "By the way, have you seen the Galaxy in recent days?"

"No, but I've seen Ivan in town, so, I think she must be close by."

Will thought a moment, then asked, "Have you seen Josef Resnic or Larry Hanson?"

"No, I haven't seen either of them. I saw Ella Resnic in town yesterday. She was driving Josef's truck, but he wasn't with her," said Steadman.

"How soon do you expect to hear from the DA?"

"She told me she would have an answer for me before noon tomorrow."

"Call me as soon as you hear anything, Dean"

Will was beginning to think it had been a good afternoon. He had slipped out of the office. He had checked several hunters for licenses, and Dean had good news about the search warrant.

>>>>>>>

The following day Josef was in Ivan's house with a sea bag sitting by his feet. Ivan was on the telephone with the air taxi company. When he hung up, he turned to his younger brother.

"OK, Josef, we will do this like we discussed. There are six men on the Galaxy. You can have my cabin and let the crew handle the boat. I have instructed the mate, you know him, Yuri Petznic, as to where to go and what to do. I will be in touch later for final instructions, but for now it will be as I said: take the boat out of the inlet and into open water. Head toward the Kamchatka Peninsula. I told Yuri to take her through False Pass to get north of the Aleutian Islands. Go west toward Russia until you cross into international waters. Keep moving west, but stay in international water. Be careful to stay out of Russian water. We have no papers and their navy would arrest you all and take the boat and cargo."

Ivan was staring at Josef, who had said nothing. "Have you heard what I have been saying?"

"Yes, Ivan, I've heard. You must remember I am leaving my family here; I'm leaving my land here; and I am leaving my life here. I will never be able to come back. That is a lot to give up. Someday, maybe, I will be able to send for my family, but where? Where will I end up living and what will I do to earn a living. I am losing my whole life." There was deep sadness in his voice and regret etched in his eyes as he spoke. "I don't like this one bit."

"This is your doing, Josef, and yours alone. You can stay if you like, but if you do, it will cost you everything you own along with your family and your freedom. You heard Stroud on the phone this morning. He said the same thing; the state is out to put you away for good. Is that what you want?

On the other hand, you can spend some time away from your family now and meet up with them later to go on with your life. I'm only thinking of your best interest. By doing it this way we keep the Galaxy, sell the cargo, have the boat renovated by skilled boat wrights and keep you out of prison. You can relocate anywhere in the world and your family can join you there." Ivan stopped talking and stared into his brother's eyes. Finally he asked Josef, "Well, how do you want it to be?"

"Yes, Ivan. You are right, of course. Go ahead; I'll listen to the plan again."

Nodding approval of his younger brother's decision, Ivan slid his index finger across the map on the table. "Stay as far north as possible in international waters until you talk to me again. After you hear from me, begin moving south toward Japan. By the time you get there, I will have found a buyer for the cargo and scheduled the Galaxy for overhaul at the shipyard. I am awaiting a call to finalize that part of the plan. Petznic has all this on his map. Your fuel tanks are full. Food and water are on board and the crew knows how to operate the boat. Relax, have a nice cruise and wait for my call."

"I will miss you, my brother. We have worked together all our lives. It will be strange that you will not be there." He reached out and gave his brother a huge hug. Both men had tears in their eyes.

"I will miss you, too, Josef. Now, get your bag and let's get moving. I want you on board and the Galaxy under way as soon as possible. Petznic will be navigating mostly at night to avoid being seen and I have instructed him to stay off the radio. I don't want anyone to know where you are until you are in international waters and out of U.S. jurisdiction. Come, I'll take you to the plane. Do you have plenty of cash with you?"

"Yes, but I won't need much between here and Japan." Josef had tears once again. "Take good care of my family, Ivan."

"I will, Brother, I will."

Josef tossed his duffle into the back of the big, white Ford pickup and climbed into the passenger seat. With Ivan driving, they headed to the air taxi office. The two men hugged again as Josef boarded the floatplane. Once in the air, Josef asked the pilot to circle around the city of Homer and over the Homer Spit one last time before heading west. This might be the last time he ever saw this sight and it saddened him. He sat silently the rest of the trip across the inlet to the shelter of Ursus Cove.

CHAPTER 30

The following morning Will was in his office early, anticipating the call from Dean Steadman. He emptied his in-box and completed his mandatory daily reports, becoming more and more anxious as the morning wore on. He thought about calling Steadman, but knew Dean would call him as soon as he had an answer from the District Attorney. He had stopped by the captain's office and chatted with him a few minutes and was back in his own office pacing the floor when the call came.

"We got it, pardner," Steadman nearly shouted.

"Great, Dean. When do you want to execute the warrant?"

"How soon can you get here? I'm ready. The last position report I had on the Galaxy was Ursus Cove. I'll have the crew warm up the engines and make ready to go. The wind is kicking up out in the middle of the inlet, but we can make some speed for about half the distance." Steadman had been busy this morning.

"Don't leave without me. I'll be there in an hour and a half. I'll meet you at your berth and be ready to go when I get there. I'm excited about this one, Dean."

"I can tell, and so are me and my crew. We didn't like it when the Anchorage judge let Josef off the hook. Even if we come up empty, it will be worth the trip." Steadman admitted to wanting some revenge.

"Put the coffee on; I'm on my way." Trippet cleared his desk and checked out with Marcy. The drive seemed slow because of traffic and Will had to remind himself that the speed limit applied to him as well as the others. From the top of the hill above Homer, he saw the whitecaps on the water outside the bay. He wondered if Dean had been too optimistic about the weather and water conditions in the inlet. Five minutes later he parked at the boat harbor and walked down to the dock occupied by the Enforcer.

Loco met him on deck and helped him aboard. "Welcome back, Will. Good to see you again. We have fun every time you come on board."

Will laughed and went into the cabin while Loco went about his business of closing the rail entry and, with Eric's help, untied from the dock. Dean saw the signal and began moving the boat away from the dock and toward the harbor entry. He kept his attention on boat traffic and gauges until they passed the marker buoy. Once in open water he tapped the throttles ahead, punched the buttons on the GPS and picked up his coffee cup.

"Howdy, pardner," Steadman said, grinning. "Are you ready for this?"

"Ready? I'm positively excited." Will was grinning as broadly as Dean was. "I think we need to get the crew together and establish a plan for boarding the Galaxy. I don't expect the crew to be too hostile. I think we will get an argument, but I don't think they'll get physical."

"I think you're right, but if Ivan orders them to repel boarders there may be a scuffle. He was in town yesterday, but he may have gone back to the Galaxy this morning."

"The Galaxy is twice the size of the Enforcer. Will it be a problem getting over the rail and on board?"

"They will probably have the rail gate closed, but Loco will climb up and take care of that. We have some experience at this, Will, don't worry."

The two men and members of the crew tried to anticipate every possibility, given the last time they boarded a Resnic boat they had been shot at by Josef. An hour out Dave got up and fixed lunch for the entire crew. He had fried cube steak sandwiches for all with French fries and Cokes. Conversation ceased during the meal and when they finished eating Will leaned back in the booth and napped for a few minutes.

Dave tapped his skipper on the shoulder and pointed at Trippet. "He doesn't seem too worried," he told Steadman before returning to his clean-up chores.

Will slept until they had passed St. Augustine Island. Behind the island, the water became slightly rougher and Dean was forced to slow the Enforcer. Cruising at a slower pace and with the weather worsening, all hands were straining to catch sight of the Galaxy. With the wind coming out of the southwest, they all thought the Galaxy would be anchored deep in the cove. Dean angled his boat north and west, staying safely offshore. He drove deeper into the cove, but saw no sign of the big fish tender. It was soon apparent the boat was not in Ursus Cove.

Dean blew an exasperated sigh and reached for his marine radio mike to call the Galaxy. There was no reply. He called the Coast Guard to inquire about a location, but they could not give one. Their last location on the Galaxy was Ursus Cove. Next, he contacted the marine operator in Kodiak to make the same inquiry. The operator said there had been no communication with the Galaxy since noon the previous day. Worried now, Dean called the Coast Guard commander on the official radio channel the troopers were authorized to use.

The response from the Coast Guard officer was the same as the one from the marine operator, no communication since before noon yesterday. Dean asked the officer to have his people keep an eye out for the tender. The Coast Guard had C-130 aircraft flying in the area. Frustrated and knowing it was fruitless to cruise around in hopes of spotting the Galaxy, Dean pointed the Enforcer back toward Homer. It was late when the crew finished mooring the Enforcer and Trippet climbed into his truck for the drive home.

The sea had been choppy, but nothing big enough to hinder the Galaxy. Petznic had been in the wheelhouse all night. With the last glimpses of Kodiak Island fading over the stern, they exited Shelikof Strait and plied the open ocean. The course kept them to the east of the Shumagin Islands and south and east of the Sanak Islands. It was now the decision had to be made about whether to stay south of the Aleutian Islands or cross through to the north through Unimak Pass. Petznic returned to the wheelhouse as the Galaxy was sailing past the Nanak Island group. He checked the weather and the radar before making a final decision. The weather to the north was deteriorating quickly. Yuri studied the map and decided to stay to the south of the islands, hoping the weather and the water would be better and knowing he ran the risk of running across a Coast Guard or Navy vessel. He entered his planned course into the global positioning system and explained his reasoning to Dmetri Kuzmin, the young, but capable, sailor at the helm.

"We are not in a hurry, Dmetri, and we won't have so much heavy sea to fight on this side of the islands. I am going below and have some breakfast. We are looking for international waters, so just keep her headed west," Yuri instructed. "Can I send you something to eat?"

"Thank you, Skipper, but Ted will be relieving me soon and I will go to the mess when I get off." He paused a second before venturing a question. "Can I ask you something, Skipper?"

"Of course, Dmetri. What is it?"

"We were told this would be a long voyage and to bring our passports. Can you tell us where we will be going?"

"Certainly. We are taking a slow route because the entry papers have not been completed, but we are going to Japan to have the boat refitted. You will be on the beach for a long time in Japan, but you will be paid just the same. Pretty easy duty, heh?" Petznic had been honest with the crewman as far as it went. "I didn't tell anyone where we were going to prevent rumors while we were in port and I don't want anyone calling home on the satellite phone for the same reason."

Dmetri grinned at his captain. "I always wanted to be on a secret mission."

Both men laughed and the captain left the bridge.

The ship's mess was small but neat. Josef was seated at one of the two tables when Yuri entered. Yuri walked to the table like a true seaman, swaying in rhythmic cadence, maintaining his balance easily with the rocking of the boat.

"Good morning, Captain Petznic," Josef greeted.

"Good morning to you, Josef." The two men had been acquainted for many years. "May I sit with you?"

"Of course, Captain. It would be my pleasure." Petznic sat. "I haven't been on deck this morning, Captain. How does the weather look?"

"I had planned to go north of the Aleutians, but the weather is dropping on that side. I plan to head due west and stay south of the islands for a smoother voyage. I don't expect to encounter any other ships with the weather deteriorating like it is. If it gets too bad, I will turn further south when we get into international waters. Just relax and enjoy the cruise, Josef."

"I plan to do just that." The cook motioned for Josef to come for his plate. As he stood, he asked the captain, "Can I order you something?"

"No, the cook knows what I want for breakfast. Thank you anyway, but you can bring me a cup of coffee, if you can manage."

The men chatted about the old days and relived some experiences they had once shared. The captain ate quickly and went back to his cabin. Josef was sitting alone drinking a cup of hot coffee when a lanky middle-aged man, with a four-day growth of beard and grease smeared on his cheeks, came into the mess. His name was John Beeman, the engineer. Josef had known the man more years than he cared to remember. Back in the days when Josef was drinking heavily, he and Beeman were in the Casino Bar in Kenai, both drunk and loud. Beeman leaned over to say something nasty about a large drunk native woman. Josef said, "She's my next wife," and hit Beeman squarely on the chin, knocking him backward off his chair. Beeman rolled over, shook his head and got up to answer the challenge. The two men were rolling around the barroom floor when two city of Kenai police officers broke up the fight and took both men to jail where they awakened the next morning wondering where they were and how they got there.

"Good morning, John," Josef said.

"Good morning, Josef. Long time, no see." He gave Josef a toothy smile. "Been in any bar fights lately?"

Both men laughed. "No, and I haven't been that drunk since that night in Kenai." They both laughed again and Josef continued, "And I have you to thank for that."

"Mind if I sit with you a while?" Beeman asked.

"I'd like that, John."

Beeman fetched his tray and returned. The two men visited and caught up on old times. Finally, Beeman looked into Josef's eyes, "I heard about you losing the Volga to the troopers. Tough break, Josef. Is that why you're going to Japan with us?"

Resnic glanced around the mess hall. Aside from the cook, they were the only ones in the room. "Yes, I got really angry when they tried to come aboard and I took a shot at one of the troopers. They took offense at that. They arrested me, took the Volga and my catch, and filed felony assault charges and attempted murder charges. They had been trying to catch me all season but couldn't do it. They made up for it all when I took the shot at them. My lawyer says he thinks I'll be doing a lot of jail time for it and that there is nothing he can do, so, under the table he suggested I leave and don't come back. Now, here I am second-guessing that decision, but it's done. I don't know where I will end up, but wherever it is, I'll send for my family. The only thing I know is fishing, so I will probably go to South America, maybe Peru. Maybe get a tuna fishing boat and start over. I don't know."

John Beeman finished his breakfast and stood to leave. "I'll be in the engine room all day. Come down and sit a while, if you would like to just talk."

Resnic walked out onto the deck. The wind was cold and brisk. The water was capping here and there, but the big Galaxy was taking it well. Josef leaned on the rail for a long time, mostly thinking of his family and wondering how long it would be before he saw them again. His son had just graduated high school and Josef wondered if he would follow his mother and sister to whatever future lay in store. He began to shiver and walked to his cabin for a jacket.

CHAPTER 31

The first call of the day was from the blue shirt troopers. They had a report of a bear mauling near Killey River on the Kenai River. The spot is relatively remote and only reached by boat. Dispatch had relayed to Trippet that a rescue team would meet him and another trooper at Bings Landing, a few miles below the Kenai/Killey Rivers confluence. Will knew the area well having fished salmon there many times. Details of the mauling were sketchy, but the call came in on a cell phone. The caller said his partner had been badly injured and needed to be taken out of the area, by air if possible. He also said the bear was still in the vicinity.

Two minutes after the call from dispatch, he was in his truck speeding toward Bings Landing near Sterling. He arrived five minutes before the rescue squad arrived with the boat. The other trooper was at the boat ramp, waiting. His name was Tom Donaldson. Like Will he had a shotgun on his shoulder.

When the boat arrived the three medics and two troopers boarded and headed up river. The Kenai River is a fast flowing, glacial stream and even with the huge outboard engines on the boat it took almost twenty minutes to make it upstream to the Killey River. There is a small, brush-covered delta where the rivers meet. The fisherman and his injured friend were on the delta. The injured man was unconscious and bleeding. The medics wasted no time beginning treatment. He had lost a great deal of blood. While one medic began bandaging his wounds, the other two started an IV to replenish the fluids lost from his injuries.

Donaldson took the other fisherman aside and began to get all the information about the incident while Will stood a few yards away, his shotgun at the ready in case the bear decided to come back. Will could hear the bear moving around in the brush a few yards up the Killey River. The thick foliage made it impossible to see the animal. There were bear tracks everywhere on the little beach and he spotted three brown bears across the Kenai River. Luckily, those were a big sow and two cubs, all intent on catching their lunch and not paying any attention to the activity on this side of the river. Will stayed on alert, knowing a bear can cover the distance he was able to see in less than two seconds. He kept the shotgun butt tight against his shoulder with the muzzle pointed slightly downward and toward the brush. He paced back and forth peering into the dense brush from different angles. He maintained this vigil until the medics began to load the injured man into the boat. The helmsman motored downstream at a slow pace to avoid further injury to the patient. One of the medics used his radio to call for a helicopter to meet them at a small, populated area called Kenai Keys.

Traveling with the current, they made it to the first destination quickly. The medics continued to treat the injured man while he lay on a stretcher in the inflatable boat. They had just started another IV when they heard the WOP, WOP, WOP of the helicopter rotors. It landed on the wide gravel beach that lay between the homes and the water. The patient was loaded and the helicopter on its way back to the hospital in a matter of minutes. Will, Donaldson and the medics climbed into the boat and returned to Bings Landing where the two troopers shared information about the incident. They agreed it was unlikely a search would be launched for the offending bear. Donaldson had agreed with the victim's friend that they had trespassed on the bear's food source.

Will drove to the hospital with Donaldson right behind him. In the emergency room, the nurses said the victim was stable and would survive, but he had lost a lot of blood and was headed to surgery to close several of his wounds. Both troopers wrote information in their notebooks and thanked the nurses before leaving.

Marcy greeted him at the door when he returned. "How is he?" she asked with genuine concern.

"The nurses said he would survive, but it's going to leave a mark. They were taking him to surgery when we left the hospital."

"I'm glad he's going to be OK," she said. "By the way, Dean Steadman called and asked to have you call him when you returned." With that, she marched back to her desk in the front of the offices.

With a fresh cup of hot coffee in his hand and sitting at his desk, relaxing, he dialed Steadman.

"We can't find the Galaxy. She seems to have disappeared. I drove out to Ivan's home this morning and talked to him. He denied knowing where the boat was. He said he thought the crew might have started for Washington State. I don't believe it, but that's what he said."

"Donavan Fleer has been flying on the west side lately. I think I'll ask him to keep an eye out for the Galaxy." Will paused a few beats before continuing, "Where do you think she went, Dean?"

"I haven't a clue. I've been thinking about it. The boat and crew simply leaving for Washington doesn't seem likely to me. Ivan would have known, and in fact, would have ordered it to leave. I think she may be hiding in some cove or bay on Kodiak Island. There are lots of places to hide where nobody looks. I plan to call the Coast Guard in Kodiak and have them keep an eye out for it. I'm at a loss, Pardner. I have no idea where to look."

"I'll have Sean Adams stop by and have a talk with Josef. He doesn't like us much, but he might get mad and say something about the Galaxy to Sean." Will was grasping at yet another straw.

"Let me know if you learn anything, Will."

Sean Adams was on duty when Trippet called. "Hey, Will, I hear you guys lost a 128-foot tender," he laughed heartily. "How can anyone lose a toy that big?" he laughed again.

"Thanks for the vote of confidence, Sean." Will wasn't laughing, "I've got a job for you, since you're in such a good mood."

"Don't ask me to find it for you; I didn't take it," Sean joked again.

"I'm serious, Sean. Nobody knows where the Galaxy has gone. Dean asked Ivan this morning and he said he didn't know where his boat had gone. Neither of us believes that. But, if you have a few minutes today, will you stop and see if you can learn anything from Josef?"

"I don't know if he will talk to me, but I'll try. Larry Hanson is still living in the cabin behind Josef's house. I could talk to him and see if he has heard anything."

"Good idea, Sean. Call me when you finish." Will hung up the phone and walked to the captain's office.

Captain Olson was grinning when Will came through the door of his office. "How's your day so far?" he asked.

"The bear mauling victim is in the hospital and is headed to surgery for his wounds. He was still unconscious when I left a few minutes ago. He's lucky to be alive; so is his partner, for that matter. They were fishing at the Killey River mouth, without bear spray or a gun, and the bear came out of the brush, took down the closest fisherman and chewed him up pretty good. The other guy said he yelled and threw rocks at the bear to drive him off. I don't know if he was crazy or brave, but in this case, it worked. I can't figure out why the bear didn't come back for dessert."

"That's the way bears are, predictably unpredictable. I hope the victim recovers." Olson changed the subject. "Have you found the Galaxy?"

"No, not yet. Dean went to Ivan's home this morning and asked him where it was and he said he didn't know. He said the crew may have started the trip south, but he didn't know for sure. I asked Sean Adams to try to talk with Josef to see if he knows where it is. Adams reminded me that Larry Hanson still lives on the same property and said he would try to talk with him also. I can't believe a big tender can just disappear without anyone seeing it." Trippet was shaking his head, "Dean and I were all geared up to make a big case when we searched the Galaxy. We not only didn't make the case, but also lost the Galaxy. It's frustrating, to say the least."

"You don't want everything to come easy, do you? It would take all the fun out of the job." Olson was grinning again. "Let me know what Adams learns."

The Galaxy continued its slow, steady course to the west. Josef was bored and had walked down to the engine room to talk with Beeman. The engineer was busy and had no time to socialize. Josef asked if he could help, but Beeman refused the offer claiming he had a routine and would rather stick with it.

Back on deck, Josef was leaning on the rail watching a pod of orca whales when Yuri Petznic came from the bridge. "How's it going, Josef?"

"I get nervous sitting around with nothing to do."

"You won't be bored for long. Look straight ahead over the bow. That ship is the U.S. Navy. They stop every vessel they come across and check papers. We're OK except for you, if you don't want to be seen. They hailed us on the radio and we had to answer or be sunk by gunfire. They will be boarding us in about a half hour. I think you should make yourself scarce for a while. You should be okay in your cabin. They usually just check our manifest and the crew passports for citizenship and tell us to have a nice day. I'm hoping that's what they do today. The trouble is that we left port without notifying anyone and that opens the possibility they are looking for us. Just stay in your cabin unless I send someone to get you. I am going to try to bluff our way out of this."

"How long will they be on board?"

"It normally takes less than an hour," Petznic explained.

When the Galaxy came to a stop alongside the Navy ship, the crew came to the open mid-ship deck with their passports with the exception of Kuzmin who remained in the wheelhouse. The captain held his passport for inspection. Six sailors came over on a small launch. Petznic had let down a boarding ladder for them to use. Five men came aboard while the sixth man stayed with the launch.

The ranking man, a chief petty officer, introduced himself and asked what the cargo was. He then asked if all the crew were U.S. citizens. Petznic said yes and produced the passports and the ship's manifest. Josef had not been listed, either as crew or as passenger. The navy man asked off-handedly where the boat was headed and Petznic answered honestly, "Japan for a re-fit."

Satisfied, the chief petty officer saluted and followed his men down the ladder to the launch. The entire crew watched as the navy crew returned to their ship. Petznic ordered the boarding ladder raised and stowed. While that was being done, he climbed back to the bridge and ordered Kuzmin to return to course and speed. Several minutes later, when the ships were a good distance apart, Petznic sent word to Josef he could return to the main deck.

The captain studied the charts for several minutes and made notes in the ship's log about the boarding. He would turn his ship south soon, heading for southern Japan. He would need to maintain a slow speed until he received word and docking arrangements from Ivan. This relaxing voyage had become a challenge to Petznic's nervous system. He had operated this boat doing illegal acts and making very good money for a long time. Doing it on the open ocean and in foreign countries with the U.S. Navy watching was becoming difficult. In Japan, he would rid himself of Josef and the illegal fish in the freezers. When that was done, he could deal with the shipyard and the overhaul of his boat. At that time things would cease to be so tense—he hoped.

CHAPTER 32

Adams drove back to Ninilchik to have lunch at home. The summer was going by far too quickly. His son had found employment at the local cannery and fish processing plant. It wasn't much of a job, but it paid well and gave him experience at working for a living. Next week he would enroll at Kenai Peninsula Community College. He had already rented a room in the new dorm facility and was looking forward to going back to school. Sean was proud of his family, and justifiably so, as both kids had avoided serious trouble and maintained good grades in school. Before eating, he called Ella Resnic to let her know he was coming over to speak with her and Josef. He arrived at their residence shortly after one in the afternoon. Adams admired the way the Resnics maintained the place. The small lawn was evenly mowed; the trim on the house neatly painted; and the only old boat in the yard was still in service as a sport fishing boat for his son. Sean tapped on the door and heard footsteps inside coming to answer his knock.

Ella Resnic showed her Russian heritage to a greater extent than the rest of the family. She was rather square-built but a handsome woman. "Come in, Trooper Adams," she greeted. "We can talk in the living room. Would you like some coffee or a soda?"

Sean waved his hand in refusal, "Oh, no thank you, Ella. I just finished lunch at home. Is Josef at home?" he asked, glancing around the room.

"I thought you knew. Ivan sent him somewhere on the big boat. He packed a big duffle when he left and said he would be gone a long time. He and Ivan have big secrets all the time they don't tell me."

"When did he leave, Ella?"

"Two days ago. He was in a big hurry. He was upset after going to court and I thought he was going to start drinking again, but he didn't, thank the Lord."

"How did he leave?"

"Ivan brought him home the first day, after court. He sat around, mad and cussing, and then the next day Ivan came to get him. He had his bag packed and said he was going to be gone and if I needed anything to contact Ivan. I knew it was serious and he was not coming back 'cause of the way he kissed me goodbye. He never kisses me like that anymore." There were tears in Ella's eyes.

"I'm sorry, Ella, I didn't mean to upset you. I didn't know Josef had gone and came here to talk with him." Sean reached out, took her hand and gently squeezed it. "You say you don't know where he went, but did he say anything about contacting you later?"

"Yes, he said he would contact me as soon as he could, but he didn't say when." Tears were now streaming down her cheeks.

"Mrs. Resnic, Josef and I have our differences, but I want you to know if you need anything, call me. I'll do anything I can to help you." It was a sincere offer by Adams as he stood to leave. "By the way, Ella, is Larry Hanson still in the cabin?"

"Yes, and I think he's home. The old pickup is there and there was smoke from the chimney early this morning."

She showed him to the door and thanked him again. Once again, he patted her hand in friendship. He stepped off the porch and walked to the cabin behind the main house. A wisp of smoke came from the chimney. Adams stepped up on the small porch and was about to knock when the door opened. Hanson stood in the doorway. He needed a shave, but he was clean, his hair was combed and his eyes were clear.

"What do you want?" Hanson asked curtly.

"Hello, Larry, I just came to ask a couple of questions about Josef. Can you spare me a couple of minutes?"

Hanson seemed to relax. "Sure, come on in."

The inside of the cabin was neat and tidy and had a fresh, clean smell. He was obviously taking good care of the place. "Have you found a job, yet?" Adams asked.

"No. People know me from before and don't want to hire me because they think I'm still doing drugs and robbing people. I try to tell them I'm through with that, but I don't think they believe me."

"Sorry to hear that, Larry. It may get tougher with fishing season over and the canneries closing down. Sometimes people ask me if I know someone who needs work. If anyone asks, I'll recommend you. Will Trippet seems to think pretty highly of you and that's a good enough endorsement for me."

"I appreciate that, Trooper. I need the work."

"It's OK, you earned it. Now, I need to ask you about Josef. Ella says he left and is going to be gone for a long time. Do you know anything about that?"

"Really? I didn't know he was gone. Did she know where?"

"She didn't seem to. That's why I came to talk with you. I thought you might have some idea."

"Boy, I sure don't. I'm surprised, though. He and I have court dates next week. I wonder if he will be back for it," said Larry, scratching his stubble.

"I hope so, for his sake. He's already facing felony charges and missing court will only compound the felony." Adams stood to leave. "Call me if you hear from him, will you?"

"Sure thing, trooper, and please, don't forget me if you hear about a job."

"I won't," he said as he went out the door. He already had something in mind, but didn't want to say anything until he confirmed it.

Will Trippet had been out on patrol on Mystery Creek Road checking bow hunters. He hadn't cited anyone, but assumed his presence kept the honest folks honest. He had just dropped his notebook on his desk and seated himself when the intercom jingled. It was Marcy saying he had a call on line one, "Somebody from the Coast Guard," she said.

He picked up the receiver and punched the button for line one. "Trooper Trippet," he answered.

"This is Commander McGowan, Commander of the Coast Guard unit on Kodiak Island. Are you the trooper trying to locate a fish tender named 'Galaxy'?"

Will sat straight in his chair, excited. "Yes sir, I have a search warrant for her. Do you know where she is now?"

"Not an exact location, but close. Earlier today, the U.S. Navy stopped her on the open ocean for an inspection. Routine, just checking crew citizenship and ship manifest. They reported the stop and I recognized the boat's name. The navy found nothing irregular about the inspection and let them go on. If you have a pencil, I'll give you the coordinates." He recited the numbers for Will. "They are in international water heading southwest, and had just crossed the international dateline."

"Did they give a destination?" Will asked.

"Yes, the navy report said she was bound for Japan. The name of the port isn't listed on my copy of the report. They are a long way out on the open ocean and out of our jurisdiction, but I review all the navy reports every day. That's about all the information I have, trooper. If I hear anything else I'll call you."

"Thank you, Commander. I owe you." He hung up and took his notes to Captain Olson.

"Do you mean to say Ivan Resnic sent his tender to Japan?" Olson asked incredulously.

"It looks that way, Cap." Will put on a devilish grin and asked, "Does this mean Dean and I have to fly to Japan and serve the search warrant?"

Captain Olson wasn't laughing. "How could he have known we were about to serve a warrant on the Galaxy?"

"Maybe he didn't. Maybe it was just a coincidence."

"I don't like coincidences," Olson said. "Look into it and see if you can find out anything at all."

Will's cell phone rang as he left the captain's office. "Trippet," he answered.

"Sean Adams. I just talked to Ella Resnic and Larry Hanson. Josef is gone."

"What do you mean he's gone?"

"Ivan picked him up a couple of days ago. When he left, he told Ella he was going to be gone a long time. He didn't say how long he would be gone, just a long time, and he didn't say where he was going but had a big duffle bag with him."

"Thanks, Sean. I have to talk with the captain about this. I'll call you later."

Trippet spun around in the hallway and returned to Captain Olson's office. "I think I have solved the question about the Galaxy," he said as he walked through the door.

"What is it?" Olson asked, momentarily startled by his reappearance.

"Ivan didn't know we were coming. He put Josef on the Galaxy and sent her to Japan. Josef wasn't on the list of names on the manifest, but I'll bet you a cheeseburger he was on the boat. Someone told me once they didn't believe in coincidence. This would prove it."

"I'm going to need a full report to take to the Colonel. I'm not sure what we can do about Josef at this point. He has a court date next week and if he doesn't show, he'll be a wanted felon. Japan is out of our jurisdiction, so we'll have to wait until he comes home; if he ever does."

"I think we should take some precautions against losing Ivan. He may decide to vanish like his brother," Will speculated.

"We have no charges against him. That makes him a free man to come and go as he pleases. Suspicion isn't a valid criminal charge, as much as you would like it to be." Olson massaged his chin a moment, then commented, "I can't see any way we can stop him from leaving if he decides to do that. We have no evidence against him. Get me a report and I'll take it to the Colonel. Good job, Will—bad result, but good job."

>>>>>>>

The Galaxy continued south and west at half throttles. Petznic was still waiting for Ivan to call. The crew was enjoying the ease of the voyage with little to do but keep the boat clean and eat. The weather was better today and Josef was relaxing on deck. He had made his living on boats of one kind or another all his life, but the circumstances made him uneasy about this voyage. He thought about Ella and his family, wishing they could be here with him. His thoughts were interrupted when Beeman called his name. He turned around to see the skinny engineer stepping out onto the deck.

"How about some dinner, Josef?"

"Sounds like a good idea to me," and the two men walked down to the mess. "Maybe some poker later?" Josef asked.

"I'll ask the others if anyone wants to play," Beeman said.

Petznic came in and asked to sit with the men. "The weather is supposed to be good the rest of the way to Japan. I still haven't heard from Ivan, but he should be calling me tonight or tomorrow. Beeman told me the number four freezer is acting up. We need to get to port before it quits altogether. One of the things we're replacing in Japan is all the freezers and compressors." He poked a fork into his deep fried halibut. "We will be getting a new kitchen, too. I wonder if it will improve the cook."

"I'll be leaving you when we get to dry-dock, Skipper. Had the circumstances been different, it would have been a nice trip." Josef liked Petznic and this was his way of thanking him.

"Think nothing of it, Josef. We don't often have the luxury of a pleasure cruise. It's been pleasant for us all." Petznic went silent then, attacking his halibut.

Petznic was the big winner at poker that night, while Josef was the big loser. He just couldn't keep his mind on the game.

Two or three more days and he would be able to call Ella.

Ella, meanwhile, was at home, lonely and crying.

CHAPTER 33

I van Resnic had bought the Galaxy at a bankruptcy auction in Louisiana at a fraction of its true value. The boat was only two years old and in excellent condition. The Louisiana Shrimp Company had made a terrible mistake in buying it. In theory, the company had planned to do exactly what Ivan was doing with it, which was to hold his catch and bring it to a better market. The shrimp market went downhill on both sides of the ledger at the time. Catches were down dramatically and, because of South American imports, prices fell. Those factors coupled with a huge debt service spelled a death knell for the company.

The Magnuson-Stevens Act mandates that the picking up of cargo in the United States and delivering it to another port in the United States must be accomplished by a vessel built in the United States. Ivan planned to use the Galaxy to buy and sell fish all season and to take a full load in the freezers to his own fish company in Washington State. The tender met his needs perfectly and, for many years, had made him a great deal of money. The boat was getting tired and worn, and it was time to have it upgraded. He had shopped shipyards all over the U.S. and was shocked by the amount they all wanted to do the job. He heard of a company in Japan, Takazumi Marine Fitters, who did this type of work at a reduced rate. They accomplished this by removing everything from the hull and recycling it all, either as scrap or by reselling it. Takazumi offered to do the job for a little more than 50% of the cost at a U.S. shipyard. Ivan had negotiated all summer and was now waiting for Takazumi Marine Fitters to contact him with a date to deliver the boat.

Resnic had not planned to sail to Japan with the freezers full of salmon and halibut, but the situation with Josef had dictated its own schedule. He contacted several fish buyers in Japan and found one in the same vicinity as the Takazumi dry docks. They wanted to inspect the cargo for quality, but offered a price more than double what he would have sold it for on the retail market in Washington State. He would need to off-load the cargo and collect the sale price before docking at the shipyard. Those negotiations had been intense and were now in the final stages. He wanted to have everything settled and a plan in place within two days.

Dean Steadman, of course, knew nothing of this plan and was thinking hard to come up with his own plan to keep Ivan Resnic from leaving his jurisdiction. Nothing he thought of seemed to work. He was at his desk in the office in Homer when Will Trippet called.

"Hello, Will, good to hear from you. What's up?"

It took Will several minutes to explain what he had learned from the Coast Guard and the supposition that Josef was on the Galaxy. "I have a hunch Ivan is about to bid us a fond farewell," he said in conclusion.

"I've been sitting at my desk trying to think of some way to keep him from leaving town, but I'm coming up empty." Steadman sounded tired and frustrated.

"Let me run something past you, Dean. He told us he didn't know where the Galaxy went. He told us he didn't know where Josef was. He lied to us. How do you think he would react if you and I went to his house and arrested him for hindering an investigation and to providing false information to a police officer?"

Steadman was silent a few seconds. "I'm not sure he would worry much about us. He's already shown he isn't afraid of committing felonies by aiding Josef. I'm not sure he would fall on his knees and beg forgiveness if we threatened him with a misdemeanor charge, but I can't think of anything at all. This could cause him to make some kind of mistake in our favor. Do you really think it will work?"

"I doubt it, but I had drawn the same conclusion as you, and it may possibly cause him to make a mistake. It would be better if we could wait until Josef and Hanson are supposed to appear in court. We could ask the DA to dismiss charges on Hanson and to issue a felony "failure to appear" warrant on Josef."

"It sounds like we're hunting grizzlies with a fly swatter," Dean commented.

"I know, but what else have we got?"

"When do you want to do this?"

"I would rather wait until the court date next week, but there is no guarantee Ivan will wait. What do you think, Dean?"

"We could just watch him through the weekend. If he leaves the house with a suitcase, we arrest him."

"That may be the way to go. I'm not sure about arresting him when he leaves the house, but we might put a kink in his plans." All scenarios seemed like weak options to Will Trippet.

"Well, lacking other options, I'll send Loco out to watch his house. At least we'll know if he leaves. I'll get back to you if anything happens."

On East End Road, Ivan had been in his house for several days. He had been on the telephone by the hour. He was tired and his body ached from lack of activity. All he could do now was wait until the final calls came from Takazumi Marine Fitter and the Japanese fish company with a final offer. Waiting was the hardest part. Ivan was used to making things happen and was finding it difficult to cope with the idle time.

The weekend passed without anything of note happening. He had been called once to investigate the shooting of a sub-legal moose. The shooter was young and had shot a cow moose. The young man was crying when Will interviewed him. He was only fifteen years old, and had become too excited when he saw the moose, shooting it before checking for antler size. The new regulations stated a moose must have a rack that is a minimum of fifty inches across. When hunting, size is a difficult judgment to make, but a cow moose has no antlers at all. It was Will Trippet's job to cite the boy and he did so after speaking with the boy's father. The boy would have to face the judge, but Will would send a recommendation of leniency along with the citation.

Moose season had opened on Saturday and the road hunters were out in force. Since he had not heard from Dean, he decided to patrol Mystery Creek Road. Hunters often set up camp along the pipeline corridor and hike the many trails crossing it. He drove in about 25 miles to the second airport along the pipeline. The airport was no longer in use, but several hunters had camps in the area. The Wildlife Trooper checked licenses and passed on advice to those who asked and arrived back in the office late. Tuesday would be a repeat of Monday only on Swanson River Road. He had managed to stay busy and not worry much about Ivan Resnic.

Late Tuesday evening Ivan had a call from the fish buyer. They were ready to meet the Galaxy and inspect the cargo. Ivan was elated. He called Petznic and passed on the telephone number for the buyer. He told Petznic the proposal and gave the skipper authority to sign a contract and sell the fish. It was late evening in Alaska, but only morning in Japan and Petznic was looking forward to a full day.

"Have you heard from Takazumi?" Petznic asked his boss.

"No, but I expect to hear either tonight or tomorrow. Go ahead, set a course for the fish buyer and unload. By the time that is done, I should have a time scheduled for your arrival at Takazumi Marine Fitters. Be aware, there will be Japanese customs agents crawling all over the boat. You won't be able to hide Josef. Have him present his passport with the others and claim him as crew. Once you dock on dry land he will be leaving you and you can wash your hands of him permanently. Give him the packet in your safe. It has contact numbers as well as bank account numbers and some cash. Tell him to call me on the telephone when he is settled."

Petznic instructed the helmsman to increase the throttles and speed as the boat made its way to the prearranged destination. A vessel was to meet them in a protected cove about a four-hour sail from the Takazumi docks. He felt more relaxed now with a purpose and some speed to help him. He knew what he was to do; he had dealt with fish buyers before, though never through an interpreter.

He called Josef to the bridge to pass on the good news to him. "By tomorrow you will be a free man," Petznic said. "I have a packet of papers and cash in the safe in my cabin that is yours. I'll get it for you later today. I've enjoyed having you with us on this trip, Josef. I'm sorry it all ends like this, but I know you will do well in the future." The two men shook hands and Josef returned to his small cabin to pack up his belongings.

Three hours later, they dropped anchor in the cove where another fish tender was anchored and waiting. A radio call came for the Galaxy. The fish buyer was sending a small speedboat over with him aboard. The buyer, who didn't speak any English, and an interpreter came on board. Introductions were made and the translator explained to Petznic that if the cargo was as they were told it would be for the agreed upon price. The total sale would depend on the total weight transferred.

Yuri led the two men to the freezers and opened each door for them to enter. He had a crewman move boxes so the buyer could see product in the lower tiers. Satisfied, the buyer and interpreter produced a contract written in both English and Japanese. Both parties signed the document. A small radio was used to order the other ship alongside to take on cargo. The manner of payment was a direct bank transfer to the account numbers supplied by Petznic. The buyer was a soft-spoken, gracious man in his sixties. When the transaction was complete, he gave a slight bow and, without fanfare, went back to his tender and motored away, leaving a plume of black exhaust smoke hovering over the smooth, calm waters of the cove. Petznic watched until the boat was out of sight before weighing his own anchor and proceeding to the Takazumi Marine Fitters dock to meet with officials there and arrange a docking time.

All personal items had been stacked on the open deck, palletized and shrink-wrapped for storage. The boat was secured to the dock and the Japanese customs agents came aboard and inspected it. Then the Takazumi personnel came to take possession of the Galaxy. It was a sad moment for the skipper, but he looked forward to getting his boat returned to him in new condition.

Josef marched down the gangway with his green duffle over his shoulder. At the bottom, he stopped to wave and salute Petznic at the rail above. This would be the last familiar contact he would have and he was regretting his decision. Takazumi officials had provided him a car to take him to a hotel.

Once he had checked into the hotel, he picked up the phone and called Ella.

CHAPTER 34

Tuesday morning saw Will Trippet and Dean Steadman seated beside each other in the Homer courtroom. Larry Hanson was there with a public defender to represent him. Although he was not yet aware of it, Hanson's charges were about to be dismissed by the District Attorney at the request of Dean Steadman. They were all awaiting the arrival of the judge, sitting quietly in the gallery, when the lobby door opened and Sean Adams came in to sit beside the Wildlife Troopers.

"I'll be right back," Adams whispered to Steadman. He then walked to the defense table and whispered to Larry Hanson. Even his public defender couldn't hear what was said. Adams returned to the last row of seats and planted himself next to Steadman.

"What was that all about?" Steadman whispered to Adams.

"I just told him to see me before he leaves court." Sean looked around the courtroom. "Have you seen Josef Resnic?"

"I saw his lawyer in the hall, but I haven't seen him. We think he skipped."

"I know; I talked with his wife." Adams was about to say something else when the door behind the judge's bench opened and the judge entered.

"All rise," called the court clerk. When the judge was seated, the clerk called, "Be seated." And everyone sat. She read the day's docket and called Larry Hanson.

"Here, Your Honor," replied the public defender.

"I have a petition to dismiss all charges submitted by the District Attorney's Office." Looking at the assistant DA he asked, "Do you still want to dismiss all charges against Larry Hanson?"

"I have conferred with Wildlife Troopers and they say one of the main witnesses has failed to appear and the State does not wish to pursue the charges further."

"I see Officer Steadman in the gallery. Officer Steadman, do you concur with this dismissal?"

"Yes, Your Honor. I do." he replied.

"So ordered," the judge noted the dismissal on his file. "Next case."

Hanson and his public defender were astonished. They spoke briefly and the lawyer left. As Hanson walked to the back of the court, Adams rose to follow him. The clerk was calling Josef Resnic.

Adams followed Hanson into the hallway outside the courtroom.

"What happened?" Hanson asked.

"Don't ask, just be grateful. You're a free man," Adams explained.

"Oh, man! Thank you, Trooper Adams. Thank you."

"You have made some friends, Larry. Stay on the good side."

"I can't thank you enough," his grin was wide enough to break his face.

"One other thing, Larry. Are you still looking for work?"

"Yeah, I am."

"Go to the City of Homer office. They need a maintenance man and I put in a word for you. It isn't an executive job, but it pays well and, as long as you show up for work every day, you have a job."

"Oh, Trooper Adams, I've never had anyone help me out like this. I won't let you down." Hanson thanked Adams again and walked away.

Adams watched the ex-fisherman walk out of the court building. He had a good feeling about what he had done. He was returning to the courtroom when he met the two Wildlife Troopers.

"What happened in there?"

"The judge issued a felony warrant for Josef Resnic: failure to appear on a felony charge. Now if we can find him, we can arrest him." Steadman had a broad smile. "Want some lunch?"

It was eight hours earlier in Josef Resnic's hotel room than it was at his home in Ninilchik. Ella answered on the second ring.

"I am in Japan, Ella. Get a pencil and I will give you my phone number here. I will be getting a cell phone tomorrow, but you can contact me here until I do. How are you and the kids?"

"It is so good to hear your voice, Josef. I love you very much, but I don't understand what is happening. What have you done?" Ella was excited to hear from Josef, but wanted an explanation.

"They caught me doing what Ivan and I have always done. They tried to arrest me and take the Volga, so I took a shot at one of the troopers. The attorney said I was going to have to go to prison for a long time, so I ran. I think I will go to Peru, buy a fishing boat and fish for tuna. I don't know yet. I will send for you as soon as I make a good plan."

"Josef, this isn't good. I can't leave here. Sergei is starting college in Kenai and Elsa has another year of high school. It would not be good for them to move now. You should have talked with me about this before you ran away." Ella was crying into the phone.

"Don't cry, Ella, don't cry. I will make it all up to you, but I can't do that in prison. I had to run. Please, Ella, try to understand." Hearing Ella cry made Josef's heart break.

"I know you will do what you want, but I have to think of the children. Sergei has enrolled in the college and he has a good job at the Tesoro refinery. This is his future. I cannot ask him to sacrifice that for your mistake. Ivan has always had you do the dirty things and he has always taken the money. We did well, Josef, but Ivan got rich. I don't trust him to take care of you or me or even the children. I can't come there with you, Josef. I love you and have always stood by you, but I cannot do this."

"Ella, you have to come and be with me. We are a family, I need you." Josef was pleading now.

"No, Josef. I will not do this. You only think of me when I cook and care for the children while you go out and do whatever you please. I cannot do this again. Maybe someday you will understand, but unless you come back here I will not see you again." Ella was sobbing heavily now.

"Ella, you cannot say this. Please, think about it and I will call you again in a couple of days."

"You can call and I will answer, but I am not going to travel around the world with you. My family will not do it either. Goodbye, Josef." Ella hung up the phone, pulled a pillow to her face and cried for hours.

Josef called the front desk and had a bottle of Chavez Scotch whisky sent to his room.

>>>>>>>

In Homer, the three troopers ate lunch and reveled in the short glow of success. The men discussed what to do next. Will and Dean were in agreement about one thing: Ivan was not going to sit still for long. They decided to pay a visit to the elder Resnic after lunch. It had been decided that they had nothing to lose and it might cause Ivan to get careless.

The wildlife Troopers arrived at the Resnic home in two marked pickups. Two vehicles in the drive might be more impressive to the fisherman than a single vehicle with two men, they decided. A little phycology may put him off guard. Dean knocked on the door with Will standing behind him.

Ivan opened the door looking tired and not at all well. He had a cell phone stuck to his ear but motioned them inside. He led them to the kitchen where he closed his cell phone and asked if the men wanted coffee.

"No, thank you, Mr. Resnic. We won't take much of your time. We came to pass on some information to you about your tender, Galaxy. Have you got a minute to listen?" Dean was using a friendly tone.

"Sure, have a seat. I have been really busy and the telephone is driving me crazy. What is it you want?"

"First of all we have located the Galaxy. You will be pleased to note she is safe and on her way to Japan with your crew. The U.S. Navy stopped her and inspected her papers a few days ago. Funny thing, though, your brother Josef wasn't listed on the crew manifest. I was sure he was aboard the Galaxy because we have been unable to locate him since it disappeared. Can you tell us where he is now?"

"I haven't the slightest idea. I hired him a lawyer; perhaps he knows where my brother is; I don't." Ivan wasn't falling for the ploy. "I plan to leave Homer in a couple of days myself. I have other company business to think about."

"You don't seem too worried about either your brother or a very valuable fish tender." Dean wasn't giving up. "Can you tell me what your boat is doing in Japan?"

"Of course, I sent her to be updated and refitted. This has been in the works for more than a year. I had planned to have the work done in the U.S., but the price was too high. And as to Josef, he is a big boy and can take care of himself."

"Then you were aware of the whereabouts of the Galaxy when I asked you about her before?" Dean was goading him a little.

"Yes, I knew," Ivan said with a smirk on his face.

"Then you knowingly gave false information to an officer," Dean commented.

"Yes, I didn't want anyone to know where the boat had gone."

"The law takes a dim view of receiving false information in the course of an investigation, Mr. Resnic."

"That's too bad. It was a business decision."

"I'll bet it was, Resnic. I think you had an idea we were about to search the boat and you sent her on her way to Japan. You stopped us from finding Josef because he went out on the Galaxy and you stopped us from searching your tender for illegal product."

"I can't help it if you can't keep track of a 128-foot boat, and I am not my brother's keeper. Now if you have nothing else, I have work to do. Please excuse me. You can find the door." Ivan was dismissing the troopers with bluster.

"Thank you for your time, Mr. Resnic. We will be back when we have more questions." Dean and Will both marched to the front door before Resnic could think of another comment.

Outside, Dean turned to Will and chuckled. "I think he just gave us what my old dad used to call 'the bum's rush'." They went to their trucks and drove away.

"I'm going back to the office in Soldotna, Dean. Call me if anything happens," he said into the radio.

"I'll stay on it," was the reply.

CHAPTER 35

Riding in the first class section of an Alaska Airlines 737/400, Ivan sat comfortably sipping a double scotch and water. It worried him that the troopers had come to see him. He was angry with his brother Josef for bringing on all this attention of the authorities. He had hoped to stay under their radar for a long time to come, but his brother's angry act had ended that possibility. They had lost the Volga, but it might still be possible to recover the boat when it was auctioned by the state. He would have to arrange for someone else to do the bidding and keep the state from contesting his bid. The Volga was too good a boat to let go of without trying.

Takazumi shipyard had assured Ivan the Galaxy would be ready for next season. He hoped this wasn't just a ploy to get the project. He had researched the shipyard's work and found that their customers, many were repeat business, were very happy with the work done by the company. Petznic and Beeman would stay in Japan with the boat until it was finished.

The work was to be extensive: new, more powerful Kubota engines installed; and replacement of all the freezers. The old ones had failing insulation as well as worn-out refrigeration compressors. The boat was to be sandblasted, top to bottom, inside and out. New interior was scheduled for the entire boat. The mess would get a new kitchen and furnishings. Two ladder wells were to be removed and replaced, making it more convenient to move about the interior. There was to be all new lighting throughout the vessel. LED would be replacing the incandescent lighting. Crew amenities were being upgraded. There would be more fuel and water storage. The ice making capability would be increased.

On the bridge there would be upgraded panels, both electronics and engine gauges. The seating and lighting there would also be replaced. Petznic, Beeman and Resnic had spent many days and nights designing the upgrades. There were plans to upgrade the docking area where boats tied up to sell and unload fish, as well as take on ice, water and fuel. This included new davits and vacuum system for transferring fish.

The paint scheme would be changed and deck storage modernized. In the end, the Galaxy would retain little resemblance to the one that left Alaska to go to Japan.

Ivan was satisfied with the decision to take the boat overseas to be renovated, but now he must go to Bellingham to meet with his Empire Fish Company. They would not like the fact that the entire catch for the season had been sold in Japan. The sale had netted nearly triple what it would have brought in Washington, but now his company would have to find another source for fish. His managers would not be happy, but he was not going to explain that the decision was made because of Josef and his criminal acts.

The stress of the past weeks had made Ivan weary. That, coupled with the drinks he had consumed, was making him sleepy. He put his head back, reclined the seat and slept until the plane began its descent into SeaTac Airport.

He had a small carry-on containing his cell phone and laptop computer as well as one checked bag. He found the assigned carrousel and waited for his bag to appear. As he waited, a man approached and said, "Hello, Ivan." It was his fish company manager, Russ Talbot. Russ was a tall, well-proportioned man who always wore a suit and tie.

"Ah, Russ, good to see you. Let me pick up my bag and we can go. Have you had dinner?"

"No, I was planning to stop on the way back to Bellingham and buy you something. I know a great steakhouse in Everett, if that's okay with you," Russ replied, always the businessman.

"Have you been able to find us any product?" asked Ivan.

"Some, but not enough. There's a group in Oregon that has been calling me and wants to sell us salmon and albacore. They don't have any halibut or cod, but they do have a lot of Chinook. I think we will be all right. I wish we had some halibut though," he informed his boss.

Ivan stepped up to pick his bag from the carousel. "I have a friend in Ketchikan who told me he could get enough halibut, but it would have to be shipped in three lots. With the new quota system, he can't get enough at one time to fill the order. I told him I would get back to him about that."

The two men walked to the parking garage without further talk of business. "How are Bernice and the kids, Russ?" asked Ivan.

"They are doing well. The kids are back in school and Bernice thinks her vacation has begun. They keep her busy all summer long."

Russ unlocked the Lincoln with the remote. He opened the trunk for Ivan to deposit his bags. Once inside the car he said, "I heard about Victor. Tragic, just tragic. How is Josef?"

"He is well," Ivan lied.

"Will he be here this winter?"

"I doubt it. He has some personal problems he must work out." Ivan was not willing to discuss it with his manager.

"And you, Ivan, how have you been? Will you be staying all winter?" Russ inquired.

"I'm not sure just yet. There is a lot going on in Alaska that may require my going back north before spring, at least for some business trips."

Russ sensed Ivan's reluctance to talk and let it go. He would press him harder when they were in the office. In the meantime, they had a great dinner at a small steakhouse in Everett where Ivan tossed back two more scotch and waters.

Russ dropped Ivan at the Holiday Inn where he had reserved a small suite for his boss. This was the first time he had ever seen his boss drink more than one drink and he made note of the fact it was affecting him.

>>>>>>>

Wilson Trippet was happy commercial fishing season was over. There was enough to keep him very busy, though his hours were almost normal now. Coho salmon were running and, for some fishermen, it was a fun time to fish. The weather was getting cooler and the majority of the guides had pulled their boats after Chinook season ended. There were more private boats on the river now, except for a couple of stretches of water, one being referred to by fishermen as blood alley, there was little boat traffic. Fishermen anchored their boats and called back and forth between boats with good-natured chatter.

Will used any free time he had to check bag limits and licenses on the river. Moose season was still open and he was sent on patrol in various areas to check on hunters. As is always the case, there were a few sub-legal moose reported killed. These cases had to be investigated. These routine duties had kept him busy and he had not had time to socialize with Gordy. Today he called his friend and asked him to meet with him at The Moose Is Loose for coffee.

Will arrived first and was inside teasing Miss Emma, the girl behind the counter. "Have you found a boyfriend yet?" he asked the smiling clerk.

"I thought you were going to find one for me," she laughed.

"I've been busy, but I'll get on it right away. I know about a half-blind, one legged, simple-minded young man who isn't too ugly. I might get him to ask you out. You have to promise not to hurt him, though. He's a nice young simpleton." Trippet teased the girl every time they talked.

Emma was about to give Will a man-size dose of rage when Gordy Ponset came in. "What will you two have?" she asked curtly.

Gordy carried the tray to a table while Trippet paid the tab with Emma glaring at him all the while.

Will sat down and put his elbows on the table. "You look tired, Will," commented his friend.

"I have worked a lot of hours this summer, Gordy. It's slowing down now, though."

"I've been wondering if you have talked to that retired warden about his bear attack."

"I haven't had time, but I am going to call him again soon." He sipped his coffee. "What became of the hide of the bear you and I shot? Is it back from the taxidermist?" Will asked.

"We probably won't get that back until next spring." There was a short pause in the conversation. "I've been hearing that you and Dean Steadman shared some interesting times together."

"You could say that, but don't ask me what we accomplished. We got Josef Resnic's boat, but he escaped. We still don't know where he is for sure. We suspect he is in Japan. I have to stop and talk with his wife in a few days. She was pretty upset the last time I spoke with her."

Gordy was still catching up, "And what about Victor Resnic's son, Vladimir? Have you heard from him?"

"The last time he called he said he was registering at college. My friend in Fairbanks, where the kid stays, calls and keeps me informed. He really likes the boy. He says the kid works hard, does good work and is neat and tidy in his habits. Doesn't sound like most of today's youngsters."

"You're right," Gordy was nodding his head. "He seemed like he was a pretty squared away young man when we were dealing with him at the time of his father's death. He impressed me."

"I have to get back to the office, Gordy. I just wanted to say hello. After moose season perhaps we can get together and do something, like have a barbeque or something," said Will Trippet.

Back in his office, Will caught up on his logbook and daily paperwork. It took several hours to complete the work he had let slide for the past few weeks. He was the last to leave the office. He had been sitting at his desk with the light out thinking about the events of this fishing season. He wondered if he could have handled it differently, if he and Dean should have been more aggressive with the Resnic brothers. Looking back, he could see where things could have been done differently, but at the time they had acted on the limited information they had and the time they could dedicate to it. He decided not to second guess his actions or those of the other officers. It is the way it is. I can't change it now, he thought.

CHAPTER 36

When he arrived in Japan, Josef Resnic was low in spirits and empty of prospects. He had taken his few belongings from the Galaxy and hired a cab to a modern hotel on the outskirts of Yokohama. There were some small shops and restaurants in the area, but he had no intention of shopping. His plan was to contact someone to help him buy a boat and establish a fishing business in South America somewhere—where he didn't know. He had called Ella when he arrived and she informed him she would not follow him around the world. She was going to stay in Ninilchik with the children to make a life, with him or without him. Josef had been devastated by the news.

In his younger days, he had been a heavy drinker. He had been arrested many times for bar fights and assaults. His reputation was that of a mean drunk. Ella had coaxed and threatened him about his drinking, but it was Ivan who had convinced him to quit. Ivan had tired of bailing him out of jail or paying the hospital each time he lost one of his fights. For many years he had been sober, but Ella's dire words had triggered something inside him.

He had called Ella every three days since he had arrived. Her message was always the same. When she suspected he had started drinking again, she became even more adamant in her refusal to join him. Each time he called, Ella chastised and rejected him and each time he would send for a bottle and stay drunk in his room for two or three days. Hotel room life, without exercise and with too much alcohol in his system, began to take its toll.

Eating had become a problem for him. He grew tired of the food from room service and began to walk the local area looking for something different. Local Japanese fare was nutritious enough, but the steady diet of rice, noodles, poultry and fish were not setting well with his body. He never considered the alcohol was contributing to his poor health.

It had now been nearly a month since his arrival and he was no closer to a solution to his future than on the first. The difference now was that his hope was nearly gone. Living in the hotel was expensive. Eating out every day was expensive. Drinking Scotch whisky was expensive. He was beginning to worry about his financial situation.

Some of the locals spoke a little English but he spoke no Japanese, making it difficult or impossible to communicate his needs outside the hotel. His depression deepened with each day and more quickly with each hangover.

He had purchased a cell phone with English lettering making it easier for him to make calls. He dialed Ivan. There was no answer. It had taken him some time to compute the difference in time zones. His ability to cope with the stresses of daily life was failing him.

It was midafternoon in Yokohama, but it was morning in Ninilchik, Alaska. His daughter Elsa answered the phone. "Hi, Dad. How are you?" It was wonderful to hear her voice.

"I'm doing well, Elsa, and you?"

"School has started and I'm getting ready to go now. When are you coming home, Dad?" Josef missed these disjointed conversations with his daughter. She was a senior this year and growing up fast.

"Maybe soon, Baby, I love you." There was a cracking in his voice betraying his emotions. "Can I speak with your mother?"

"Sure, Dad." He heard her call, "Mom, it's Dad." Then she added, "Gotta go to school, Dad. Love you." And she was gone.

There was silence on the phone for a moment. Finally, Ella came on the line. "Good morning, Josef."

"Good morning, Ella. I miss you. It was good to talk to Elsa. She is growing up so fast."

"She asks when you are coming home, but I can't give her an answer, can I?"

"I'm sorry, Ella, I think you may be right. I think running away was a big mistake. I haven't talked to Ivan, but if I can't get a line on a boat and a permit to fish somewhere, I am thinking of coming home and facing the charges. It is too lonely here without you and the family," said Josef.

"Finally, you are making some sense, Josef. It is lonely here, too. But I think it is better to be lonely here in my own house with my family than to be lonely in some foreign country without even a friend." He knew Ella was right. "How long before you make up your mind?"

"I don't know. I will try to call Ivan after a while, and I have a number for the fishing commission in Peru. I will try to get a permit and buy a boat there. I have been putting it off because I want to come home, but even if I come home, we will not be together. They will put me in jail for a long time. At least here or in South America I am free."

"Josef, you are not thinking right. How can you be free when you cannot come home and be with your family? How can you be free if you must go to the other side of the world to live? How can you be free if your children never see you again or you see them?" Ella was crying.

"I love you very much, my wife, but this is the fight I am having inside myself. I know all these questions, and I have no answers. I have to know you will be there when I decide. Please say you will be there, Ella." Now Josef, too, was sobbing. He said goodbye, hung up the phone, and sat on the edge of the bed for a long time. He could not live like this, he decided. It was too difficult.

In his duffle bag was a large manila envelope with his important papers. He searched the pages until he found the numbers for the Fishing Commission of Peru. He dialed the number and waited for several minutes for the phone to ring on the other end. For a long time, there was no answer and when it came, it was in a language he didn't understand. When the voice on the other end paused he interjected, "Do you speak English?" The answer came in the same unintelligible language. After several more tries, he gave up. It was a revelation to him, one he had never before considered. He had just learned that not everyone speaks the language of North America. He didn't even know what language the voice in Peru had spoken. Was it Spanish? Portuguese? An ancient Inca dialect he didn't even know existed?

Tired, frustrated and lonely, he hung up the phone. Josef considered pouring himself another drink and then changed his mind. He had made a commitment to his wife and he would do his best to honor it. He tried Ivan's cell phone again. This time there was an answer.

"Ivan Resnic," answered the gruff voice without checking the caller ID.

"Ivan, it's Josef. How are things going for you?"

"I am doing well, Josef, and you?"

"I am not doing so well. I haven't been able to make any business connections either here or in Peru. The language barriers make it difficult to communicate."

"I understand, my brother. I have found it the same when I tried to deal in some countries. That is why I use an agent when I do business in a place where English is not spoken. You should do the same." Ivan was still giving instruction and advice to Josef. "Are you OK? Do you have enough money?"

"Yes, I have enough for a while, but that is why I called. I think this was a bad idea. I am thinking of returning to Alaska. I am thinking of going home. I miss my family."

Startled by the revelation, Ivan didn't like the idea. "Why would you want to do that, Josef? If you come back, they will arrest you and put you in prison. This way you are free to go anywhere. You had better think about this."

"I have thought about it. For a month, I have thought about it. I am here and have no friends, no income, no boat and no family. It is lonely." Josef was trying to explain, but he knew his brother didn't understand his plight.

"Now you know how I live," Ivan explained. "This is how I have had to keep our business going for all these years. You have gone home to a family every night and I have traveled from one end of the earth to the other, keeping the money and business coming in. It is why I never married. This is a lonely way to live, Josef. It is profitable, but lonely."

"I admire what you've done, Ivan, but I have responsibilities to my family. I cannot just desert them."

"You can't help your family from prison, Josef. You can't earn a living from prison. You can learn a new language and you can find new fishing grounds. You can learn. That is how you survive in the big world."

"All right, Ivan, I will try. I will get an agent and try to find a boat in South America." Josef had lost the argument to his brother. He would try to find an agent to represent him.

"Stay in touch, Josef. We are brothers. We look out for each other." With that they ended the call.

The next day Josef contacted Takazumi Marine and asked for the man he had met when they arrived. He spoke English and had knowledge of boats and business. Surely, he would know of an agent to represent him in finding a tuna-fishing vessel and permit somewhere in the world. The company representative came on the line and was helpful in every aspect. He knew an agent who dealt in just such transactions. He would call his friend and recommend Josef to him.

Within an hour, Henry Yamamata called. Josef nearly laughed aloud when he introduced himself on the phone. They agreed to meet in the hotel restaurant for dinner and discuss the venture. When they met, Josef was pleasantly surprised to meet an American-educated Japanese/American.

"My father was an American soldier stationed here in Tokyo. He married my mother and took her back to America. I was raised in Southern California and went to college at Stanford. After graduation, I was hired by a firm here in Japan because of my language skills and my MBA. Life here is good to me, but I miss the U.S. of A."

There was small talk where the two men became acquainted and grew confident in each other. When they finally got down to business, Henry wrote several pages of information on his legal pad. He determined the type, size and expectations of his new client. When he left the hotel, he told Josef he was confident he could find just what he needed.

Two days later Josef received a call from Henry Yamamata detailing his findings. He told Josef that he had found several boats suitable for tuna fishing in the waters off Peru. He also had some news about a permit. These are closely regulated by the Peruvian Government and not easily obtained. As a non-citizen he would not be allowed to apply for a permit; however, he would be allowed to file for a joint venture and become a partner in a permit owned by a Peruvian. Josef said he was not inclined to enter such a partnership but would read the agreement and give Henry an answer in a few days. Henry said he would send the papers to the hotel by courier.

When the papers arrived, Josef studied them intensely for three days. Josef found the language in the contracts to be ambiguous and with loopholes big enough to drive a tuna boat through. In the end, it amounted to him providing all the financing and the Peruvian partner having all the control, including control of all revenues; however, the foreign partner was liable for all debts and taxes. The more he read it the less he liked the proposal and called Henry to tell him so.

"I'm sorry, Henry. I cannot sign this agreement. It leaves me nothing," said Josef.

"This is a standard agreement the Peruvian government allows," Henry explained.

"I am not going to give control of a company I own and am financially responsible for to someone I have never met. I don't need him. I am a fisherman. I know what risks are worth taking and which aren't. There is nothing in this for me. There is nothing guaranteeing I will even receive my legal share. I'm sorry, Henry. I can't do it. Goodbye."

Josef spent the evening in his room, sober. His western style hotel had a cheeseburger and fries on the menu for a modest $31.50. The price was bitter, but the burger was delicious. He sat in his room pondering his situation and concluding that the next morning he would buy a ticket to Anchorage. He was going home to face his fate. He checked his wristwatch and decided there was still time to make one more call. He knew the number by heart.

"Wildlife Officer Will Trippet," the friendly voice on the other end answered.

CHAPTER 37

"Trooper Trippet, this is Josef Resnic. Do you have time to speak for a moment?"

Will Trippet could hardly believe his ears. Their resources had failed to find the fugitive fisherman and now he wanted to talk on the telephone. "Of course, Mr. Resnic, what is it you want?"

"First, I want to apologize to you," he began. "That day on the Volga when I shot at you fellas, I never intended to hit anyone. I was just angry and upset and ashamed for being caught doing that illegal halibut fishing. I know you probably won't believe me, but I mean it. It was the end of the season and I let things get out of hand. I have a bad temper and sometimes I don't control it well. I'm not making an excuse, I'm just telling you I'm sorry it happened."

"I thank you for the apology and I accept it, but you committed a serious offense and I can't make that go away just by saying I forgive you. You will have to come back and face the court. The judge is a fair man and I think he will consider your apology, but it will have to be made in court, Josef, not on the telephone. Where are you now? Will you tell me?"

"Yes, I'll tell you. I am in Japan. I was going to leave America and go somewhere you would never find me. I have been here thinking about it and I think I was a fool. I think I should come to Alaska and go to court. My lawyer says I will be going to prison for a long time. I don't care. At least I could see my family sometimes." There was a great sadness in Josef Resnic's voice.

"For what it's worth, Josef, I believe you. I am not allowed to make promises, but if you come back, I will do what I can to help you. I don't know what I can do for you except to put in a word with the District Attorney, but I will do that for you if you come back here and meet me." Will thought Resnic sounded sincere, but he had been fooled before. "I have to tell you that when you failed to show up in court they issued a felony arrest warrant for you. Any officer who sees you will arrest you on sight. If you come back, I will arrange to meet you when you land in Alaska and take you into custody. This will assure your safety and be good for your case when you go to court. Will you agree to those terms?"

"That is why I am calling you. I don't want my lawyer or my brother Ivan to know I am coming back. I think it would be dangerous for me if they knew. I know I did what I did and I am willing to pay the price for my stupid acts, but I need your help. If you promise to tell the judge what I have said, I will come back and meet with you. One other thing, Trooper, I don't want you to tell Ella or the kids I am coming home. Will you promise me?"

"I will do what I've said, Josef. I can't promise anything else. When do you plan to be back?" Trippet didn't want to push the issue, but he had to get precise information. He also noted when Josef spoke that his Russian background was causing him to speak with a more pronounced accent. "I want to help you, Josef, if you will let me."

"This is a big decision. It is not easy for me to make it. I know you are doing your job and I respect you for that. I will pay for what I have done. I just want to be treated fairly. I want to someday get out of jail and be with my family, if they will have me." All the bitterness in him had died and only the remorse and shame remained. "I will make arrangements for a flight to Alaska. I will call you when I know the flight numbers and the time."

"I want to give you a different number, Josef. This is for my cell phone. I carry it all the time. The number you are calling is my number in the office. I will answer my cell phone wherever I am and whenever you call." Will gave him the number.

"Thank you for everything, Trooper. I need some help and I think I can trust you. I will call you back as soon as I have a ticket."

Will could hardly believe what had transpired. He picked up his notes and walked down the hall to Captain Olson's office.

"I've got some news, Captain," he announced as the entered.

Olson seemed to have been daydreaming when Trippet entered. "I hope it's good news for a change, Will. What is it?"

"I just had a phone call from our good friend Josef Resnic."

The words got the attention of the Captain immediately. "Where is he?"

"He's in Japan and wants to come home. He wants me to meet him when he gets here and to keep his return secret from his lawyer and his brother. I think he's afraid something may happen to him if they find out he is coming back to Alaska.

I told him I would, and I hope you let me keep my word to him. I think he is tired of running and misses his family. I think he is really ready to come home."

"We will have to see about that, but we may be able to make some arrangement if the Colonel agrees. How soon will he call you back?" Olson was showing some excitement about the prospects.

"I gave him my cell phone number and told him to call me at that number. He was going to make a flight reservation and call me back. He didn't say when exactly." Will looked at his watch. "What time is it in Japan, anyway?"

"I have no idea what time it is in Japan, but you make the arrangements and I'll call our boss and see what we can work out. Don't plan on any other duties until we make these plans. We need to catch this guy when he sets foot back in Alaska." Olson had another thought, "Get a printed copy of the felony warrant and keep it with you. I want you to serve it as soon as he arrives. He will be arriving at the international terminal and I want you and two other officers on hand when he comes down the ramp. There will be many people present, many of them foreign nationals and we don't want to give them a bad impression of our police powers. I want this low-key and I want it done safely. Got it?"

"I've got it, Boss," Will said as he headed back to his own office.

It was 11:00 p.m. when his cell phone rang. Resnic was calling with his schedule. He had excitement in his voice as he passed the information to the trooper. "The day after tomorrow. I'll arrive in Anchorage on Japan Air Lines at three in the afternoon. I will come through customs and meet you at the customs entry. Will you be there, Trooper?"

"You can count on it, Josef," Will replied while writing information in his notebook.

The following morning Will Trippet was in Captain Olson's office with the news. He passed on the time and flight number to his commander.

"OK, I talked to the Colonel and he said he would go along with your plan with some provisos. First, you will take an officer from here to back you up and aid in the transport back here. Second, you will meet with Lieutenant Dumont from headquarters. He works with customs a lot and has experience in that area. He will be in charge of events inside the customs area of the international terminal. Once you have Resnic in custody and out of the building, Dumont will leave you and your partner to your task. We will bring him to Kenai and book him into the Wildwood Correctional Center. We will arrange for his court hearings to be held in the courthouse in Kenai since it will undoubtedly be a long period before trial." Olson could see Trippet understood, "Now, who do you want to take with you to Anchorage?"

"I've thought about that, Captain, and I would like to have Sean Adams go with me. He knows Resnic and I can trust him."

"I'll call him and let him know. What time do you want to leave in the morning?" asked the captain.

"Assuming the flight is on time, we should leave no later than ten o'clock. It will take three hours to drive up and an hour to meet with Dumont and set up a plan with U.S. Customs officials. Sean and I will want to have a bite to eat before we start back. I think ten will be good."

"I'll have him here before ten, then. Good luck." Olson was making notes and dialing his phone.

Will cleaned up his desk and left the office for the day. He went to the gym for an hour and then home to relax, hoping he was covering all his bases. If Resnic were genuine in his desire to make amends, it would be enough; but if he was just setting up a plan to run again, it could get complicated. He was glad the captain had let him use Sean. He had done these types of things before and could improvise if the need arose.

Sean came into the office fifteen minutes early. He greeted Will and Marcy then turned his attention to Will and asked, "We're taking my car, right?"

"Yes, it has a cage and a backseat. It wouldn't look good to make Resnic ride in the back of my pickup from Anchorage to here."

"Let's stop at The Moose Is Loose for coffee and a donut for the road. You're buying," Sean quipped.

The pair met Lieutenant Dumont in front of the International terminal an hour before plane time. Dumont had already arranged with the customs agents to take Resnic aside and into a private office to serve the warrant and make the arrest. Dumont showed the two men to the office where they met a customs official for introductions and where the copy of the warrant was presented for verification.

The three troopers watched Resnic walk down the stairs to the ramp and into the terminal building. They had seen him coming and alerted the customs officers. The customs officers took him aside and spoke with him quietly. Two customs agents escorted Resnic to the small office where the three Alaska State Troopers waited. Resnic recognized Will and Sean when he entered and a small grin came upon his face.

"I was hoping you would be here when I came through customs. Thank you, Trooper. Thank you."

They greeted him and waited while the customs agents inspected his luggage and passport. Once this had been done, they gave Resnic over to the trio. Will explained the need for handcuffs and said they would wait until the other passengers had left the area. They handcuffed him behind his back and marched him out to the waiting patrol car, covering his exit from the eyes of people in the lobby as best they could. Will put him in the rear seat of the car, said goodbye to Dumont and thanked him for his help. With Sean at the wheel, they began the three-hour return trip to Kenai.

Once out of town and on the road Resnic asked Trippet, "Have you told my wife I was coming?"

"You asked me not to say anything, Josef, and I haven't."

"I have something I want to ask, but I don't know if it is proper," Resnic said.

"Josef, I admire your coming back to face the music. There are just the three of us here and we will keep any secret you ask. So if you have a question, now is the time to ask it." Will was speaking in a friendly tone.

Josef Resnic seemed reluctant to speak. Sean, driving and keeping his eyes on the road, looked into the mirror and asked. "Josef, would you like me to stop in Girdwood and get you a sandwich or a cup of coffee?"

"That would be nice, thank you. I haven't eaten since yesterday."

Will again coaxed his prisoner. "You said you had a question, Josef. What is it?"

Resnic gave a huge sigh, "I want to know if it would help me to give you information about my brother Ivan. I know the things he does and how much money he makes. I know how he hides his fish and where he sells them in Washington State. He is my brother and I love him and I owe him much, but he left me to take all the blame for everything. If it will help me to get out of jail sooner, I will tell you these things. If it will not help me, I will never say anything."

"Josef, I am surprised. I was not prepared for this. I can't promise you anything, but I will take what you said to the District Attorney and ask her to help you if she can. It will be up to her." Trippet was almost afraid Josef would say things that he would later be told he could not use because of the circumstances.

Josef had eaten his sandwich and drank his Coke. The conversation was less formal now and he wanted to know how his wife and family were. He asked about his brother's son, Vladimir. Will told him all he knew about the family and how he admired Vladimir for his efforts to educate himself. The time passed quickly and they soon pulled into the sally port of the Pretrial Facility of Wildwood Correctional Center.

CHAPTER 38

Will signed the remand slip and turned his prisoner over to the jail authorities. He went inside the booking office to speak with the shift supervisor, Sargent Givens. He explained the circumstances and asked Givens to give Resnic a little break in making phone calls and such. Givens said he would do what he could.

It was late when Trippet called his captain. He gave Olson a brief report and explained what the fisherman had said about turning on his brother. Olson said he would contact the District Attorney's office in the morning.

Sean Adams drove home feeling good. This had been a good break from the routine he was used to in the small community of Ninilchik. Sylvia had his dinner ready and served it with a dozen questions about his day.

The following morning an assistant DA came to the jail and asked to speak with Josef Resnic. The two were left alone in the attorney's conference room where Assistant District Attorney Lynda Bloom introduced herself. She explained Josef's right to have an attorney present during this interview, but Josef declined, saying he knew what he was doing and what he wanted to say.

"It is my understanding that you have knowledge of serious game violations and illegal commercial fishing acts you wish to report. Is that correct, Mr. Resnic?"

"No, not exactly. I have information about these things, which I will share if it will help me to get out of jail sooner to be with my family. I guess I would like to trade," Josef corrected her.

"I see. Are you sure you don't want an attorney present while we discuss this?" Bloom asked.

"I'm sure. The attorney who represented me on the fishing charges and the assault was my brother's attorney from Anchorage. I think he gave me some bad advice and I don't want to have him doing that again."

"You don't have to retain the same lawyer, Mr. Resnic. You can hire any lawyer you want or, if you cannot afford one, the court will appoint one for you. Are you sure you understand this?"

"Yes, I understand. It is you who doesn't understand. What I say to you now you cannot tell to anyone. I just want you to know what I am thinking. OK?" Josef was trying to get her to understand what he wanted.

"Mr. Resnic, I cannot offer you any sort of a deal, especially since I have no idea what you are willing to trade. I can give you the names of a number of attorneys here in Kenai with the experience in these cases to help you. I am advising you to call one of them."

"I have told you, I don't want an attorney. I only want to deal with one person. If you have the authority to do this, then I will talk to you. If not, you will have to send someone who can do what I ask."

"OK, Mr. Resnic. If that is what you want to do business, then let's do it. I'll keep everything off the record for now. You and I can talk about this and if we can come to an agreement then we will go on the record. Is that alright with you?" a frustrated Bloom asked.

"That is what I want," Resnic agreed.

Bloom closed her notebook and shut off her recorder. "All right, Josef. What kind of deal are you willing to make?"

"Before, when I was in court in Homer, my brother had his attorney come down from Anchorage. After court, he said there was nothing he could do and that I should go away before they put me in prison for a long time. My brother, Ivan, was getting his fish tender ready to go to Japan. He hurried the boat and put me on it and I went to Japan. My family is here and if I stayed there, I would never see them again. That is no good for me. I love my family. The point is that Ivan was not protecting me—he was protecting himself. I know all his dealings and fish sales. Some are with the cannery and legal, but most are not legal and the fish are taken to Washington and sold through his fish company there, Empire Fish Company. I catch halibut and salmon; Ivan processes the fish; and when he leaves in the fall, he takes them to Bellingham to be sold. There are no fish tickets for any of those fish. He makes millions of dollars doing this. Now, is this worth making a deal with me?"

"If you can prove any of this, I will see what I can do. Do you have proof, Mr. Resnic?"

"Yes, I have a logbook with all the dates and times of the fishing, as well as the weights and dates and times that he took the fish on board the Galaxy. For those fish, I was paid after they were sold in Washington. The fish I caught this year were sold when he took the Galaxy to Yokohama. Some Japanese fish company bought them. I have the name of the company and the agent written in my book."

"You will be taken to court today, Josef. It will be an arraignment on the felony failure to appear charge. I will have a public defender in court to represent you for this hearing. I want you to plead not guilty when the judge asks. They will bring you back here after the judge sets a new court date. This will give us some time to work out a plea bargain for you. Is your logbook available?" Bloom asked.

"I have it in my duffle bag. I have to tell you one more thing, Ms. Bloom. My brother is a ruthless man who has done away with people who were a danger to him. It would not be good for me if he knew you and I were talking." It was a caution to Bloom, but a real fear for Josef.

"Don't worry, Josef. I will keep our conversations private. I will discuss it with my boss because he has the authority to say yea or nay to a deal between us." Lynda Bloom saw Josef stare at the floor, worried. "You will be safe in here, Josef. Legal proceedings take a long time to play out. You will have to be patient. Would you like me to call you wife and ask her to come visit you?"

"No, I don't want her to know I am here until we have a deal."

Bloom stood to leave when Josef spoke again, "I would like to tell you something you can put on the record, Ms. Bloom.

"What's that, Josef?"

"About the time on the boat, the Volga. The time I shot at the trooper. I was angry and upset at being caught doing illegal fishing. I didn't want to hurt anyone. I just wanted to scare them away. It was stupid and I am sorry. I already told Trooper Trippet, and I mean it, I'm sorry."

Bloom gave him a pleasant smile, "That means a lot Mr. Resnic. I'll include it in my report. I won't be able to talk with you much in court today, but you do what I said and things will work out for you. I can tell you I don't think you'll get off Scott free, but I think I can get the charges reduced to misdemeanor with a fine and a short jail term. If we can put your brother, Ivan, in jail for his misdeeds, the threat to you will be eliminated and you can go on with your life. I'll be talking with you soon."

At just after noon, a trooper came in a van with caged window. He was the Judicial Services Officer. Josef was trussed up in handcuffs and leg irons for the trip to court. There were two other prisoners in the van with him. None of them spoke during the short trip. The van parked inside the court building and the officer marched his little chain gang to a holding cell inside the court. Josef was first on the list to appear. He was led to the courtroom by the judicial services officer and made to wait in the gallery during the proceedings. A young man with acne and a painfully young face met Josef in the courtroom.

"The Assistant DA told you what to say?" he asked in a whisper.

"Yes," replied Josef, also in a whisper.

Everyone stood as the judge entered. The court clerk read the charges. The judge looked at Josef and his attorney and asked, "Do you understand the charges as read?"

"Yes sir," replied Josef.

"How do you plead?" asked the judge.

"Not guilty, Judge," Resnic answered.

"I will set a court date two weeks from today, 10:00 a.m. Any other business?"

"The matter of bail, Your Honor?" the defense attorney asked.

The judge looked at Ms. Bloom, "What does the DA have to say as to bail?"

"The District Attorney's office is opposed to bail at this time due to the danger of Mr. Resnic being a flight risk as demonstrated on a previous occasion."

"What does the Public Defender say?"

"We will not argue the point at this time."

The judge made a note, "I order the prisoner returned to custody without bail, to be delivered to this court two weeks from today." He banged his gavel. "Next case."

Josef was taken back to the holding cell where he waited for the others to finish, and then the prisoners were all taken back to the jail in the same van that had brought them. They were searched and sent back to their cells. The correctional officers kept Josef in the booking area and placed him in the attorney visiting area where he waited without knowing why. The door opened a half hour later and Lynda Bloom entered.

"You did very well in court today, Josef. I opposed bail because I thought it may be safer for you in here than out on the street where your brother could get at you if he chose to do so."

"It was what I expected," Josef said, calmly. "What did your boss say to my offer?"

"If you give us everything you say you can, he agrees to drop the felony assault charges to a misdemeanor sixth-degree assault. You will still have to deal with the fishing charges and I suspect they will give you a large fine for those. As a bonus, the DA said if you gave us the information on Ivan and it details several years, as you said to me, he would try to return your boat, Volga. That is not a promise, only he would try. The troopers have a say in that. Although, I spoke with Trooper Wilson Trippet and he said you had been cooperative and came back on your own with arrangements for them to meet you and he told me if we decided to give back the Volga, he would not oppose it. I think he likes you, Josef."

"How soon can we start?" he asked.

"As soon as you can get me your notebooks. Where are they?"

"They are here in the jail. I can ask the jailer to get my bag. They are in there."

Lynda Bloom was stunned, "If you can do that, I'll have him get the bag for you now."

"OK," was his only reply.

The DA called an officer and asked for the duffle. He said he would bring it, but that he would have to stand by while Josef took out what he needed. They both agreed to that. Minutes later the two were building a history of illegal fishing practices going back more than ten years. The story included income tax evasion, keeping undersize fish, fishing closed season and closed waters. They documented fishing without a permit in several fishing districts. There were notes and dates of bullying other fishermen and one case where a complaining deckhand went over the side, never to be seen again. The more notes Bloom took, the more charges she could file. She documented reports of interstate transport of illegal fish and transporting illegal aliens—fish cleaners who worked on the Galaxy. The list continued to grow as the hours passed. Lynda Bloom had changed the tape in her mini recorder several times. It was late now and she was exhausted. In her opinion, this would be a monumental poaching case.

Late in the day, she told Josef she had enough information for the time being. She said she had to go to the office and type her notes into a case file. She thanked Josef repeatedly.

"All this amounts to more than I ever expected. If the DA agrees with me, I think there is a very good chance you will get your boat back. What the State will do about your permits, I can't venture a guess. If I were you, I would not expect to ever fish again. But the boat is valuable and it would give you a nest egg to invest in another business." Lynda gave him a kindly look. "Would you like me to contact your wife now, Josef?"

"Yes, I think it is now time. I want to see her, if she will see me."

"I'll see what I can do."

With that, she stood and motioned for the guard to come for Josef. They took him back to his cell and she returned to her office. They had both missed dinner.

CHAPTER 39

It was late afternoon when Lynda Bloom called Will Trippet to inform him of Josef Resnic's revelation. The DA was, indeed, willing to make a deal with Resnic and offered to throw in the Volga as a bonus. The evidence was rock solid, documented in the logbooks of the brother of the accused. Once the logs were reviewed, the final list of charges ranged from illegal fishing to transporting illegal aliens to illegal interstate commerce and fish trafficking to a possible murder. The murder charge was without evidence at this point. Assistant DA Bloom was almost giddy with excitement.

"I may be able to find out some details about the man overboard incident. I think I know a person who was there at the time. Give me a little time to investigate." Will liked Lynda and had dated her on a couple of occasions in the past. Recent events had renewed his interest, but he would try not to let it interfere with business. "How soon will you be filing charges on Ivan Resnic?"

"It will likely be a few days. There are so many charges and some fit different laws, depending on jurisdiction. We think it would be beneficial if we kept this quiet until Ivan returns to the state. Josef said he talked to him a few days ago and he was in Bellingham, Washington at that time. It will be safer for Josef also. I called his wife, by the way. She was surprised he was in the U.S. and was going to drive up from Ninilchik to see him. I called the jail and asked them to put her on the visitor list."

"Thanks, she is a nice lady. Life hasn't been easy for her. I think and I hope Josef has seen the light and really changes his ways. I guess parting company with his brother Ivan is a big step in that direction. Anyway, I'll get busy on finding information about the missing sailor. Thanks for the call."

"I just thought you would want to know. I'll be talking with you soon." Lynda hung up, secretly wondering if Will would ever ask her out again.

Will sat at his desk wondering how to go about approaching Larry Hanson on the subject of a murder. Hanson had indicated he was aware of the incident, but he did not want to be involved in the prosecution of Ivan Resnic.

Will called Sean Adams.

"What's on your mind, old buddy?" Sean asked.

"Just how friendly are you with Larry Hanson? Do you think he would talk to me about the time a man went over the side and was never reported or seen again?" Trippet inquired of his friend.

"Boy, I really don't know. He has always shied away from the subject. We helped him with the court and I helped him get a job with the city, so maybe he would say something off the record, but I wouldn't guarantee it." Adams was doubtful.

"I have to try. What time does he get off work?" Will asked.

"I see him coming home around 4:30 every day."

Will checked the time. Hanson should be home by now. "Can you meet me at his place in a half hour?"

"Sure, but, like I said, he might not want to talk about it"

"I'm on my way; meet me there." Will hung up and hurried to his pickup. Traffic was light this time of the year and he was able to push the speed limit a little.

When he arrived, Adams was waiting along the street and followed him into the cabin. Resnic's old truck was parked in front. Hanson was still using it to get to work. They walked up the steps to the porch together. Hanson heard them coming and met them at the door.

He gave them a friendly greeting and invited them inside. They all sat at a small dining room table. Hanson offered coffee, but both men refused. "What can I do for you?" Hanson finally asked.

"I'm looking for some information and I think you have some knowledge of the incident. Before we start, I want to tell you I am only looking for information and have no reason to believe you were involved. I'm telling you this just so you can relax." Will tried to put him at ease.

"This is beginning to sound serious. Should I have a lawyer here?"

"We aren't here to investigate or arrest you, Larry. If you don't want people to know where we came up with the information, they will never know. It stays between us." Will tried to explain without giving him any information.

Hanson was silent for a few moments before speaking. "I don't know what you want, but the two of you have been fair with me and I think I can trust you. If I get to where I don't want to say any more, I want you to understand. Is that okay with you?"

"Yes, it is, Larry. And for what it's worth, we don't want you to say anything about this conversation to anyone, either. We don't want anyone to know about this investigation. Are you good with that?" Will wanted it to be clear with Larry.

"I guess we understand each other. What is it you want to know?"

"Josef Resnic is back home and in jail in Kenai. He is here to face charges of illegal fishing and assault. You had your day in court and I hope you feel good about the result. Josef has the same thing to look forward to with the charges being more serious.

"In the course of this investigation we came across an incident which involved Ivan Resnic aboard the Galaxy. I think you were present when this happened and was hoping you would be willing to tell us about it. Remember, this is between us, no one else."

"If I gave you anything, it would get me killed. There's no way I can tell you about it." Hanson had a look of terror on his face.

"I understand your reluctance, Larry, but no one will ever know where we got this information and, if it leads to Ivan's arrest, he would be put away for a long time and unable to do anything to either you or Josef." Will was still trying to convince Larry. "We think a mortal crime has been committed and want the person responsible to pay for his acts. Our job is to protect the public, and the dead man was part of that public. Today, you are a part of that public and we need your help to put the guilty person away."

Larry was shaking his head and gave a huge sigh. "You have to keep my name out of it. I think he should have to pay for what he did, but I don't ever want him to know where this came from." He stood up and walked to a small bedroom in the back of the cabin. A minute later he returned with a large manila envelope containing a notebook and several loose sheets that looked to be time sheets. "This is my record from the time I was on the Galaxy." He opened the spiral notebook. "I keep a diary of sorts with the dates, times and locations of things that happened. It's all in here and I will tell you about all of it, but I won't give you my book."

"OK, Larry, but can I record it so I can type it up later?" Will asked.

"That's okay with me, but I won't give up my notebook." He opened the book and searched for the right page. "I had worked on the Galaxy for a couple of years. I was doing drugs at the time and lots of my friends were druggies, too. I worked with a guy names Denton Fox. He was a dealer and big-time user. He was a mouthy sort of guy and he and Ivan didn't get along. Ivan had promised us a big payday if we stayed on the boat until we reached Bellingham. Denton kept after Ivan to make it even more. The two fought a lot. One evening Denton was whacked out on cocaine and got into a fight with Ivan. He was screaming and carrying on and took a swing at Ivan. Ivan is a big guy and outweighed Denton by more than fifty pounds. He decked Denton, but Denton got up off the deck with a steel bar in his hand. Ivan was furious. He grabbed Fox by the shirt and started hitting him. Fox went limp and fell to the deck and Ivan kept kicking him and hitting him. There was a small Davis anchor with about thirty feet of chain laying there. Ivan wrapped it all around Denton and hiked him on his shoulder, walked to the rail and dumped him in the channel. We were between Petersburg and Wrangell. When Ivan turned around, he saw me standing on the deck. He looked at me with a crazy look on his face and said, 'keep your mouth shut.' He stormed back to the bridge and I didn't see him again until the next morning. He never said a word at breakfast, only gave me a mean stare. This is the first time I have ever said anything about it to anyone." Larry Hanson fell silent again.

"That is an amazing story, Larry," Will commented. "And you have all this documented, dates, times and locations?"

"Yes, I'll give you all the details and you can write them down. Like I said, I'm keeping my book."

"Did anyone else see this happen? There were other crew members on board the Galaxy; did any of them see it happen?"

"No, just me. The rest of the off-duty crew was in the mess hall playing poker, and the helmsman was busy with the boat."

Both Will and Sean were taking notes as fast as they could write. The three men went over the details several more times before Will decided he had what he had come for.

"Larry, you have no idea what a help this is to me and the DA. I know there will be other questions, but I promise I will keep your name out of the investigation. When this goes to trial, you may be called upon to testify, but that decision will be yours. I think, by that time, we will have Ivan in custody and unable to inflict any harm on you or anyone else."

It was late and Will wanted to get home. On the way he called Lynda Bloom to tell her he had good news for her and he would talk with her in person tomorrow.

CHAPTER 40

I van Resnic was in his Empire Fish Company office when his cell phone rang. Annoyed with the interruption, he answered gruffly. "Resnic," he said in a caustic tone.

"Ivan, Calvin Stoddard. I have some news for you and I don't think you will like it very much." He spoke without preamble.

"Well, spit it out, Cal. What is it?"

"Your brother Josef is back in Alaska and he was arrested. I had a report that he was in court yesterday and plead not guilty to the charges, one of which was attempted murder of a police officer. Bail has been denied and he's in jail."

This was shocking news to Ivan, "What? When? Where is he being held?"

"I've told you all I know. I wanted to call you as soon as I heard. What do you want me to do? Do you want me to go down to Kenai? That's where they have him. He will need a lawyer." Stoddard had been Ivan's lawyer for many years doing mostly contracts and corporate work. His knowledge of criminal law had grown in recent years due to the frequency of violations by Ivan and his employees.

Ivan thought for just a moment, "I'll call you back as soon as I book a flight. I want you to meet me at the Anchorage Airport and to fly to Kenai with me. We will go together and if he needs a lawyer, you will be there to take the job. Josef is smart and he'll keep his mouth shut. I'll call you back in a few minutes."

Resnic called Stoddard, "Meet me at the Anchorage Airport. My flight gets into Anchorage at 2:05, flight 155. I have us booked on ERA for Kenai at 2:30. Don't be late."

The two men landed in Kenai at 3:10 and went directly to the Budget car rental agency in the airport. Ivan had reserved a car and in minutes, they were driving the four miles to the correctional facility. They were not on the visitor list, but Ivan convinced the guard to let them in and to call Josef to the visiting room. He was sure Josef would see him and his lawyer.

The two men waited in the outer waiting area until Josef was seated in the visiting room. They were escorted into the secure visiting area to find they were separated from Josef by a thick pane of glass and had to talk to him by telephone. It was inconvenient, but necessary for security. Once the guard left them alone and with the door closed, Ivan picked up the telephone.

"Why did you come back here?" Ivan asked, without saying hello.

"I had time to think about it and decided I would be better off coming back. I made a deal by turning myself in and I hope to get the charges reduced. I'll still go to jail probably, but at least I'll be able to see my family."

"This is very dangerous for both of us, Josef. I don't understand you. I did everything to help you. I even got you out of the country and now you come back and put all of us in jeopardy once again. How could you do this to me? You know I risked everything for you."

"You talk very loud, Ivan. You are not the one who was sitting in a hotel in a foreign country with no one to talk to, not even my family. You left me out there all alone, without help to start up again. I am better off here in jail."

"Don't be crazy, Josef. I brought Calvin with me. He's your lawyer. He will help you get out of here. Now be reasonable. You are my brother. I'll take care of you." There was desperation in Ivan's voice.

"I don't want your lawyer. Look what he did for me in Homer. I will get a lawyer of my own. I have already made a deal to get the charges reduced. That's more than this shyster did for me. Go away, Ivan. I don't need you to protect me. You only want to protect yourself. Take him with you," Josef pointed his chin at Stoddard. "Go away."

Ivan couldn't believe his ears. Josef had never gone against him before. Josef hung up his phone and motioned for the guard to come back. Ivan was devastated. He was going to have to rethink his intentions for Josef.

Outside and back in the rental car Ivan spoke to Calvin Stoddard. "Go back to Anchorage. I don't need you here now. I'll do something else about Josef. I'll be in touch with you soon."

At the Kenai Airport, he turned in the rental car and sent Stoddard back to the city. He booked himself on a flight to Homer and took a cab to his home. His only luggage was a small carry-on, which he left in a chair in the living room. It took only two phone calls to locate Larry Hanson. Hanson was now working for the City Of Homer as a maintenance man. He went back out and started his Suburban for the drive to Ninilchik. His informant had said Larry was living in the cabin at Josef's place.

Larry was home when he arrived. He knocked on the door. When Larry answered, Ivan told him he had a job for him. Their meeting took only a few minutes and Ivan was on his way back to Homer.

The taillights of the Suburban were hardly out of sight when Larry Hanson called the cell phone number for Wilson Trippet. When Will answered, Hanson was nearly shouting into the phone.

"Ivan Resnic just left my place. He said he would make it worth my while to be arrested and to be put into jail with Josef. He wants me to beat him really bad or even kill him. He didn't seem to care which. Ivan scares me, Trooper. I told him I would, but I can't do it. You've been too good to me and I have a fresh start. I want to keep it going. You gotta help me, you gotta."

"Calm down, Larry. Tell me exactly what he said. I'm going to help you, but I have to know the details. Did he offer you money?" Will was asking.

"Yeah, he said he would give me his lawyer and pay me $10,000 to do the job. He said when I get put into jail I should get friendly with Josef and use the first chance I have to club him 'to death,' he said. He said he would get me bailed out and get me out of Alaska and that I would never be put into prison. I ain't going back to prison, not for him or anybody."

"OK, Larry. I'm going to call the DA and get a warrant issued for Ivan. Stay by the phone until I can call you back. They will need you to make a statement before they can get the warrant. Stay put, Larry, and I'll get right back to you."

Will called Lynda Bloom. Luckily, she was still in her office, working late. At first, she was pleased Will had called, but then heard the urgency in his voice. "What's the problem, Will?"

"I just had a call from Larry Hanson. Ivan Resnic just hired him to kill Josef Resnic. Hanson agreed to do the job out of fear of Ivan. If I get Hanson to write a statement, will that be enough justification to have a warrant for Ivan's arrest issued? Contracting a killing is still against the law, isn't it?"

"Oh, wow, Will. When did this take place?"

"A few minutes ago, Lynda. Ivan had just left Larry Hanson when he called me. This needs to be expedited. Ivan has a lot of money and a lot of resources. He may be home packing to leave right now. If he thinks Larry is going to do the job, he won't want to be in Alaska when it happens. I think he'll go back to Bellingham and be sitting in his office there when it goes down. The perfect alibi. We need to arrest him before he leaves the state."

"I'll call the DA and talk to him. In the meantime, have Larry Hanson come to your office and write a statement for me. If the DA sees the urgency as you do, I'll draw up the warrant and we'll get a judge up to sign it and you can serve it tonight. In any case, I'll need that statement."

When she hung up, he called Larry Hanson. "I want you to come up here tonight, right now, to make a statement for the DA. We're trying to get a warrant for Ivan Resnic. This is a big deal, Larry, and I need you here as soon as you can get here. I'll be waiting for you."

Forty-five minutes later Hanson came in looking pale. "How about a cup of coffee or a Coke, Larry?" Will offered.

"I could use a cup of coffee," replied Larry. He was shaking from fear.

They were the only ones in the office and Hanson walked to the coffee pot with Will. "I think he will kill me, too. I don't think he intends to pay me. He doesn't know I talked with you before or he might have killed me today. He is a dangerous man."

It took more than two hours to put the statement together. Marcy wasn't in the office, leaving Will the task of typing up the statement. The document was four pages long when finished. Will sat Larry in front of his computer screen to read the script. When he had finished, Larry said it was correct and agreed to sign it. Will punched the buttons to print the document and walked over to the printer. It took a while for the paper to finish spitting from the machine. When it did, he picked up the pages, handing the top four copies to Hanson.

"Read these and check them for mistakes. I'll do the same." Both men sat in the office reading for about five minutes. Will finished first and waited for Larry.

When he finished, Larry looked up and said. "Looks good to me. I'll sign it."

"You're sure everything in the statement is accurate?" asked Will, handing Larry a pen from his desk

"Yes, it looks right to me," Larry said as he picked up the pen and began to sign.

While Larry signed the documents, Will dialed Lynda. "I have your statements on my desk."

"How do they look to you?" she asked.

"I think everything is covered and Larry has just finished signing them."

"Great, can you bring them to my office? I'm working on the warrant now. The judge said he would read them and sign them off tonight," she informed him. "It will take the judge a while to read and think about this, so when you bring them over, I'll buy you dinner at Louie's."

"You know me, Lynda. I work for food." They both laughed. Will said he would be there in twenty minutes.

Will sent Larry home, assuring him he would be safe there. He told him it would be safe to go to work the next day because he intended to locate Resnic and arrest him tonight. When Larry was gone, Will gathered the statements and drove to Kenai to meet with Lynda Bloom. She read the document, nodding her head in satisfaction.

"This looks really good, Will. Let me call the judge and we'll drop these papers at his office in the courthouse. After that we can get some dinner."

After a short stop at the courthouse where Lynda went in alone to give the paperwork to the judge, the two met at Louie's Restaurant. Louie's is a small place with hometown atmosphere and some of the best steaks you ever ate. They sat in a booth near the hotel lobby door in order to have some privacy. Will was still in uniform and didn't want it to appear that he was sitting near the bar. The two had kept an on-again, off-again relationship for quite a long time. Will liked Lynda a lot and had told her so in private many times. She wasn't interested in a serious relationship because her secret ambition was to step into the District Attorney seat if her boss was appointed Attorney General, as he planned. They were just finishing a second cup of coffee when the judge called to say the warrants were signed and ready.

"Go and pick them up," Will said. "I'll take care of the bill. I know you have student loans to pay." Will was grinning at her and pleased with himself for getting the warrants so quickly.

While he waited for Lynda at her office, Trippet called his boss. He explained what had taken place, saying, "I want to get Sean Adams, use Homer PD as a backup and arrest Ivan Resnic at his home."

"OK, Will, you have my blessing, but I will want you to stay in touch with me throughout the entire operation. I don't want anyone hurt. I'm going to go back to the office and wait. You can contact me there."

Next Will called Sean. "Get out of bed and meet me at the Homer PD. We have a warrant for Ivan: conspiracy to commit murder. I want you to go with me while I arrest him."

Immediately Adams was excited. "See you in Homer," he said.

The night was cool with the feel of frost in the air. Will had driven as fast as he could to meet Adams and the Homer police officers. He led the little parade out East End Road to the home of Ivan Resnic. No lights were visible from the yard. Will sent the two Homer officers to the back to cover any exit. With the warrant in his hand, Will bounded up the steps of the front porch with Adams close behind. They had noted the Suburban parked in the yard and the hood felt cold.

Adams took a position beside the front door, his back against the thick log wall. When he was in position, he nodded to Will who moved to the left side of the doorway and knocked loudly. There was no answer. He knocked again. Still no answer and no lights came on inside the house. Will stole a look through the living room window. He saw no one inside. He called one of the Homer officers on the radio to ask if they saw anyone or any sign anyone was home. The answer was no. After several minutes, he relaxed and called Captain Olson on the phone to explain the situation.

"What do you want to do, Will?" asked the captain.

"I want to force the front door and get inside to serve this warrant."

"OK, do it."

Will took a steel bar from the toolbox in the back of his truck and came back to the porch. He knocked again and again there was no answer. He jammed the bar into the wood next to the fancy brass door lock and pried hard. It took some effort, but the door finally gave in.

Both troopers cautiously entered the room. Nothing moved. Switching on the lights, they began a systematic search of the residence. Minutes later, they had determined no one was home. He called one of the Homer officers and asked him to check with the local cab company and see if Ivan had called them for a ride.

Will and Adams had just finished securing the front door when the officer returned with the answer. "Ivan took a cab to the airport three hours ago. He caught a plane for Anchorage and left town. I checked and the air carrier said he had a reservation on Alaska Airlines for Seattle leaving an hour ago. It looks like we missed him," said the Homer officer.

CHAPTER 41

At the time of the attempt to arrest Ivan Resnic, there had been a mad scramble to catch up with the fleeing criminal. Seattle has a small contingent of troopers to deal with just such contingencies as this. They were dispatched to SeaTac Airport to intercept Ivan. Somehow, he had eluded them in the crowds of the terminal. Everyone involved was disappointed but believed he would be picked up at his office in Bellingham. Everyone was wrong. Ivan had taken his carry-on bag with him when he deplaned in Seattle. Instead of exiting through the baggage area, he had gone down to the underground railway and boarded, getting off at the international terminal. He marched boldly through the customs inspection and passport check to get on a Japan Airlines 747 headed to Tokyo, Japan. In fairness, the troopers noted that neither he nor the customs officials knew he was being sought for crimes in Alaska.

Today, only days away from the Thanksgiving holiday, Josef Resnic was sentenced for his misdeeds. True to her word, the charges were all misdemeanors and the sentence moderate. The judge fined him $10.000 for the fishing violations, forfeited all the seized catch and, the biggest revelation, returned the Volga to Resnic. In the matter of the charge of assault on an officer, the judge was harsher in his judgment. Resnic was sentenced to one year in jail with credit for time served. When he heard the sentence, he gave a sigh of relief and turned around to see his wife in the gallery. She was nodding at him with tears flowing down her cheeks. At the end, the judge ordered the sentence be served at Wildwood Correctional Center where his family could come to visit him.

Josef leaned ahead to look at Lynda Bloom, caught her eye and mouthed the words, "Thank you." She gave him a small smile. The lawyer seated at the defense table turned to Josef and said he could appeal the sentence, but Josef declined.

Trooper Judicial Services took Josef back to the pre-trial jail where correctional officers helped him gather his belongings and transferred him to the main building next door. Officers there completed the booking process and assigned him to a room on the second floor. Things were relaxed in the sentencing facility where inmates had a certain amount of freedom inside the fences. The food was good and he could visit his wife often, but the time went very slowly. He had a calendar with his release date clearly marked on it and crossed out each day as it passed. Fish and Game had revoked his commercial fishing licenses and he had would sell the Volga. His plan was to buy a small business selling fishing gear to commercial fishermen. He knew about nets and such. His wife thought he would do well in that business.

His big worry was Ivan. He was still out there somewhere. There had been no word from him since the day he came with the lawyer. Will Trippet had told him about the offer to Larry Hanson to do him harm and Hanson's call that made it possible to have a warrant issued for Ivan. He had also told Josef there was no word of where Ivan had gone. Ivan was not one to forget or to forgive. He would be back and try again to do him harm. Josef knew he would be out of prison before the next salmon season started, and he relished the thought. He would fall to sleep thinking, 'maybe my son will finish his education and come to work with me in the new business.' It was a pleasant thought and it helped him sleep.

Will Trippet was busy with his normal duties for this time of year. Background checks for license residency was the most time consuming. There had been no word of the whereabouts of Ivan Resnic. Immigrations and Customs had been notified to be on the lookout for him, but unless he came home before his boat was completed, he would not be coming through a regular customs entry. It was likely he would ride home on his newly renovated fish tender and enter Homer without any customs check at all. The Galaxy would ask for a customs inspection, probably in Kodiak, but Ivan would be gone when it took place, of this Will was certain.

The winter passed slowly. It was a mild winter with only a small accumulation of snow and moderate temperatures. It was now late April and the snow was melting fast. This was the period, known in Alaska as break-up. Most residents felt it was the worst time of year, with muddy yards and bad roads with rutted side roads all making access to fishing or hunting very difficult. The temperatures were rising and the sun was shining many hours each day. The birch trees were showing signs of leafing out again. Pussy willows bloomed and the moose population browsed happily.

In Yokohama, Yakazumi Marine Fitters had worked around the clock all winter. Their operation was efficient and professional. Ivan had joined Petznic and Beeman in assisting the Yakazumi engineers during the renovation. This company was experienced in this type of re-fit and needed little guidance in its completion. When the work was completed and the final inspection done, Ivan hired two Japanese men to help unpack the palletized personal goods and make the boat ready to sail. Only a small amount of water was put into the tanks and the fuel that had been pumped out in the beginning was now back on board the Galaxy. Ivan had paid a sizable deposit to Yakazumi in the beginning and now, with the work complete and Ivan very pleased with the outcome, final payment was made from a trust account set up for this purpose.

Four days after payment was made and all the new equipment tested, they set out for the ocean crossing to the U.S.A. Ivan took his turn at the helm and became familiar with the new systems. The updated radar was wonderful. The depth finder and fish locater was much more efficient and easier to read than the old one. New engine gauges were digital and direct read. The new engines were strong, quiet and without vibration. Every system was new and easy to use. The color of the Galaxy had been changed to a pale gray and the deck structures had been changed. Crew quarters had been upgraded and the mess had been replaced. The Galaxy was essentially a new boat.

Everything about the overhaul made the boat better and faster. She was a delight to handle. The Japanese crewmen both spoke passable English and worked hard. Once at sea, they were more relaxed but kept to themselves. They were told at the outset that they would return to Japan by air when the trip was concluded.

Will had been dead wrong about the return of the Galaxy. He supposed the boat would come directly back to Alaska. It didn't. The Galaxy made straight for Bellingham, Washington. Once they were close, Petznic notified U.S. Customs he was coming and wanted a customs inspection. As he did that, Ivan was on the telephone to Russ Talbot. Russ had a 45-foot Carter pleasure craft where he entertained customers and clients. Ivan asked him to come out to deep water and meet the Galaxy right away. Thirty-five miles out of Bellingham, Ivan stepped off the Galaxy and onto the private boat. Russ greeted him and they talked while the Galaxy picked up speed and moved on toward a mooring where she would take on fresh water, fuel, food and supplies needed for the new fishing season.

Talbot set the speed at a slow pace and followed the big boat toward port. Once they were under way, he began to inform Ivan of the warrant and the investigation by the Alaska Wildlife Troopers. They had actively looked for Ivan all winter and Talbot suspected that they would be notified by Customs about the return of the Galaxy. Police would surely be there to look for Ivan when she docked.

"What do you think my options are, Russ?" asked Resnic.

"With all the TSA checks, it's much more difficult to get on a flight than it used to be. However, if it were me, I would drive to Portland, Oregon and catch a flight out of there. The troopers have looked for you all winter, but by now, they may not be looking as intensely. I wouldn't guarantee it, but you might be able to fly back to Alaska without being noticed just by using a different airport. I think you would double your chances if you flew to Fairbanks instead of Anchorage. You can get a charter or a rental car there and get back to Homer."

"I didn't know about the warrant. That makes this a little more difficult. I've been watching the news on the internet and can't find where anything has happened to my brother or Larry Hanson. Have you heard anything about either of them?"

"Not a word," replied Talbot.

"Would you mind if I spent a few days with you before going home? I would like the Galaxy to get back and draw attention away from me." Ivan was shaking his head. "I can't figure out why Hanson didn't take care of Josef. He knows I'll settle with him when I get there. He was always a good crewman and I thought I could count on him. It only goes to show, you can only trust them when you're looking them in the eye."

"You have to get this taken care of, Ivan. You and I have too much at stake. We lost an entire season last year and it cost us a lot of money this winter. We made a little profit, but not enough to keep us going. We can't stand another winter like this. I really don't know how you will manage to run the business under these conditions, but we have to find a way." Talbot was worried and expressed his concerns.

"I know, Russ, I have the same concerns. Petznic will run the operation until I can work it out, but if I'm arrested, there could be some serious problems. I'm not willing to go to prison like my brother." Ivan knew he had to get back to Alaska to solve each of his problems. Angry now, he resolved to solve them permanently.

"I need a steak and a drink, Russ. Let's worry about this in the morning." Ivan was tired and had no answers.

Russ Talbot expertly inched the cruiser into its slip in the marina. Ivan tied the lines and went back on board to help Russ close up the boat. Russ drove to their favorite steak house where they each had a Porterhouse and drinks. Once at home with Russ, Ivan showered and retired for a long night's sleep.

Three days later the Galaxy, with the old crew back on board, began its trip back to Alaska. The weather cooperated and it was a quick trip, shaving two days off the usual passage time. Petznic took the Galaxy to anchor in Kachemak Bay a mile east of the Homer Spit. He dropped his anchor and was shutting down the systems when the Enforcer, with Dean Steadman at the wheel, pulled along side. Eric and Loco secured the Enforcer to the side for the Galaxy. Petznic came to the rail to ask what this was all about.

Dean Steadman had come to the back deck. "Alaska State Troopers, Mr. Petznic. We have reason to believe your boss, Ivan Resnic, is aboard this boat. We have a warrant for his arrest and will be coming aboard to look for him. Are you willing to let us on board?"

"Come aboard, but you won't find Mr. Resnic here. He didn't come on this voyage, but you are welcome to look."

Steadman waited on the Enforcer while the other three crewmen searched the Galaxy for its owner. When they returned and reported finding nothing, Dean saluted Petznic and said, "Thank you, have a nice day." They untied the lines and slowly moved away from the Galaxy. Dean reported the contact to Will Trippet by telephone.

Will took the information to the captain in his office. "I'm beginning to get worried, Captain. Josef Resnic will be getting out of jail in a few days and we haven't found Ivan. He and Larry Hanson will be in danger of being killed if we can't find Ivan."

"Remember, Will, you didn't create this problem and the result isn't your fault. You have to take comfort in knowing you did everything within your power to prevent injury to these men. You have to keep looking and remain vigilant, but the responsibility of the criminal acts lies with the criminal, Ivan Resnic." This was today's lesson according to Captain Olson.

"Thanks, Captain, but I'm not sure I'm comforted in that." Will returned to his office thinking he should pay a visit to Josef Resnic—maybe later today.

CHAPTER 42

Five mornings later, Will was driving into the office when his phone rang. It was Sean Adams in Homer. "Can you get down here in a hurry, Will?" Adams asked in an excited voice.

"I guess I could, what's happening?"

"I'm sitting across the street from Duncan's Café. I was driving into the Homer office and spotted Ivan Resnic getting out of an old pick-up here. He has one of our old friends with him."

"Hold on, Sean." He paused, reaching down and flipping on the switch for the overhead flashing red lights and pressing hard on the throttle pedal. "I'm on my way. Who is the person with him?" He pressed the button on the speaker phone to enable him to pay attention to his driving.

"Do you remember the guy a couple of years ago that you busted on East End Road out at the village for poaching a moose?"

"Do you mean the one who beat his neighbor so bad he nearly died?" Will inquired.

"That's him, Alexi Christov, a huge man, meaner than a snake with a sore tail. I thought he was in prison, but he must have got out 'cause he just went into the restaurant with Ivan."

Will was driving fast passing through Kasilof now. "I'm getting off the phone now, Sean. Call me back if he makes a move. I'll be there in less than an hour." Shutting off the cell phone, Will devoted all his attention to speeding south. Traffic was light and moose were scarce this morning. There had been a few patches of black ice, but he made it into Homer forty minutes later. He found Sean still parked across the street from the café.

"How do you want to handle this, Sean? I don't think we should try to take him here with all these people around, someone could get hurt." Will knew Sean had more experience at this sort of thing than he did.

"I think we should stay out of sight until they leave, then follow them until they go somewhere we can safely approach them. We don't have anything on Alexi, so if they split we only have to follow Ivan. I think it's entirely possible he will either run or fight. If he fights, he may use a weapon. Either way it could be dicey."

"OK, I'll park near the back of this store and wait. You get where you won't be seen and wait. Call me when they leave and I'll follow you. When they get to a secluded spot, we'll take them." Will outlined his plan for arresting Ivan Resnic.

Ten minutes later the two men came out of the restaurant. Ivan said something to Alexi and they each went to their own vehicle. Alexi drove away first with Ivan close behind. Both vehicles headed out East End Road past Ivan's home. They drove several miles, nearing the village of Kachemak Silo. A mile before reaching the Russian settlement, the two trucks turned right down a steep road toward the bay. Sean had been on this road many times and knew there were three houses—one of them belonging to Alexi Christov.

"It looks like they are headed to Alexi's place. We can take them there." Sean was speaking into his shoulder-mounted microphone.

"Sounds good to me," replied Trippet.

The road was rough, but the trooper car sped a little, closing the distance between it and Ivan's pick-up. All four vehicles drove into the spacious yard at nearly the same time. Neither Ivan nor Alexi had seen the troopers following and were surprised when they exited their vehicles.

"Alexi, it's the troopers," shouted Ivan Resnic, startled by their sudden appearance.

"Ivan, take my motorcycle and head down across the field. They won't be able to follow. I'll keep them here. Get going."

Ivan ran to the dirt bike while Alexi walked quickly toward the officers. Sean tried to sprint toward Ivan, but was blocked by Alexi who held him around the waist, lifting him off the ground. Will ran the few steps to the aid of his partner. It was all the two troopers could do to subdue the big man. While they were wrestling with Alexi, Ivan sped away down the hill, through the soft muddy field, past a house a half mile away before getting out of their sight. Once Alexi was handcuffed, Sean called on his radio for assistance from Homer police. Two city police cars started out East End Road to where they were, all the while keeping an eye out for the motorcycle. When the Homer officers arrived, they took custody of Alexi and took him to the Homer jail. Sean and Will continued the search for Ivan.

Ivan, meanwhile, was riding fast. He knew every road and trail in these hills. He kept away from the road, angling back toward town and up toward the ridge. He made his way to Bald Mountain and from there, using snow machine trails; he made his way across the countryside to the Anchor River. Finally hitting the road, he sped down the Old Sterling Highway to Anchor point. He had friends there. He hid the motorcycle and did his best to brush the mud from his clothing. At the Anchor River Inn, he went into the restroom to wash his face and hands and clean more mud from himself. He went into a stall and sat, relaxing, trying to collect his thoughts. He didn't fully understand what was happening, but it was clear the troopers were after him. He had to get out of town or be arrested.

Ivan found his cell phone in his shirt pocket and made two calls. The first was to Yuri Petznic. When Yuri answered, Ivan quickly explained he was on the run and needed help to get to the boat. Petznic agreed to come to Anchor Point to get him.

The second call was to Calvin Stoddard. When the lawyer answered the private line, Ivan nearly shouted into the phone, "What's going on, Calvin? The troopers are chasing me and I'm on the run. What is this about?"

"I told you there was a warrant for your arrest, Ivan. You shouldn't be here. I haven't been able to find out what the warrant is for, but I know it is a felony warrant. If they have you in their sights, they will chase you until they get you. My advice is to get out while you can. I don't know how, but get out now."

"You're a lot of help, Calvin. For all the money I pay you and this is the best advice you can give me?" Ivan was angry and hung up the phone without any further conversation.

Yuri Petznic told Beeman he would be gone for a short time and put him in charge of the boat until he returned. He slipped into a light jacket and went down the boarding ladder to a small skiff tied there. It was an 18-foot outboard-powered craft that the crew used to commute to the Homer harbor. He didn't go into the harbor, but beached the small boat near the breakwater. The boat would be safe here as long as he returned before the high tide swept it away. The company truck was parked up in the parking area near the launching ramp. It took only a couple of minutes to climb to the truck, get it started and begin the drive to Anchor Point fifteen miles to the North.

Little more than a half hour from the time he made the call, he recognized his old pickup pulling into the front of the inn. Checking to see if any troopers were in sight and seeing none, he walked quickly to the rusty old truck. He jumped into the passenger side and told Yuri to go.

Once they were on the road, Ivan asked Yuri if any troopers had been to the Galaxy.

"Yes, Sir. The Enforcer has been there. They were looking for you. They looked us over and left. They told me to call them if you came aboard." He smiled and looked at Ivan. "Not a chance," he said.

"How long will it take to get the boat ready to shove off?" asked Ivan.

"We're ready to go. Everything is on board and we have full fuel and water. Beeman has repaired the couple of little glitches we had on the ocean crossing. The boat is beautiful and ready to pull anchor. Where do you want to go, Boss?"

"I have to think about that. I had made other plans, but they were interrupted. I need a little time to decide what to do. If the Enforcer has been to the Galaxy, it seems likely they won't be back unless they see me coming aboard. I might just wait it out here in Homer before making a decision."

"I'm ready, the crew is ready and the boat is ready. You tell me where and when you want to go and we'll head out." Petznic was curious. "What's this all about, Boss?"

"Truthfully, I can't answer that. All I know is that the troopers said they had a warrant for my arrest. I'm not sure what for. I ran before they could tell me. My lawyer didn't know, but said it was a felony charge. I can't imagine what the charges could be," Ivan lied. He had a pretty good idea what had triggered the warrant. Either Josef or Hanson had talked. It didn't matter which one, but one of them had snitched him off. He had been meeting with Alexi for help with the problem when the troopers came. Now he was at a loss as to what to do. He needed time to make a plan. "Let's just stay at anchor in Homer until I can make a new plan. I wish I had more information."

The tide was beginning to rise quickly when they returned to the parking area. The two men walked to the skiff without drawing attention. Minutes later, they were on the Galaxy feeling safe.

Every police officer on the south end of the Kenai Peninsula was on the lookout for Ivan. Sean's opposite shift relief found the dirt bike stashed behind a building at Anchor Point. Sean was at the police station questioning Alexi Christov while Will Trippet drove to Anchor Point and began driving subdivision roads on the off chance he would get a glimpse of the fugitive.

He patrolled all day on every road between Anchor Point and Homer with no success. Late in the day, he met Sean at Duncan's Café for something to eat, the first meal today for either man.

When they had finished, they decided to call it a day. Sean drove back to Ninilchik and Will drove to his office to file some reports before going home. He called Captain Olson, gave him a short verbal report and said he would see him the next day.

Next, he called Lynda Bloom to tell her they had tried to serve the warrant and had been outwitted by Ivan and Alexi. Again, he told her he would give her a full report the next day.

"You sound tired, Will," she said over the phone.

"It's been a long day," he replied.

"Do you want to come by and have a glass of wine with me? It might do you some good," she offered.

"That sounds great, but I had better just go home and lick my wounds. Tomorrow is going to be a busy and, I suspect, unpleasant day. Thanks for the offer, anyway. I'll take a rain check."

"Any time, Will. Good night."

Will hung up and drove home, but couldn't help thinking about Ivan. "Where the devil could he have gone," he wondered.

CHAPTER 43

There had been no sightings of Ivan in four days. Patrols were intense with every officer from every agency looking. Back roads and neighborhoods that had not seen a patrol car in years were now seeing several patrol units each day. The overall crime rate had dropped by more than fifty percent. There had not been a burglary on the south peninsula in nearly a week. The jail had seen only one booking in that period, for driving under the influence. Officers being officers were becoming bored with the chase.

Ivan had sequestered himself on the boat and only appeared on deck after dark. He was becoming nervous from the confinement. This evening he would speak with Petznic about going ashore and going to his home to get some personal items he would need when he made his break.

Ivan, Petznic and Beeman were in the newly renovated mess hall eating dinner when Ivan spoke of his plan. He wasn't looking for approval, only telling his men what he planned to do.

"I have decided to go to the house and get some things. Yuri, I want you to drive me there. I need some money I have in the safe, some clothing and a couple of other items. I want to trade vehicles with you for a while. You take the Suburban and I'll use the old pickup. As soon as you drop me at the house, I want you to take the Chevy and come back to the boat. If anyone stops you just say the Suburban had been sitting too long so you were going to use it awhile and that I had told you to use it."

"Are you sure you want to go to the house? They may still be watching it." Yuri wasn't at all sure this was a good idea.

"Yes, I'll be OK. The truck may need to be jump started at first. John, I want you to send a pair of jumper cables with Yuri."

"I'll get them as soon as I finish dinner," said the engineer.

Ivan continued his instructions, "I want you to drive me to the house, Yuri, and as soon as we start the Suburban I want you to come back to the boat. Someone will surely see my truck on the street and call it in. Just come back to the Galaxy and wait. It won't be long before someone comes out here to investigate. I may not be back for a few days, but I will be back. When I return I am going to have you take me on the boat to Washington. As soon as you fuel up there, you will run it back here and get ready for the salmon season. You know how we do it."

"It seems to me the Galaxy is going to be the center of attention for quite a while. How do you want to operate this summer? Shall I try to run another fishery on the side like last year?" Petznic wanted clarification on this issue.

"No, keep it legal. We will still make money and, as you said, we will be watched. With Josef in jail and having lost his boat, it would cost more than it would be worth. We will find another boat and other fishermen later on." Ivan liked both these men and trusted them to do what was best for him. "I want you men to have a good summer and make some money. I don't know what will happen to me, but I'll find you at the end of the season in Bellingham."

"We wish you luck, boss." Petznic and Beeman shook hands with Ivan, and Beeman went down to the engine room to get the jumper cables.

It was late and dark when Petznic and Ivan Resnic took the skiff to shore. The two men walked slowly to the truck with Petznic carrying the electrical cables. Petznic drove and Ivan sat quietly in the passenger seat. They made it to Ivan's home and found the Suburban was dead and in need of an electrical assist. Three minutes later, Yuri drove out of the yard and back to the harbor. He let the truck run for several minutes to assure it would start the next time he turned the key. There was no one on the breakwater when he walked back to the skiff and returned to the Galaxy.

At the house, Ivan had erred badly by turning on the light in the kitchen, thinking it would not be seen from the street. He was wrong. A Homer police officer, patrolling East End Road, was driving by and noticed the light in the back window of the house. He stopped his patrol car and walked up onto the front deck. Through the window, he could see someone walking around in the back portion of the house. The front door had been secured with screws after the troopers had broken into the house to serve the warrant. Realizing whoever was inside would have to exit through the rear door, he went around to the back and waited below the rear deck. It was cold and he was shaking from standing motionless. He was holding his Glock automatic when the door opened. He was able to see it was Ivan, but Ivan couldn't see him. The officer waited until Ivan was out of the house and had closed the door, giving him nowhere to retreat before confronting him.

Stepping into view the officer identified himself, "Homer police, Mr. Resnic. Drop your weapon and raise your hands." Until Resnic was in the open, the officer had not seen the shotgun in his hands.

Without hesitation, Ivan swung the barrel of the gun in the officer's direction and pulled the trigger. The 00 buckshot struck the officer in the chest. He was wearing a bulletproof vest, but at close range, though the shot didn't completely penetrate the vest, the blunt force trauma from the blast killed the officer immediately.

Ivan ran down the steps to where the officer was lying on his back dead. He could tell immediately that the man was done for. He ran to the top of the steps and grabbed a large suitcase he had packed. He hurried to the old pickup in the front yard and started the engine. As he went around the house, he could hear the sirens of police cars coming from town. He backed out of the drive and headed toward the downtown area.

Four police cars sped past in the opposite direction. Ivan held his breath, but none of them stopped or turned around. They had been too intent on getting to his house. He drove slowly through downtown Homer, not wanting to draw attention. Once he reached the Sterling Highway, northbound, he relaxed a bit. He hadn't counted on this situation, but now he was committed. The consequences were going to be the same whether he made it to Hanson's home or not.

Will Trippet was having dinner with Lynda Bloom at her apartment when he got the call. A Homer officer had been shot down at Ivan Resnic's home on East End Road. Without explanation, Will ran from the apartment building and jumped into his state pickup. Turning on the red lights and siren, he left Kenai, turning right on Kalifornsky Road speeding toward Kasilof. He didn't stop when he reached the Sterling Highway, but drove as fast as he dared toward Homer. He was going past Clam Gulch when the thought struck him, "What if he decided to get Hanson, since he had already killed one man." He pressed harder on the throttle, wishing he could go faster. Traffic was pulling over for his red lights and he took advantage of the space. He weaved in and out of the cars until he reached Ninilchik. He slowed when he reached Kingsly Road, turned left and hurried to the Josef Resnic home where Larry Hanson lived in his small cabin.

The old truck Larry drove was parked in front when Trippet slid to a stop. He got out of his truck and ran up the steps to the front door. Banging hard on the door, he shouted, "Open up, Larry. It's Will Trippet."

The door flew open and a half-dressed man opened the door. "What is it, Will?" Hanson asked in a sleepy voice.

"Get your shoes on, get in your truck and drive to Kenai. Ivan just killed a police officer in Homer and I think he may come here next."

Hanson spun around without answering and grabbed a pair of shoes. He slipped them on and picked up a jacket, shut off the light and closed the door. He ran to his truck and started the engine. "I'll call you in the morning," he said, closing his door and spinning his tires. Seconds later he was gone.

Next Will went to the main house in the front. Ella and her daughter were watching TV when Trippet knocked. "What is it, Mr. Trippet?"

"I don't want to alarm you, Ella, but Ivan may be headed this way and he is looking for trouble. I don't think he would do you any harm, but I would rather not take the chance. Would you take Elsa and drive to Soldotna and get a room for the night? Just to be safe." Will was nervous about standing in the open on the front porch.

"If you think it is necessary, I will." She turned to her daughter, "Get your coat, Elsa. We are going to stay in Soldotna tonight." Without hesitation, Elsa stood and found her coat.

"Call me in the morning, Ella. Now go. Please hurry."

When she was gone, Will climbed into his truck and shut off the red lights. He turned around and drove out of the yard to a spot about a city block up the street where Ivan wouldn't notice him if he showed.

Twenty minutes went by. Sean had heard the news and called Will. They met where Will was parked, both with their lights off, waiting. Adams gave Will more details with regard to the shooting in Homer. Both agreed it seemed Ivan had gone wild in the past few days. They waited.

It was midnight when an old pickup with the lights off slowly made its way toward the Resnic home. It rolled slowly to the back and stopped in front of the cabin.

Before it stopped, Will and Sean drove slowly to the front of the house. Will blocked the driveway with his truck, stepped out and quickly moved to the rear for cover. Adams went behind the corner of the house with a huge spotlight in his hands. When Trippet exited his truck, Adams turned the spotlight on a surprised and angry Ivan Resnic.

Blinded by the light, Resnic shot in the direction of the light source, firing his shotgun for the second time that night. The shot went wide and left Ivan cursing.

"Trooper Trippet here, Ivan, drop your weapon. You don't have a chance."

Adams propped the big spotlight between the house and a trellis at the side of the house. It lit the whole front of the cabin. It also gave Sean a chance to move away from the light in case Ivan decided to take another shot at it.

"Get out of here and leave me alone, Trippet. I'll shoot you if you don't," shouted Ivan Resnic.

"Don't be stupid, Ivan. We don't want to do you harm, but we have a warrant for your arrest. One way or the other we are taking you in." Will didn't really think he would give himself up, but he had to try.

Ivan caught a glimpse of Adams making a move near the front of the house and fired from the waist. Will didn't wait to hear the result. He fired his .40 Smith and Wesson, two shots. Both projectiles struck Ivan Resnic in the chest, but both were a little high. Ivan went down, dropping his shotgun. Both Adams and Trippet rushed the cabin. Adams kicked the shotgun out of reach while Will checked Ivan who was alive but in bad shape. Both bullets struck the left shoulder and there was extensive bleeding. Adams reported the shooting to dispatch and ordered an ambulance. Will pulled off Ivan's jacket and used it as a compress to stem the bleeding. Three minutes later the ambulance was on the scene and trained medics took over the treatment.

"Did he hit you when he fired in your direction," Will asked Adams.

"No, but it was close. He shot right behind me. Makes me glad I'm a small target," he said, laughing a little.

CHAPTER 44

When the medics took over the care of Ivan Resnic, Will backed away and called Captain Olson. Olson said he was already on his way to Ninilchik and would arrive in fifteen minutes. Homer police were now on the scene of both shootings as well as state troopers. The Colonel had been called and the state twin-engine aircraft had been dispatched with the Major and an investigator from the Anchorage Police Department. The latter was an effort to conform to the policy that an agency shall not be the investigating group for an officer-involved shooting involving its own officer. It must be investigated by an outside agency. In this case, both the troopers and the Homer police department were excluded. The major and the state plane were due at the Homer airport in ten minutes.

Meanwhile, the medics were franticly attempting to control the bleeding and stabilize the vital signs of the patient. They were in contact with Central Peninsula General Hospital where doctors advised, after determining the condition of the patient, they were sending a Life Flight helicopter to transport the shooting victim to Providence Hospital in Anchorage. They had been advised of the extent of the wound and decided that the local hospital, as good as it was, did not have the expertise or the trauma surgeons needed for this wound.

Will and Sean were seated in Sean's patrol car when the captain arrived. The two had been busy documenting the sequence of events leading to the shooting of Ivan Resnic. Olson found the two men, who told him first hand of the events of the evening.

"Sean, do you have room at your house to take in Will for the night?" asked the captain. "The Major and the APD Investigator will be here soon and they are going to want to see you both. You really shouldn't be here any longer."

"I sure do Captain. Sylvia and I will be glad to have him. You know where I live," Sean said, pointing a finger in the direction of his home, three blocks away. "Send the Investigator over when he gets ready to talk to me and Will."

"Thanks, Sean." He turned to Wilson Trippet. "Will, I am going to ask you to unload your weapon and place it in an evidence bag and seal it. The investigator will want it. By policy, you are off duty as of now. The protocol is three days. I don't expect any questions about the shooting that would extend that time line. I would appreciate it if both you and Sean would write an account of the incident while it is fresh in your minds. From my perspective, you two did an outstanding job by getting bystanders out of the area before Resnic showed. Great job, men."

All three men turned as they heard the helicopter arrive. It landed, stirring the rocks and dust in the street in front of Ella Resnic's home. The medics working on Ivan loaded him into the ambulance and drove to the waiting helicopter only 75 yards away. They watched as the local medics transferred the victim to the helicopter and the IVs and monitors were packed inside. Within minutes, Ivan Resnic was being flown to Anchorage for treatment. Once the helicopter took off, one of the ambulance medics walked back to where the three troopers stood.

As he approached he said, "You guys did an outstanding job of keeping this victim alive. His collarbone is shattered and his left shoulder joint is blown away. The blood loss could have killed him. The bullet took out a big chunk of artery, but the compress you applied kept him from bleeding to death before we could get here." He gave a small wave and as he turned to leave he said, "Just wanted you to know that."

Will asked Sean to open the trunk lid of his patrol car and get an evidence bag. Will did as the captain ordered and unloaded the Smith and Wesson, placing the shells, gun and clip in the bag. He sealed it with red evidence tape and handed it to the captain.

"I'm tired, Captain. I think three days off will feel good. I'll take my truck over to Sean's house and we will be there when you need us." The adrenalin was draining from his body leaving him without energy. Will felt like a rag doll when he sat in his pickup.

Both men drank coffee, and then dozed fitfully during the early morning hours. Finally, the investigators came to the house to interview them. Major

Thomas Dunn was the number two man in the department, directly under the colonel. He had brought Bill Morrisey from the Anchorage investigators office of the Anchorage police department. Morrisey was a tall man with thinning blond hair and a winning smile. It was easy to see why he made such a good investigator by his manner of interrogation.

Major Dunn introduced Bill Morrisey, opening the interview.

"I'm here to document the events of this evening. State procedures require an outside investigator when a trooper is involved; that's why I'm here. I'm familiar with events up to the point where Ivan Resnic came to this property. I want to hear your version of what took place when he arrived." He placed a recorder on the table in front of Will. "Start by giving your name, rank and occupation."

"My name is Wilson Trippet. I am a Wildlife Trooper for the State of Alaska." He went on to chronicle the events from the time he received the call from Sean Adams until the arrival of Captain Olson. This portion of the interview took just over an hour. Then it was Sean's turn. The major sat quietly sipping coffee while the interviews were done. It was daylight when they finished.

The major stood and addressed Will and Sean, "I want to make it plain that this is not a suspension, and you will be paid as though you were on duty. You are on administrative leave. It is not a punitive action, only a procedural requirement. From what I have heard from everyone involved in this event, you two did an outstanding job. You kept bystanders from being involved, isolated the shooter and attempted to apprehend him without violence. He initiated the actions that caused him injury. I'm grateful the two of you were not injured in the gunfire. We'll be in touch once the investigation is complete. I've talked to the Colonel and he passes on his congratulations and thanks as well."

Once they were gone, Will turned to Sylvia, "Can I crash on your couch a couple of hours before I go home?"

"Of course you can, Will. But we have a spare bedroom and a nice bed for you to sleep in. I'll show you where it is. It has its own bathroom and you can wash up before you lie down. Would you like some breakfast?" Sylvia was a sweet lady.

It was noon when Will Trippet stirred and began to get out of bed. He stumbled to the front of the house where Sean was sitting at the kitchen table. Sylvia said, "good morning" and brought him coffee.

"Does bacon, eggs and hash browns sound good to you?" she asked.

"It sounds wonderful, Sylvia, thanks," replied Will.

"I haven't heard anything from the office," said Sean. "There was a little blurb on the local radio about a shootout in Homer where they reported the death of the Homer police officer. My guess is that the department isn't releasing any information yet."

After breakfast, Trippet began the drive home. Still weary from the events of the previous night, he dialed the cell phone number for Lynda Bloom. She was excited when she answered.

"Oh, Will, I have waited all night for you to call. Are you alright?"

"I'm fine, Lynda, just tired. Are you busy this morning?" asked Will.

"Not really, what is it you want?"

"I want you. I shot a man last night and I need to have a friend close to me right now. Can you come to my place for a while?"

She paused a few moments before answering, "How soon?" she asked.

He had showered and changed into sweat pants and a sweatshirt with Wildlife Trooper emblazoned on the front and was drinking a Coke when the front bell rang. When he opened the door, she flew into his arms, crying. He held her with one arm while closing the door with the other.

She looked up at him, tears streaming down her cheeks. "Oh, Will, I realized, when I got your call that this relationship has turned into more than just friendship. I think I love you. I was so frightened. I worried all night about you and didn't dare call. I didn't sleep all night. I was so relieved at your call this morning and I didn't understand my feelings. Please don't be mad at me for saying this, but I couldn't help it."

"That was one of the reasons I called. I am having the same feelings. It seemed important to call you and tell you I was okay," explained Will. "Until you came along, I never felt responsible to anyone but myself; but this morning I had to call you. I knew I had to hold you. I think this must be what love is like. I have always been afraid of the feeling, but this morning I can't live without you. I love you, Lynda."

They stayed in the house all day, just being together and liking it a lot.

CHAPTER 45

Six weeks after the shooting, life had returned to what Will considered normal. He had returned to duty and both he and Sean Adams were given letters of commendation for their part in the arrest of Ivan Resnic. Ivan himself was in a jail cell in Anchorage where he was still under the care of the surgeons who had saved his arm. Ivan's left arm was no longer functional, but was better than a prosthesis. He would soon be transferred to Kenai where a trial would be scheduled. The list of charges had grown with the death of the Homer officer. Another charge of murder would be added for the killing of the deckhand he threw overboard tied to an anchor. This man would never again see freedom.

Josef Resnic had finished his sentence and was at home with his wife and daughter. Their son was finishing his first year in college at Kenai Peninsula College. When he was released from Wildwood Correctional Facility, Josef sent word to Will Trippet he wanted to see him. Will agreed to see him in the office. Ella was driving the day they came. Josef looked fit and well when he came into the office. Ella looked happy. Both Resnics were smiling when they came into Will's office.

When he came through the door, Josef stuck out his hand and said, "Trooper Trippet, I want to thank you for changing my life. Ella and I will be forever grateful for what you did for us. If not for you, I would be out on the inlet, fishing illegally, worrying about being caught, and my wife would be home worrying, too. My son is proud of me now. My wife is proud of me, and my daughter loves me again. Today I have paid my debt and I feel good about it. I'm sorry for what happened to Ivan, but, like me, he made his world and he must live in it. Mostly I thank you for getting my wife and daughter out of the house before Ivan came that night. I think he was insane enough to do them harm that night. I owe you a great deal. If there is ever anything I can do for you, just ask. Thank you, Trooper." He shook Will's hand again and left the office.

Vladimir Resnic had just finished his first year in college at the University of Alaska, Fairbanks. Will's friend, who had given Vlad a job and housed him for the school year, reported on a regular basis that the boy was doing fine. He seemed happy and often spoke of Will and Sean in glowing terms. He also reported that Vlad's grade level at school was steady at 3.9, nearly perfect.

Vlad, too, stopped at the office to visit with Will Trippet. He had grown and put on some muscle. He was a good-looking young man, well groomed and well spoken. His calm demeanor belied the violence that had shaped his life. He too had come to thank his benefactor. It made Wilson Trippet feel good to have been a part of this young man's future.

Early May had been eventful and satisfying. This morning he called Gordy Ponset. When he had Gordy on the phone, he said, "Good morning, Gordy. I looked at the calendar this morning and this is an anniversary of sorts. How would you like to go out to Mystery Creek and patrol for bear baiting stations with me?"

Ponset laughed aloud. "I knew it was about this time of year, but didn't realize this was the date. Sure, Will. I'll meet you at the gravel pit at Mile 63. Is 10:00 good for you?"

"Perfect, Gordy, but don't hang up. I have to ask you something. Lynda is planning a June wedding and I need a best man. Are you willing to chance taking the job?"

"Congratulations, Will! She is finally going to house break you, eh?" he laughed.

"That is her aim. I went willingly after watching you and your wife. If Lynda treats me half as well as you get treated, I'll go willingly."

"The answer is yes, old friend. I would be mad if you hadn't asked."

"Thanks, Gordy. I'll call her now and let her know. She has a checklist and is marking off the things I am supposed to take care of. See you at Mile 63."

Today he would think a lot about the gruesome sight he had encountered one year ago today—the dead poached moose, the dead half-skinned bear, the little clearing with blood on every living thing. Mostly he remembered the partially eaten body of Victor Resnic. This single thing had triggered the events of the past year. Strangely, he could remember every detail in vivid color. It was something he never wanted to encounter again.

As he drove to Mile 63, he thought about his up-coming wedding. It came to him that he might talk Lynda into visiting Al "Bear Bait" Thompson and his wife, Joyce. It would be an honor to meet them.